JAY TINSIANO & JAY NEWTON

Black Horse

Acknowledgement

We would like to extend huge thanks to everyone who helped craft this book. Your contribution helped us make Black Horse the best story we possibly could.

A special thanks to Jim Newton for his considerable support.

Also, thanks to the following beta readers:

Diane Velasquez
Dorene A. Johnson USN (Ret)
Mr Maff
Lynn Hallbrooks

Join the Jay Tinsiano Reader Group

Free Thriller Starter Library
Books and stories
Previews and Sneak Peeks
Exclusive material

To join the VIP Jay Tinsiano reading group, head to:

www.jaytinsiano.com/newsletter

Revelation

"And when He opened the third seal, I heard the third living creature saying, Come. And I saw, and behold, a black horse; and he who sits on it had a balance in his hand. And I heard as it were a voice in the midst of the four living creatures saying: A choenix of wheat for a denarius and three choenixes of barley for a denarius; and do not harm the oil and the wine."

Chapter 1

Ed Flanagan had it all – the sleek Audi, the stylish apartment, and the six-figure salary. But behind his polished exterior, Ed was plagued by a gnawing sense that it was all spiralling out of control. Despite his high earnings, the bonuses and the stellar month for the bank, he questioned how much longer he could maintain his façade.

He killed the ignition to his Audi Sport RS5 and made his way across the underground car park to the private elevator. The bitter coldness of the concrete surroundings clawed at him, making him shiver.

Ed nodded and mumbled a greeting to another resident walking to their vehicle before sliding a key into the lock next to the number 38. The elevator rose, the floor numbers steadily climbing up to the thirty-eighth floor. Checking his phone, he saw a message from Zoe.

"Sorry, hon. Don't think I can make dinner now. Work's been a shit show. Ring in ten."

"Damn. Guess I'll order a cheeky delivery, then," Ed muttered to himself.

He stepped into the duplex, hung up his cashmere wool coat and kicked off his cap-toe Oxford shoes, glad to be inside where the smart heating had already kicked in.

"Lights," he said aloud, and spots from the ceiling came to life.

Panoramic wall-to-ceiling windows revealed the London Docklands. Reflected in the tranquil water of the river, the shimmering city lights of the illuminated metropolis.

The open-plan apartment contained a huge black sectional leather sofa that dominated one corner of the room, with a sixty-five-inch LED TV screen built into the wall. A retro-style rug nestled under a glass-topped coffee table, completing a space dynamic that demanded full couch potato mode.

"Goya, give me the business news on One," he said to the room.

The voice of a male news reporter kicked in: "— following investigations into the Tehran dirty bomb explosion. The state secretary also said that "we hadn't been this close to the cliff edge of global war since the Cuban missile crisis of the sixties."

"Meanwhile, there is the continuing global food crisis, with vast areas of Asia still experiencing unprecedented drought. The death toll is currently over one hundred thousand due to food shortages. In China, there is a similar crisis, and although the figures cannot be confirmed due to state secrecy, experts believe their death toll to be close to half a million."

The thought of feasting on tagliatelle and meatballs from one of the Italian restaurants at the Robot Rooftopia restaurant complex immediately sprang to mind, and Ed began scrolling through his food delivery app. However, he soon found it to be glitching.

He already had the number as it was one of his favourites, so he tapped through and called the restaurant directly. He spoke briefly to the young woman, gave his details and order, and ended the call.

Ed glanced at the stock market prices scrolling across the bottom of the TV screen, then continued into the kitchen area, brushing past an oak table with six chairs to entertain his City friends.

He selected a crystal whisky glass from the cabinet and a few cubes of ice from the dispenser on the fridge door before pouring a generous Laphroaig Lore Single Malt. He took the first pull, savouring the warming burn sliding down his throat; loosening his tie, he walked over to the sliding doors before stepping onto his private balcony.

The view always made Ed glad he had bought this flat. It had cost a modest sum, which was nothing compared to what some of his work colleagues had paid for their plush properties. Many strived for the Ferrari lifestyle, champagne party binges and cocaine nights. He had seen too many young and thrusting cocksure boys flush it all away, throwing money around like it was confetti and being proud of their profligate lifestyle.

No, Ed had a different plan. He preferred to tuck away as much money as possible: invest, diversify, sure, but be sensible while the good times lasted. After all, it would all end at some point. Ed was sure of it. Zoe felt the same, and if they were going to get married one day, which felt like a real possibility to him, they needed a way out of the meat grinder. They needed to invest in something that was real and tangible. A farm somewhere or maybe a vineyard. They had discussed it like a favourite movie repeatedly and figured it would only take another year to be able to have the cash to make their dream a reality.

He was smart, and so was Zoe, and they were going to be set with their unborn kids. It was going to be a beautiful life together.

The London skyline shimmered under a reddening sky, the cold autumn wind from the Thames buffeting the glass chrome tower block. He glanced over the edge onto the plaza, the scurrying people below looking more like ants than people.

Ed lit a cigarette and looked across at the ultra-modern office blocks of the Wharf. Many of the window lights were still blazing from late-night worker bees. His phone vibrated in his jacket pocket, and Zoe's caller ID came up on the screen.

"Alright there," he said in a light Scottish accent. "How's paradise?"

Zoe sighed at the end of the line. "Hasn't even ended for me yet. I'm buried in data sheets for this report. Deadline is tomorrow."

"Anything I can help with?"

"No, it's OK. Just have to plough through it. We'll go out this weekend. We can relax more then, anyway."

"Aye, you're right," he said, settling on a low seat. "Shall I let you get on then?"

"It's alright, hon. I've got a minute. Managed to take a walk around the other end of the building," Zoe said, her voice softer. "So, how was your day? Or shouldn't I ask?"

Ed focused his attention on the plants near the balcony rail, rubbing the leaves with his fingers. The plant Zoe had given him was dying already. Need to reverse that shit, or she'd label him a plant killer for life.

"Don't ask. I'll give ya the full gory details on Friday, eh? Something ta look forward to, baby."

Zoe chuckled. "Can't wait. You sure know how to work a girl up."

"Aye, been practising especially."

Zoe laughed again, and then her tone changed, "Damn.

4

Hodges has seen me. I better get on. See you at work tomorrow?"

"For sure. See you in the pit."

"Yes. Bye. Love you."

"Love you too."

The line disconnected, and Ed stubbed his cigarette onto the deck of the balcony and stepped back inside. Slumping down on the sofa, he closed his eyes and took several deep breaths. He wondered how long he could keep all of this going. Juggling so many balls in his job was getting so stressful. But the money was flowing. He just needed a little longer, and then he, and hopefully Zoe, could exit the whole rat race.

The door entry system buzzed, and Ed glanced at his watch with surprise.

That was quick.

He went to answer. A delivery guy appeared on the video screen, his face partly obscured by a baseball cap as he looked down at something in his hand out of view.

"Food delivery. Ed Flag-agan?" the man said.

"Yep. Come on up, floor thirty-eight."

Ed released the front building doors and walked back into his apartment. He took out a plate and cutlery and laid them out on the glass-topped dining table, just in case he needed it. Chances were he'd wolf it down straight out of the box. Then he picked a bottle of Argentinian Malbec, opened it, and left the wine to breathe on the kitchen island.

There was a tap at the door, and Ed strolled over and swung it open. The man standing before him was tall and well-built, with a rugged face still obscured by the cap. He looked more like an ex-army character than a delivery man. As he rummaged around in his shoulder bag, Ed glanced down at his shoes. He wore boots with some cling film wrapped around them.

Before he could process this oddity, a food box was shoved into Ed's hands, and he took it, but something was wrong. It was too light. There was no food in it.

The man moved swiftly toward him, jerking a hand towards his face as if he would hit him. Instinctively, Ed flinched, backed away, and the empty food box fell from his hand.

"What the fu—"

The man had a syringe in one hand, and Ed felt a pain, like a bee sting, in his neck. The stinging rapidly grew into a numbness that spread across Ed's neck and throat. It felt like his flesh was turning into concrete.

Get the fuck ou— Ed tried to shout, but no words came. The man pushed him back into the apartment and shut the door.

Ed's head swam. His vision tunnelled and slid into a vortex of darkness. He felt his heart beat like a jackhammer, then his legs gave way, and his body slumped to the floor. The last thing he saw was a pair of boots wrapped in cling film immediately in front of him. Then, vision slowly fading, he watched them move out of sight.

Ed felt his body shutting down, the edge of his vision darkening as his conscious mind fell away from his body, and he knew he wouldn't get that vineyard after all.

Or see Zoe again.

He clung to the thought of her as his body gradually succumbed to the chemicals coursing through his veins like a slowing tick of a dying clock.

Chapter 2

The pounding shriek of Goya's morning routine alarm shook Zoe from her slumber, but as she opened her eyes, she realised something was wrong. The haunting melody of the whale song she had heard moments before had morphed into something else entirely, signalling that she had overslept and was already running late.

Suddenly alert, she bolted upright, rolled from under the duvet, and then sat on the edge of the bed, holding her head in her hands for a moment.

"Shit!"

Activated by the sound of her voice, a smooth male voice chimed in with the good news. "Good morning, Zoe. You've overslept again but can still make it if you shift serious ass." He spoke that sentence in an American accent, a play at ironic sarcasm, one of the extra Goya features she had installed. Zoe was beginning to think it was getting old quickly and vowed to delete it later.

"Alright, I'm moving. Play me some old-school rock while I shower." As she shuffled off to the bathroom, the intro to one of her favourite tracks drifted out from hidden speakers around the apartment.

Her intention to strive for a better lifestyle had been fuelled by her recent reads, such as *The Zen Approach*, *Start the Day with Serious Intention*, and *Extreme Power Habits*. All these inspiring books had been read to her by Goya's soothing, husky tones (a voice option she'd had specially created, loosely based on her favourite actor, Ben Coney). Ed, her boyfriend, hadn't been too impressed with her choice and called Goya her other guy.

She was determined to establish new habits. According to her latest audiobook, it took at least three weeks to make or break any pattern of behaviour. That thought crossed her mind as she walked by the unused yoga mat set in the living room and walked into the wet room. The daily itinerary was a cold shower at 6 a.m., followed by exercise (she had spent nearly a grand on equipment that, to date, had stood idle in her bedroom). Another option for her was jogging around the Quays, which she did often, but this was England, not sunny California, where it rained ninety per cent of the time. So, she tended to skip the jog some days. Then, some stretching or yoga, finishing her routine with a protein-rich breakfast, something like brown rice oatmeal with blueberries and coconut sprinkled over the top.

So her plan, and it was a detailed plan – scheduled down to the exact minute with Goya –involved giving her a good twenty minutes to do her morning pages: a recommended daily exercise stream of consciousness, writing or speaking her thoughts, no matter how trivial or stupid. This was her way of getting all the shit that readily accumulated from her head. Goya would store it all and scan it using an algorithm she designed to see if anything was useful. Secretly, she wanted to write a book, but that was a very distant dream. It would be something to work on when she and Ed had their farm or vineyard in the warmer climes of Europe or whatever they were going to do. Such thoughts fleetingly came in her happier moments, usually when the wine was flowing. Ed had been very encouraging about her book writing; apparently, his father had been a writer.

Once again, she would be rushing straight into the bullpen of her job and into a maelstrom of noise and confusion.

Within ten minutes of waking, she was out of her building on Surrey Quays, which bordered the Thames and the Isle of Dogs on the far side, dressed in a fitted bomber jacket, jeans and boots. Zoe walked around Greenland Dock that her apartment overlooked, and past the still moored boats, their lights reflected in the still water. Passengers were already boarding the ferry at Greenlands Surrey Quays pier, and she had to run down the walkway to catch it.

Once on board, she found a seat on the small boat, and, as was her habit, she began scrolling through the endless financial news hub feeds. There, she found footage of a drought gripping China and Asia, dramatically affecting rice crops. The price per ton had risen by forty-two per cent in the past week alone. To Zoe, this wasn't just a passing news item. She was fully invested in information such as this.

Just another day in the merchant trading division of ZEOS bank; another busy, hectic day.

***

Zoe glanced at her G-shock watch as she rushed into the central trading zone on the fortieth floor. 7:40

She slipped in through the glass doors, clutching her boutique coffee house refillable mug, and walked up to the team standing in front of the market screens. They displayed the last closing figures, a sea of ominous red that jarred in contrast with the jolly expression on the face of Bill Keen, the floor manager holding the morning meeting. He glanced at Zoe the second she entered before continuing: "—what we have are happy clients. It may be grim out east, but the trades are going well, and everyone is doing great numbers. So, keep up the good work."

Zoe moved into a gap among her fellow traders and focused on Keen. "The environmental agency in China published the annual crop report, and it looks like China is set for the third year of very low yield. I suggest everyone give it a look. Thanks to Ed." Keen looked around the faces in front of him and muttered, "Where the hell is Ed? He kept us in the loop on this one." There was no response. He focused on Zoe, who could only offer a shrug, her expression as clueless as anyone. "He's not in yet?"

Keen smiled at her knowingly and gave her an exaggerated wink.

"Come on. You must have been celebrating last night after the last few days, eh? Don't tell me a few bottles of bubbly weren't flowing, eh, Zoe?"

Zoe's face reddened. She hated her relationship with Ed openly being discussed on the floor. Everyone was now looking at her as if they might also gain some juicy titbits from her personal life.

"No, I was working." She managed, flatly, quickly dispelling the banter. "I didn't see Ed last night."

Keen's face fell with disappointment, and he turned and glanced at the wall clock. "Alright, the party's getting started in five. See you after the bell."

The traders dispersed and spilt out into the open-plan area

clustered with an array of glowing monitors and screens, the beating heart of the trading division against a backdrop of the ceiling-to-floor glass that peered across the grey London skyline.

Zoe slipped into her chair, fired up her machine and immediately sent a text to Ed. He was an efficient man, clock loyal, he called it, and the fact he wasn't at his desk seemed odd.

A bell sounded through the building, and Zoe's screens were immediately filled with the visual dancing rhythm of multicoloured graphs following the fluctuating FT100. The morning would no doubt follow the adrenalin-fuelled rush climaxing with the opening of New York after lunch.

Her head had been packed with the subject of rice crops: types of rice, processing and quality. Rice growing had always been subject to monsoon conditions in Asia that resulted in varying yield and supply. The recent weather across the globe had shown dramatic increases in unpredictability, almost tearing up the rule book on seasons. There had been unprecedented droughts in Asia as if the taps had been switched off. And it was Ed who had cleverly predicted the whole scenario, almost down to the ratio of failure country by country.

Pundits had inevitably screamed that all this was all due to climate change, but something about it all seemed too sudden and too precise that much was clear to her.

She was busy logging on and then making sure all the account links were refreshed when her main outside line phone rang, and she answered.

"Zoe?"

"Yes, who's this?

"It's Julia, Ed's mother." She could hear her struggling to hold in her emotions but then broke into uncontrollable sobbing.

"There's been a terrible accident."

Chapter 3

Leob Runeshield Estate, Aspen, Colorado

The sleek black Mercedes-Benz S600 limousine glided through the grand automated gates set in the high perimeter walls and sped along a winding paved drive leading to a sprawling manor house. Hidden cameras planted in the vegetation and surrounding trees alongside the road silently rotated as they tracked the vehicle's progress. A row of pines followed the contoured slope down the rolling meadow of the estate, where a branch from the driveway led to a lake shimmering in the evening sun.

The manor house was majestic, set against the distant mountains of Aspen. Jason Runeshield's family had the estate built in the style of the seventeenth-century aristocracy to honour his grandfather, Leob I, who had taken control of the banking system in the United Kingdom after the Battle of Waterloo. Although the British had won, Runeshield's couriers had returned before the official government couriers got there and spread the rumour that the French had actually been victorious. The resultant panic caused a catastrophic crash in the newly formed stock market, making property prices tumble.

Jason smiled at the thought. An absolutely genius move.

With the resulting drop in prices, his family bought up entire companies and stocks for literally pennies on the pound, thereby establishing dominance in British society and Europe.

The chauffeur picked up speed, following the road up to the front of the main entrance, then pulled up in front of the broad steps leading to the brass-studded oak door. Jason exited the vehicle with barely a nod to the driver as he opened his door and ascended to the high doorway, where a butler waited to take his coat.

Inside the grand entrance hallway, a series of paintings of Runeshield's ancestors adorned the oak-panelled walls and carried alongside a sweeping spiral staircase that led up to the upper echelons of the manor.

"Jason!"

Jason turned to see Henry Oberman, his friend and associate, standing in a doorway dressed in a crisp black suit, dark features hidden in the low light.

"Henry. Are you early, or am I late?"

Henry smiled. "Ha. I think for once you're on time."

They moved into a side drawing room. The decor here, too, matched that of the hallway, with more huge paintings overshadowing pieces of antique furniture kept in the family for years. A multicoloured Persian rug, soft under their designer shoes, silenced their footsteps as Jason closed the door behind them for privacy and then moved to stand by the window.

"Finally, the day has arrived," Oberman said quietly.

"I thought it never would," Jason said, nodding as he gazed out of the window. "The old man is in a constant state of illness. His third heart transplant apparently went well, but I often wonder what keeps him going."

Oberman whistled through his teeth. "Yes, well, we all know how the old guard loves to keep their health going with the latest advancements in nutrition. It's not like we eat any of the mass-produced crap that's shovelled out to the masses."

Jason glanced across the meadow towards the lake. The sun had begun to set, and streaks of reds, yellows and pink spread across the sky.

"Let's get this over with. Then we can begin our plans. I'll see you in there."

***

Jason Runeshield moved down the stone steps into the lower levels of the manor house, past torches set in the wall, the naked flames flickering, sending dancing shafts of light deeper into the abyss. He soon reached the entrance to a small chamber set with the same ancient stones made with this part of the mansion so long ago. A secret dungeon that Jason's father had constructed especially for ceremonies such as this.

A line of black hooded cloaks hung on ornate brass hooks and a small lodge door at the end. Other figures came into the hall, respecting the code of silence. Jason put on the cloak over his suit and pulled the hood over his curly blond hair, grateful for the warmth the cloak provided against the chill of the outer hall. He stepped through the doorway into an antechamber where other figures stood waiting, their faces cast in shadow. Jason could barely see who they were but recognised Oberman's dark-skinned fingers constantly entwined in nervous agitation.

After a few minutes, a figure opened another door ahead of them, and they filed into a larger hall with a stone-vaulted ceiling that rose high above them. More open metal torches fixed in brass sconces sent the light of their flames flickering onto the stone walls. The air was musky and scented with traces of frankincense. In the centre of the room sat an elegant oval table carved from the finest oak, around which were placed thirteen matching chairs. On the headwall, flanked by two tapestries depicting the Runeshield family crest on one and the family tree on the other, hung a solid gold statue of Baphomet, the half-human, half-goat figure taken as the cabal's emblem. The reflection of the burning torches danced across its face as it glared down at those assembled beneath it.

The figures took their places and sat in silence, some pouring themselves glasses of water from crystal water jugs. Jason and Oberman exchanged sideways glances from under their ermine-edged hoods.

There was a series of heavy knocks at the door through which they had entered, and all twelve of them stood up. The door opened, and a stooped figure walked in, shuffling to his seat at the head of the table. Jason's father, Leob Runeshield, reached the head of the table and settled himself into the vacant chair next to Jason. With a gesture of his hand, the others followed suit and sat down again in silence.

Almost simultaneously, everyone in the room pulled back their hoods, revealing their faces in the chamber's uncertain light. Jason looked around at the assembled Council of Thirteen, a gathering of the most powerful people on the planet in one place at that moment. More powerful than most of the presidents and prime ministers put together, many of whom were puppets of this Council, controlled and manipulated through numerous and nefarious means.

His father, frail-looking with thin strands of silver hair

combed back across his freckled skull, spoke into the stillness, a low, guttural whisper revealing an intensity and sharpness of mind belied by his appearance.

"Greetings to all. Welcome to the 249th meeting of the Council." Heads leaned forward to catch his words. "We are gathered together at a momentous time in our history. Our bloodlines have worked together for hundreds of years, and now we arrive at this momentous point of our long-awaited plan. It has not been easy. There will always be challenges, bridges to build and obstacles to overcome. This is to be expected when so many enemies oppose our vision of the light we will bring. With that said, let us go through the motions of order," The old man paused and took a sip of water before glancing across the table at a tanned silver-haired man at the far end.

"Brother Helms. Please speak about White Horse."

Natan Helms, a regal-looking man, stood up and nodded towards his colleague, then addressed the assembly:

"Thank you, Brother Runeshield. The operation was one of those challenges that we had problems with. The original tests in 1918 proved successful, but after large parts of the formula were destroyed, we had to begin again from the ground up. Recently we have had a breakthrough with new information on the coding of the virus, and we currently are on target to include this as an option, but it still requires further field testing."

Helms glanced around as he paused in his delivery. All who were there were heavily invested in the plan that was now revealing itself in more detail.

"And Red Horse?" Runshield asked.

Clearing his throat and taking a sip of water from the crystal glass before him, Helms went on. "Red Horse is progressing, but you know how these things work. War is a hard beast to control and manipulate; not just the act of warfare itself, but the selling of approval of that war to the public. Certain elements in the current administration are baulking at a full invasion. The Iranian forces are stronger than we thought, and although the UIS made ground, it isn't a big enough catalyst to ignite the situation. Even with the recent dirty bomb incident we instigated in Tehran proved inadequate, I'm afraid it may be a much longer game than we first thought."

Leob Runeshield held up his hand. "It may not matter in the end. Please continue."

Helms continued with an evident look of relief, "Which brings me to Black Horse. Everything is proceeding well so far. There are numerous assets in place to support this operation, but it's too early to tell you more at this stage."

"Good. This is critical. Make sure it proceeds smoothly. What about our setup here in Colorado?"

Helms broke into a self-assured smile. "The main facility at Denver is almost ready. There is certainly much more to do, but we should be ready for October. I'm not directly involved in logistics, but I'm assured everything is good."

"Make sure it is!" the old man suddenly snapped, surprising everyone with the sharpness of his tone, especially Helms, whose smile suddenly faded. "We cannot afford to be complacent. We cannot simply reverse our actions and make it right if we miss anything. It will be too late after October. We will all be in a very different world by then. So, I want you to double-check absolutely everything in Denver – every single detail." Pausing for a moment to let his words sink in, he continued, "Make sure the military is on track and all our arrangements are watertight. There will be no turning back when we get to 'Pale Horse'."

Helms shifted. "Let me assure you, Brother Runeshield. Everything will be ready," he said with renewed certainty.

Jason stifled a smile at the flash of grit that defined his father. The old man had not displayed it so much in recent years, but the same steely determination had brought the Council so far in the preceding decades. Jason knew that in the same tone on display today, his father had spoken to the next secretary of state; he had also spoken to presidents and prime ministers in years past.

And it was very true, thought Jason, that his father had done much in service to the council, but the time was right to hand over the reins.

"Good," Runeshield said. His expression softened as he looked over at Laurent Wolf, a man well into his eighties, with piercing pinpoint green eyes set against pale, almost translucent skin.

"Laurent. How are things with the Exodus?"

Jason knew this was about what the insiders nicknamed the 'sell-off'—the secretive disposal of assets, stocks, bonds and other financial instruments. Since the crash of 2008, the governments and banks under the Council's influence had been propping up the financial system as best they could with a constant printing of money while secretly stockpiling physical assets such as precious metals and the takeover of vast farmlands.

Laurent Wolf leaned forward, placing his hands flat on the oak table. "Well, closing down an entire financial system in secret isn't easy."

There was a light chuckle around the table—a welcome relief

at the break in tension.

"There is only so much we can do," he continued, "Every one of us, along with our affiliated brothers, has long prepared for this. We will lose much in terms of the control we had with the old system, but we will retain our absolute power in the new system we are putting in its place. That much is certain. There has been a constant stream of disposal, well hidden by our best minds through market manipulation." Bringing his fingers together is a steeple before him, Wolf concluded his contribution, "Without going into all the pedantic details, I will just say we are indeed on schedule to reduce our exposure to the scorched earth operation."

This information brought a murmur of approval from the Council. Runeshield continued to request progress reports from each member. When finished, he leaned back and spoke above the noise. "Now," he said, "I know that today everyone was expecting an announcement regarding our going forward," He paused, avoiding Jason's gaze that now darted to him. "Our Council is the leading light for the illuminated higher pillars of humanity. We are saving everything we have passed down through generations: the knowledge of our forefathers, our righteous place to inherit the world and use the power we possess to forge the new era in our own image. The lower echelons of humanity will be severely reduced. The remaining will serve the Baphomet. The populations have failed themselves; those suckling too long on the breast of the state will taste bitter venom instead of milk." He smiled at his own choice of words, then continued with words that crackled with another display of steely determination. "With that in mind, I have realised we are in too critical a phase for there to be significant changes in the Council. Therefore I am postponing changes and will retain my position as head of the Council of Thirteen during the transition."

Jason blinked, his eyes betraying his anger for just a moment as he stared at his father, who still did not look in his direction. He looked over at Oberman, his trusted ally, who also struggled to mask his shock at what he had just heard. Others of the Council glanced between Jason and his father.

Silence prevailed as the chamber digested the news that Jason Runeshield would not succeed his father on this day.

Or any day soon.

Chapter 4

Station 12, Denver

Haleema watched what seemed like the thousandth simulation scenario play out on her thirty-four-inch curved monitor. Overlaid on a map of the East Coast of the United States, a silent animated wave expanded out from the epicentres of New York, Boston and Philadelphia.

The casual representation of millions of lives lost in an instant.

Small text boxes on her second screen displayed rapidly changing figures from the cities as the simulation software calculated the fallout speed, covered areas, and potential safe zones between blasts. Whoever she was working for seemed keen to know the worst scenario possible. Her new brief was to find these gaps and run different scenarios, positioning the blast centres at various points around the larger cities to see if there was any way of carpeting every section of the map, leaving no place untouched. A scenario her superior Leone Caine called 'decimation zero.'

There were thousands of other variables to consider. How long would an individual city take to run out of food and water when its supply infrastructure stopped working? How many people could be supported by the local resources if national transportation broke down? Where would the population migrate to? How quickly after would the death toll start rising? How long did the government have to react to minimise civilian casualties?

The questions about all these scenarios and variables seemed endless. And so they worked repetitive, long days, crunching the numbers and codes to try and get the most accurate data possible.

Haleema focused on her current task and fed the data from each scenario, saving them to different folders ready for her report. Although the AI on their system did most of the heavy lifting, Haleema's role had been to 'sanity check' what was happening on the screens and the numbers. Machines were great, but sometimes they missed something only a trained human eye could see.

Haleema stretched and then sat back in her chair, looking around the operations centre. She was surrounded by dozens of monitors and computers that adorned the walls and oc-cupied every available surface, their screens flickering in a mesmerising dance of data and information. In the previous few months, her routine had fallen into a pattern of working to this impossible deadline with one month to go until the latest reports needed to be finalised. Her new home, Station 12, did have limited facilities for relaxation and exercise, and perhaps that's what she needed right now before lunch.

She logged off, stood up, and approached her supervisor, Leone Kaine.

"I'm taking my lunch now, Mr Kaine."

He nodded without looking up, and Haleema headed across the room to the green-lit exit doorway and left the darkened atmosphere of the operations room. She walked past the hunched forms of coworkers entirely focused on their screens. This was partly to do with the intensity of their tasks but probably also to avoid looking in the direction of Fagan, the head of security, whose eyes she had felt on her in the previous weeks.

With the cloned access card she had stashed away, Haleema was desperate to explore as much of this complex subterranean hub as possible, if only to piece together some of the puzzle. Still, it was dangerous, and the last thing she wanted to do was compromise her mission. She headed along the metal lattice walkway to the elevator as if to go to the recreation room.

Instead, she walked past the elevator and along a curving corridor that came to a junction where more Station 12 operatives moved around, heading to different parts of the base. She headed along the eastern corridor, past misted-glass doors, until she arrived at the gym and swiped to enter.

Inside was a circular room, set in ambient light, with more high-resolution screens of Scandinavian forests and rugged landscapes beyond the state-of-the-art gym equipment.

A few other workers were hitting their regime hard. One muscular Afro-Caribbean man benched weights while a blonde woman wearing earphones pounded the running machine.

She saw another woman from her team at the water cooler, the quietly confident Laura, a tall woman with auburn hair who stood in her latex suit replenishing her hydro-flask. Friendships were actively discouraged in the Station, but the two women tried to keep each other in the loop. For now, they merely nodded in each other's direction.

Gym visits had never been a thing for Haleema in her previous life. Tinkering with software code, solving complex computing problems, or building elaborate hacks had always been vastly more appealing to her. But incarcerated in this synthetic, industrialised environment miles below ground, she felt the urge to push the machines until her muscles screamed.

Once the shock of arriving at this place had passed, after allowing herself to be kidnapped and then the nightmare journey through the transatlantic Maglev tunnel, Haleema marvelled at the vastness and the technology. The joy of being reunited with her father was a brutal contrast to finding out the news about her brother, Amir.

Now, she had grown weary, wondering if she had done the right thing. Yes, she had found her Dad, but now they were both trapped at the bottom of a pit, unable to help each other escape.

She had to trust Joe on this – and she did, ultimately. There was an end game, a plan, but she still felt fear that she might be stuck in this place for the rest of her life.

Haleema walked past rows of exercise bikes and into the changing rooms. When she was back out, in gym gear, she went through a simple warm-up and some stretching exercises, climbed onto a bike, and set the machine for her usual twenty kilometres that simulated cycling up and over a series of steep hills.

Laura finished her treadmill and walked toward Haleema, mopping her face with a towel. She climbed onto a bike alongside Haleema and tapped on the control panel with a series of bleeps.

"Hey," she said casually before slowly escalating her ped-dling routine.

"How's it going?"

Laura sighed and said with a straight face, "Brain overloaded with datasets—can't wait to see the last of 'em. I have to be straight with ya. I can't wait for my vacation to Hawaii. Really gonna enjoy sipping those margaritas on the beach."

Haleema sniggered. They both knew they weren't walking out anytime soon, but Laura had always shown that dark sense of humour.

"I'll be on the next flight right behind you," she replied, joining in with the theme of wishful thinking.

"Seems to be getting busier here—something's afoot," Laura said, her voice low.

"Busier?"

"A lot of trucks coming into the base, almost continuously."

Haleema nodded slowly. What could that mean?

"Supplies?"

"Yeah, could be—" Laura responded, not sounding convinced. "I did hear a few of the Alphabet agencies were relocating here."

"Right," was all Haleema could mutter, her mind ticking over at the rumour.

They both continued cycling in silence, focused on the consoles in front of them as the kilometre numbers slowly crept upwards. After twenty minutes, Haleema said goodbye to her colleague and headed to the shower, still mulling over the meaning of the intelligence agencies relocating underground.

Chapter 5

London, UK

It was a busy day at Tulip Lawn Cemetery. A stream of black hearses passed them on the way in, and Zoe felt an all-too-familiar lurch at her stomach. After cruising around the streets near the cemetery for ten minutes, she finally found a place to park, killed the engine, and slowly took a long breath. Still unwilling to continue with the process of going to Ed's funeral, Zoe remained in her seat for a few moments. She fished around in her handbag and found her meds, the Buspirone pills for anxiety. She took a capsule, swallowing it with a sip from her water bottle.

She felt numb; her eyes were sore from the tears she had shed since hearing about Ed's death, and her stomach was in knots. She had hardly eaten a thing for days.

There was a chirp on her phone. Her father, Frank, was calling from inside the funeral parlour.

She stepped out of her car and brushed down her attire, checking her appearance in the reflection of the vehicle's windows before slowly making her way to the double doors of the building's main entrance. Members of other bereaved families milled around in the reception area, looking up at a large electronic board that displayed family names and times for the service for their 'dearly departed'. Just like displaying train times in a railway station, Zoe thought. Another set of double doors led into a large communal hall, where waiting families sat at round plastic tables, some forming a queue for the cheap coffee and snacks at a concession booth run by a couple of elderly women. Inoffensive music drifted from speakers in the ceiling, topping off the surreal scene.

She looked around the room for a woman called Anne from the bereavement services office who had been the greatest comfort in her recent, hellish days. She had become her personal organiser, making all the arrangements and helping Zoe choose the service's music, poems, and readings. Ed's brother, Euan, had come down from Edinburgh, which took some weight off her, but no other family were scheduled to be present.

It was evident Euan had opted for the cheapest of options, a revelation which irked Zoe. Ed deserved far better. A more stylish send-off in line would have been what he would have wanted.

Ed's brother had been clipped and business-like with his conversations on the phone. Saying the right things to be sure, however, Zoe also got the distinct impression he was actually nonplussed on how to respond to the death of his brother. Zoe knew that he and Ed had never been close, even in childhood, but even so... "Perhaps he was still in shock about it all," she wondered. It had all happened so quickly.

"Organised chaos by the looks of it," came a familiar, rich, baritone voice.

She turned and erupted into a broad smile.

"Dad!"

She gave him a long hug and studied his face. It had been at least a year since she had last seen him. Apart from the few grey streaks at his temples and craggy lines, he looked well. She sensed from the strength of his hug and the hardness of his body that her dad was still the influential figure that gave her so much comfort in her childhood.

"Thank you for coming over. It means a lot."

"Least I could do, hon. I'm really sorry."

She looked across at a dark limo arriving outside and tried to put the last few days of tears, anger and confusion to bed.

"I've been over it again and again. We had a conversation. Totally normal. We had just made plans—" Zoe felt herself about to break, then took a breath. "—for dinner this Friday. There's just no reason he would have jumped—no reason at all. He'd just opened a bottle of wine, for God's sake! I can't understand it, Dad."

Frank Bowen nodded, held his daughter's arm comfortingly, and then asked, "What did the coroner say?"

"His verdict was an 'accidental death'." She was shaking her head in disbelief and went on, "Everyone says he either jumped or fell.' She paused as an image of the balcony and the height of the railings at Ed's flat came to her. "You'd have to climb over and make a deliberate effort to fall off." The thought made her feel sick to the pit of her stomach. Breaking into subdued sobbing, she whispered, "God, what he must have felt? Falling all that way to—" Her voice trailed off as the images of Ed falling came to mind.

She shook it out of her head. 'You have to hold it together, Zoe,' she told herself. The tears would come again, but she had to steel herself to survive the coming service without breaking down completely.

She looked up and realised from the bewildered expression on her father's face that he was lost for words. Uncertain, strained. It was a look she had never seen on her father's face.

Then he stretched out his arms again and gave her another hug.

"You'll get through this," he said, finally. "I know it's hard to believe right now, but trust me. You will."

Zoe wiped the tears that had welled up again and nodded.

"Yeah, thanks, Dad." She exhaled in one long breath and looked around the crowd. "Come on, let's find Euan. He's somewhere around." She led the way to where the service was to be held.

Chapter 6

According to the geo-location screen above the pilot's cabin doorway, the Gulfstream G500 was an hour from their New York stop.

Eva Villar finished another call, put the satellite phone down on the polished mahogany table next to her and cracked her bony knuckles with a distinct click. She leaned back in her cream leather seat and drained her iced water, then gazed out of the porthole window across an endless bank of cotton wool clouds, trying to switch her mind off.

As the Faben & Xael Group security chief, Eva had barely been off the phone and conference calls since the aircraft had left Heathrow Airport. A series of complexities around Operation Black Horse needed her full attention. The logistics were vast and complicated. Secretly winding up thousands of trades and tracking associated assets required the most intelligent and devious minds spanning multiple positions of power. There hadn't been this level of planning over the previous decades involving so many compartmentalised groups since their 9/11 event.

The day of the New Era was fast approaching. Everyone, from their members in the government, intelligence agencies, military, banking and media, all worked on their specific agendas without any knowledge of other operations. Like most of her fellow 'illuminated', Eva didn't know all the specifics that were in motion or even when the actual 'switch' was to be 'pulled'.

All were working in segregated unison to bring about the Order of the Baphomet.

Kacper Fagan, the only other passenger on the flight, was sitting further down the aisle facing her, glasses propped on his forehead and in a deep sleep. Once her CTO at Faben & Xael, Fagan had been shuttling between London and Station 12 at Denver for over a year, and he was now to be based permanently at the secret underground facility.

Well, good luck with that, she thought. She had no problem staying above ground for as long as possible rather than being transferred below ground. For her, feeling sunshine, breathing fresh air, and hearing birdsong connected her to nature. It meant something real, something truly tangible. The thought of the sun on her skin pushed away the darkness that settled on the seabed of her mind.

Eva suspected more and more personnel would follow the same route as Fagan and be re-deployed underground in the following months. Ultimately, she didn't know the plan's final details. Only the Council of Thirteen steered those high and lofty decisions.

Eva Villar knew one thing for sure: the end days were coming. There was no doubt.

***

"Mommy?"

Sobbing, the girl held her doll by the arm, letting it hang

loosely by her side as she carefully walked through the house.

She had discovered her older brother first, face down on the floor, his white T-shirt soaked in a deep red pool of thick blood. His stuff: CD player, speakers, schoolwork papers, all lay in a scattered mess like there had been a big fight. She screamed at the horrific sight and ran back to her room, crying and sobbing, wailing for her mommy, who never came. Eventually, the girl summoned the courage to find Dad or Mom. If they hadn't heard her, maybe they were outside. She left her room, doll clutched to her chest, hurried past her brother's room without looking again and climbed the steps that led to a single door to her parent's room.

The door was open just a notch, and she hesitated just outside it.

"Mommy? Daddy?" The words stuck in her throat as she choked out the words.

Finally, she peeked through and saw his dangling bare feet first. With a gaping open mouth and face flushed with tears, the girl looked up at her father hanging from the central beam of the loft room, his eyes bulging and his face contorted in the horror of death. A snake-like rope was wrapped around his throat. His legs dangled lifelessly, and she gawped, confused. She hoped he was just asleep, but deep within, she knew he wasn't.

"Daddy?" she said with a trembling voice before hurrying back down the stairs again. She kept going to the ground floor and paused in the hallway. She hugged her doll, squeezing it as tight as if it would comfort her.

She wanted Mommy. She needed her.

The girl crept towards the kitchen door and pushed it open before letting out another scream at the sight. Next to the kitchen island, Mommy was lying on the floor on her side, head twisted at a strange angle, eyes open but not seeing, not alive, just staring into space.

A dark pool of blood had formed on the tiled floor just beyond her mother's still body, spreading before her eyes. She stared at it with horror. Then a sickly smell crept up her nostrils and hit the back of her throat, making her retch, and she vomited over her tiny feet and the floor.

Stepping back to the hallway, the little girl somehow understood her parents and brother were dead and never coming back, just like when their pet dog, Scoot, had been hit by a car. Daddy carried him into the house, wrapped in a blanket, and the dog was never seen again.

Her parents had then explained death to her for the first time.

She turned and rushed back towards her room, screaming over and over. Wailing, she closed the door and crawled under her bedclothes, still clutching the doll. It was all she had now, and she was determined not to let go.

It seemed like an age later that she heard a noise followed by a knock at the door. Kind voices called her name,

"Eva? Are you in there?"

It was a woman's voice, and, in one brief moment, Eva wondered if her mother was OK after all.

Eva peeped from under the duvet, still scared but hopeful, longing for comfort.

The hope faded as the woman called again, and the door slowly opened to reveal a different woman, thin-faced, dressed in black overalls with brown, tied-back hair. She came across to the bed, gently asking Eva how she was.

"Mommy and Daddy..." Eva started. "My brother?"

The woman shook her head sympathetically. "I know, I know, Eva, I know. Listen, I need you to be a courageous girl and come with me and my friend before the bad people come back. Do you think you can do that?"

Eva shook her head. "Daddy said not to trust strangers."

The woman smiled thinly and then, crouching down next to her, stroking Eva's arm while looking closely at the little girl's bewildered face, continued speaking in a low, sing-song voice. "That's very good advice from your daddy. However, I'm the only person who can help you right now. Do you understand, Eva?" She paused, waiting for her words to register and continued to comfort the child with more stroking of her arm.

"Yes, I suppose you're right," Eva eventually replied. "I don't want the bad people to come back."

The woman smiled more broadly this time. They were correct.

This little girl was very bright.

Chapter 7

Zoe and her father, Frank, took the short flight back to Dublin from Heathrow. She was due to go over in a week anyway, as all the family were heading there for Frank's birthday. Her boss was sympathetic to her request for extra vacation time, at least for now. After all, Ed had been one of their star employees, so he wanted to show appreciation for all his efforts. No one at the bank could believe that his death was the suicide implied by the investigation. 'Ed was riding a gravy train. We were on the cusp of something great,' his boss had told Zoe, as if their activities were actually creating something of value rather than betting on misery and bad news experienced by others.

That was how it all seemed to her now. It wasn't meant to be like this when she took her Economics degree, and she had visions of being involved in a project to eliminate poverty or at least influence decisions at a government level. The promise and hopes of a young woman who had freshly graduated vanished. The banking internship had exposed her to a culture she could barely believe existed, but it was what it was when she held it to the light. The soulless existence couldn't be disguised as anything else: a complex web of dark trades that couldn't be heading any other way except for creating widespread disaster.

At the airport security station, Zoe had nearly walked off

without her laptop, and in the coffee bar, she could barely speak. Her father attempted to show her some compassion, but then his attention drifted to the opposite bar.

"Look, have a drink if you want one, Dad."

He looked at her with an expression of hurt in his eyes and shook his head.

"I'm that transparent, huh? No, no. I'm good." He sipped his coffee and rubbed his hands together. "Look, if you want some time alone when we're home, I won't get in your way. I've got plenty to get on with anyway," he said.

She stared into the mid-distance. "Sure." Then she smiled at him faintly.

"I spoke to your mum. She'll be coming over in a few days," Frank said in a more upbeat tone.

She nodded. "Yes, she told me. So, everyone will be there—"

"If you don't want to do this, you don't have to, Zoe."

"It's good— Everyone being there is good," she said again, but whether this was true, Zoe wasn't so sure as she tried to sound.

From Dublin airport, Frank drove them in his 4x4 down the winding coast towards the city of Cork, then turned off the main motorway past the darkening fields and scattered bungalows.

Frank cranked the gears and turned off into a long, spindly single-track road punctuated with patches of overgrown grass growing between the wheel tracks. On either side lay vast empty fields, broken up by the sight of several half-built houses. Their completion had been abandoned during another recent recession. Now, they were just relics of failure on the landscape, slowly being reclaimed by nature and degraded by the wild weather. The sky was an expanse of blue, and a light frost had covered the landscape, giving the surroundings a surreal, almost a picture-postcard feel. A murder of crows let fly as they drove along, the wheels kicking up rainwater and mud as Frank drove aggressively ahead.

After around ten minutes, the road curved behind a group of high conifers, and they entered thick woodland. Slowing down, Frank drove past an old stone-built farmhouse with an outside staircase leading to the roof, an old tractor parked outside, and then, a few metres up the road. They came to a rusty gate set back behind a group of trees.

Frank got out and yanked the gate back, its rusted hinges squealing in protest. He jumped back into the vehicle, drove through the gate, and then exited the car again to close it behind them.

They continued along a narrow road with high hedges arched around towards the old farmhouse Frank had bought many years before.

The place held good memories for Zoe. Since her parents had split, it was a safe haven away from London. With her father's birthday days away, her siblings would soon join them. Even Zak was travelling over from the States. But she was glad of the few days' grace when it was just her and her father. Could she handle this gathering at all? It was debatable. Part of her wanted to curl up with a blanket and not do anything. On reflection, she appreciated her father's offer to give her space.

"It's nice to be home," she said, letting out a long sigh.

Frank looked at her with contentment. "I'm so glad you think of it as home, love," he said with his eyes full of fatherly affection.

Chapter 8

The sleek black limousine that had driven straight from the airport pulled up in front of a glass-fronted three-storey building, and Eva Villar stepped out from the back. The institute was a building set deep into the hillside, its curved steel contours gleaming in the afternoon sunlight. A line of blue spruce trees formed an arc at the front, set around a perfectly immaculate garden border.

Her driver handed her the wheeled travel case from the trunk, and Eva began walking up the winding path towards the building, heels clicking on the stone heading towards the entrance. As her reflection loomed larger in the double glass doors, they parted with a whisper of sound, and the figure of Klaus Klasfeld stepped out to greet her.

Doctor Black.

Her controller.

Klasfeld, dressed in a dark navy short-sleeved shirt and linen slacks, reached out his hand as she approached.

"Eva, good to see you again," he said.

Villar nodded, smiling as she took his extended hand. A vaguely familiar emotion welled deep inside her. Fear. Hate. But also devotion to the father figure whose life was now very much intertwined with hers.

"Hello, Doctor," she said passively.

His face, deep-set and pale against jet-black hair, always triggered some internal, hidden fears that she could never consciously define. She wanted those things to be left unfound, hidden, buried deep within and not to surface. Klasfeld's presence was like a fishing line pulling at these unseen memories in those dark, murky waters of Villar's inner world.

With a sense of dread, she knew only too well that the line would be tugging hard within her, pulling up who knows what over the weekend ahead.

"Journey good?" Klasfeld asked casually.

She nodded.

"Fine, thanks," she replied, trying to emulate his casual tone.

"How are things in London?"

Her hesitant demeanour instantly changed to being fully confident and brisk.

"All on track. Going very well."

"Excellent." Doctor Black then gestured past the reception and the waiting area adorned with sofas and chairs to wide, circling steps that led up to a slanted glass roof and the deep blue sky, saying, "Well, I look forward to hearing more."

"We have some time before the meeting. I'd like to have a brief update first."

A young man, immaculately dressed in buff crème slacks and a waistcoat, appeared from a nearby side door and approached them as they stood at the bottom of the stairs. "Can I store your case for you?" he asked Eva.

She nodded and stepped back as he took the travel case and began wheeling it down a corridor towards the back of the building.

They ascended the steps, and on arriving at the top, Eva was shown through a glass door to another set of narrow steps leading into the panoramic roundhouse like a bird's nest at the top of the building. Through the clear glass panels, 360° views of the Colorado Pikes Peak mountains led to the shimmering views of the distant Denver skyscrapers.

"Take that seat," Klasfeld said casually as he pointed. She obeyed and perched on the recliner, one of three surrounding a hexagon-shaped ivory coffee table.

He then removed a glass from under the half arc-shaped bar, placed it on top, poured in tonic water, and added ice before adding a sliver of lemon with tongs. He walked over to Eva with the glass and handed it to her, whether she required it or not. She took it and thanked him.

"So, as you know, the Council is meeting later this week. I need an outlined report. Tell me what you've been doing in London."

Not wishing to look up at him, Eva stared into her drink, watching the bubbles make the lemon slice and ice swirl around her glass, feeling the moisture in the air condense beneath her grip.

"The trades are all going as planned—rice, wheat and soya commodities across the board are at all-time highs. Every indication suggests that they will continue to go up." Eva paused and took her first sip of tonic. Tentatively, she continued, still avoiding the gaze she felt upon her. "...as long as this unprecedented crisis with the droughts continues. The natural devastation in China and India is piling on the pressure. The banks are all doing their part."

"Good, good," he said soothingly as if praising a child. Eva, however, sensed he already knew this information. How could

41

he not?

She continued, "Pithcore Gen trades are continuing as advised—"

"And there are no security issues? Nothing to cause any nasty surprises?" Klasfeld suddenly asked, interrupting her.

Eva looked at him, a questioning frown on her face.

"No, no, everything is under control," she stammered, disconcerted by the tone of his voice.

He smiled down at her and moved a hand over her face, caressing her cheekbones before lightly squeezing his thumb and forefinger around her jaw and twisting her face, making her look directly at him. The doctor seemed to stare deep into her soul with his dark eyes, and Eva felt like that little girl again, lost, frightened and alone with her family gone.

Finally, Klasfeld released his grip, drew away, sat in the opposite recliner, and leaned back, still appraising her.

"And do you feel you are playing your part for the awakening?" he mercilessly continued.

"Yes, I feel good, very much part of the team," she replied, almost too quickly.

"Are you one hundred per cent efficient and working to your full capacity?"

"Absolutely," she responded more confidently.

"There is no room for error, especially now."

Klasfeld smiled, but his eyes lacked the glint of emotion.

"You always were one of the smarter ones. Ever since we found you, Eva."

Eva subconsciously shifted in her chair, his tone making her uneasy, as if he triggered some hidden secret within her that she didn't know was there.

Even when the memories were boxed away and locked, they

always seeped out, like the decomposition of a corpse within its pine container soaking into the earth around it.

***

Eva had woken early after sleeping restlessly. Yet another nightmare had pulled her from sleep, and she now stared at the dark burgundy wall and the painting depicting decaying earth that dominated her small room in the Institute.

These dreams were always the same. A knife, pools of blood. Dead bodies, contorted in their final repose. Snippets of disturbing memories that had blurred over time. But she had superimposed their faces on strangers, and then, in the years that followed, the bodies had no identities at all. Just faceless corpses strewn throughout images of her old childhood home.

Her new mother had, she recalled, made her deliberately erase all the faces and memories of her once real family: her mommy, daddy and her big brother. They did not matter anymore.

There were more important things now. She had been repeatedly told. And yet the disturbing dreams wouldn't go away, no matter how much Eva tried to bury and hide them.

Casting away the bad feeling, she rose from her bed and put on a red dress, cardigan and flat shoes. The spartan room had a table with a standalone oval mirror on top, which she used to brush her hair every morning. When she was ready, she left the room and stepped out into the cold stone floor hallway of the massive house. Eva was always the first to arrive downstairs in the large basement kitchen. She said good morning to Mother and took her place at the long wooden table.

She liked to be first. It pleased Mother, and that was all that

43

mattered to Eva.

She was soon joined by her sister pupils, five young females on the cusp of puberty like herself. They all had sad stories, just like Eva, but never mentioned any details. Mother had saved them all and now cared for them, and in return, they served her.

Their Blood Rose cohort had the same routine every day. Anyone who made mistakes or errors would endure twenty-four hours in an empty isolation cell. Eva had experienced it once and ensured she was never returning. So, she worked hard and excelled in her studies, training and other work.

Mother, dressed in a one-piece jumpsuit with her short jet-black hair tied back, stood by the stove and dished out porridge into metal bowls, then ordered the girls to come and collect them.

Once they were all sitting down, Mother began a chant that the girls soon joined in. They all offered their blood, loyalty and souls to the almighty Baphomet and the power that this beast wielded.

Then, Mother gestured with her spoon for them to start. "Eat it all up. We need you to be strong, to fight the bad people."

They all knew who she referred to. The 'bad people' who had murdered their families when they were small.

They all ate silently, and the girls waited until their bowls were cleaned. Eva gazed at Mother, hoping for a gesture of some kind that she cared or loved her, but none came.

Mother clapped, and they all stood and headed for the door, moving quickly up the steps with their guardian following close behind. They walked through the mahogany-panelled corridors adorned with dark paintings before entering an old stateroom that had been transformed into a classroom.

The central focus could not be missed: a vast collage of the Baphomet goat's head made out of hundreds of pieces of broken-up coloured glass stuck onto a plaster base. Eva remembered the cuts on their little hands while making it for a Hallow's Eve ritual. She had been told off for getting blood on the plaster.

Surrounding it were vast world maps and several boards plastered with diagrams, data and pictures covering every subject, such as maths, languages, and science. Other random items included a periodic table of chemical elements, next to which was a photograph of a slaughtered pig and then a collage of symbols, including an all-seeing eye and an assortment of pentagrams.

At the end wall, tall sash-cord windows overlooked a vast estate, with other smaller houses and a scattering of lodges and huts in front of a distant woodland that appeared grey in the morning mist.

The six girls took seats at a row of plain desks before the blackboard. Then, Mother walked up and down in front of them and began to bark questions aimed at individuals. She focused on one of the girls called Mahaska.

"Mahaska. Which king built the tower of Babel to eclipse God?"

The little girl thought, then said, "King Nimrod."

Mother smiled warmly at that response, which greatly reassured the girl, who looked relieved.

As Eva looked on, she felt jealous of this girl and a yearning for Mother to hug and hold her close. It was something that had never happened—only smiles and words, but sometimes those felt empty to her. For now, all Eva could hope and yearn for was a gesture of Mother's approval.

At that moment, the door opened, and a tall man in a light linen suit with pale skin and jet-black hair walked straight in. A palpable tension immediately filled the room.

He nodded at Mother. "Ms Hagan."

Mother bowed her head slightly in his presence, "Doctor."

She then turned to the girls and, with a hint of irritation, said, "Say good Morning to Dr Black."

In response, the girls stood up and mumbled good morning.'

The doctor barely acknowledged them with a faint quiver of his upper lip and waved his hand at Ms Hagan.

"Please continue," he said quietly.

The girls sat down again, and Mother turned to Eva.

"Eva. What years were those of the Great War, the one said to end all wars fought?"

She cleared her throat and replied, "1914–1918."

Mother did not smile.

"According to the history books, yes. But our secret war continued on the masses with the great flu. That lasted from 1918 until 1920."

Eva felt a rush of shame and confusion. Her stomach fluttered wildly. She hated being wrong more than anything, but, at the same time, she felt tricked.

The doctor walked slowly around the row of desks, ignoring Ms Hagan. He stopped behind Eva and moved his hand down around her neck. Terrified, Eva held her breath and felt the bony fingers stroke her skin before settling his hands on her shoulders.

"Ms. Hagan. Why don't you try another question?"

Mother lowered her head slightly in agreement and fixed her gaze on Eva again.

"How will the era of the Black Horse evolve?"

46

Eva took a deep inhale. The cold hands of Doctor Black were still resting on her, but she knew this story well.

Taking a calming breath, she began, "It will start with the collapse of all the money lenders, the banks, by our own hand. The food crops will be destroyed, and this will cause a great collapse as, without food, people will die." She hesitated and looked to Mother for a sign of reassurance, who indicated with a slight nod of her head for Eva to continue.

"...then there will be chaos, and then the Pale Horse will ride...and we will reset the world in our own image," Eva added with renewed confidence.

Mother briefly smiled then, and Eva felt great relief flooding through her at this token of approval.

Chapter 9

Aspen, Colorado

A fleet of dark limos, their tinted windows shielding their occupants from outside observation, snaked away from the manor house towards the main gates across the meadow soon after the close of the Council. Meanwhile, Jason had stormed just ahead of Henry in a different direction, making his way to the helipad along the rear of the mansion grounds.

"I should have fucking known he'd do this," he barked, eyes fixed on his destination.

Jason waved an arm at the waiting pilot, who quickly clambered inside the cockpit and started the engine. Soon, the whomping thuds from the rotors began slowly building momentum.

Jason felt his anger rising as he clenched his fists. He wanted to get away from his father's estate as quickly as possible. His meticulously thought-out plans were now ashes.

Henry came alongside, placing a firm hand on Jason's back as he opened the chopper passenger door. "Where are we going?" Henry asked as both men took their seats and belted up. The helicopter lifted from the ground.

"My Fort Collins residence," Jason said, looking out at his

father's vast mansion grounds as it became a series of patched squares below.

"We need to re-evaluate and figure out how to fix this," he added.

The tension was palpable, and they didn't speak for the rest of the journey. The helicopter quickly crossed the metropolis of Denver, skirting the edge of Rocky Mountain National Park. Jason let his focus blur at the rolling green meadows and forests spread out below, the snow-peaked mountain range just ahead.

***

The sprawling forests below brought back a childhood memory of a similar redwood forest.

Settling down in his seat, he remembered the reddish dusk light spilling down through the canopy like rays from a laser. Maniacal laughter echoed around them as his father drove the pickup, one of his associates in the front, Jason in the back.

The laughter had come from his father. What puzzled or irritated Jason was that he had never heard his father laugh. There had never been a smile in his direction nor any words of praise.

His friend, a tall man with an accent, slicked-back hair and high cheekbones, laughed with him as he raced the vehicle down the track.

Several other vehicles joined them from converging tracks, causing a dust trail that whipped large clouds through the trees. After ten minutes, they arrived at an open area that appeared to be a makeshift parking lot, almost full of vehicles.

They parked the pickup truck by a wooden sign crudely

daubed with the Baphomet symbol, and a simple arrow showed them the way.

Their dusty path led to a group of huts as more men streamed down the pathway, chatting, laughing, and joking as if on their way to a Boys' Club meet-up.

Jason was taken inside one of the huts. Flickering oil lamps cast morphing shadows along the striped wooden walls, giving him a strong sense of being in a dream. They entered a small room where men were stripping off and changing into dark robes. Men that Jason later discovered were senators, high-level bankers, CEOs of large corporations, generals and even presidents.

Leob had him strip and change into one of the robes. Then they filed into another room, with masks piled up on a trestle table. Jason recognised the Baphomet goat as one. Another was the Spanish fighting bull and a great horned owl—all had a symbolic reference for the cabal, just like the signs, statues and paintings around their various homes.

Jason felt a palpable sense of fear when the masks went on people's faces, transforming them into an other-worldly image. Leob placed one of the masks over Jason's face and nudged him towards an exit door.

The light faded into the night by the time they stepped outside, and the gathering crowd moved down the slope to what looked like a setting for a performance. Hundreds of seats were arranged in an arc facing a wooden platform. Oil lamps attached to surrounding trees were the only source of light.

The crowd of masked figures began to take their places as a hushed silence fell on the scene, only the hum of insects in the background. A line of figures moved in front of the audience, all in black robes and wearing the masks of the high priests. They stopped, facing their audience. A loud knocking accompanied them from a speaker that remained out of sight.

One of the men began to speak. His voice was loud, piercing and frightening to the young Jason.

The Owl is in His leafy temple
  Let all within the Grove be reverent before Him.
  Lift up your heads, oh ye trees
  And be lifted up ye everlasting spires
  For behold, here is Bohemia's shrine
  And holy are the pillars of this house.
  Weaving spiders, come not here!

The words continued for what seemed like an age before the scene once again fell into silence.

Then Jason was led to the front, alongside the makeshift stage and made to wait, his father's hands on his shoulders. Several figures in black and red hooded cloaks brought a small figure dressed in white from the opposite side.

Jason was soon to realise it was the figure of a boy. Not much older than six or seven, he looked straight ahead in a transfixed state as if drugged.

The child was made to lie on the ground. A high priest stepped forward with the object of the sacrifice. The murmurs of the man speaking turned low, the words joining each other as if turning into a chant. The other men began to join in until a growing drone rose and fell in tempo like a writhing snake.

He remembered his father's hands gripping his shoulders tightly and the low whisper.

"Look, Jason."

51

The knife struck like a striking viper down into the small figure's flesh. A single muffled scream filtered through the surrounding trees before the cries and groans faded to ragged breaths before silence returned to the forest.

*****

Twenty minutes later, Jason was snapped out of his reverie as the helicopter touched down on a pad situated inside the walled property. It was a sprawling converted farm with several outhouses, surrounded by lush green fields and trees, well away from the main highway.

Once inside the sprawling open-plan interior, Oberman closed the French doors that looked out onto the terraced grounds. Runeshield began to pace around, then turned to face Henry again.

His words were filled with vitriol and hatred for his father. "He has done this on purpose—that fucking snake."

Henry opened a cabinet in the corner, taking hold of a crystal decanter and matching glasses, poured a couple of drinks, and then brought one over for Jason, who grabbed it from him.

"Well, there is nothing we can do. It is your father's decision for the order. I guess it is out of our control," Henry said in a placatory tone.

Henry stroked Jason's arm with his hand as if calming a wild animal. Jason clenched his jaw, gripping the crystal glass filled with brandy.

Now Jason spoke again, this time more slowly, in measured menacing tones.

"Not if I can help it. We change the fucking world every day. We control events. We initiated 9/11 to push our agenda forward. We created the whole financial system that enslaves humanity with debt and servitude, playing by our rules while pushing our agenda right before their eyes. We feed them the shit food, pump them with drugs, traffic their children, and through our manipulation of the media, they even thank us for it." He stopped, face flushed, and looked up at Henry, who was staring at him expectedly, clearly impressed.

"—So why should I stop being in control now?"

Jason continued, voice even and low, "If my father was out of the picture, what would happen to the Council?"

Oberman looked at him with surprise before realising his meaning. He carefully sipped his drink and moved his gaze to the sheepskin rug under his feet.

"If that happened, there would have to be a vote. The new Head of Council would have to secure more votes than any opponent." He looked up at Jason. "With the right swing on the vote, it's possible—" He paused, then added, "—but only if your father is dead."

Chapter 10

Ireland

When they arrived in Ireland, Zoe had taken a few days to check out mentally. She went for solitary walks in the nearby woods and tried to make peace with herself now that Ed was gone. Their plans and dreams were all dust and ashes. It felt like her future had been ripped from her hands, and the cycle of thoughts kept returning, reinforcing the belief that the Ed she knew would not have killed himself. And if he hadn't, then what had actually happened?

While Zoe tried to come to terms with her new reality, Frank had cooked the meals and kept the fuel for the open stove stacked as the nights were getting colder. He also focused on doing some building maintenance work on the outhouses.

When Joe arrived, he let himself in, threw down his carry bag and wrapped Zoe in a long hug. She shook in his arms, unable to hold back her grief, and the tears came again.

"I'm so sorry, Zee," he said quietly in her ear. She pulled back, composed herself, nodded, acknowledged him, and whispered, "Thank you."

"How was the funeral?" he asked after a pause.

"Horrible," she said dryly.

"No, of course. The worst—"

Frank walked in and hugged his eldest son before they all sat down at the old oak table that dominated the dining room.

"Coffee is brewing," Frank said.

"Great, bring it on," said Joe, rubbing his hands together.

"I heard Zak was coming over," said Joe, looking between his father and sister. Frank glanced at his watch, "Early tomorrow, he said. Then your mum arrives at some point."

"All together again," mused Joe out loud. "Well, it's been a while."

"I'm so grateful you've all come over, but you shouldn't have, just for my birthday."

"We all wanted to do this, Dad," Joe said. Frank got up, poured three mugs of coffee and put them on the oak table with milk and sugar.

They sat silently, just the crackle of wood from the fire and the smell of coffee drifting through the house around them.

"Let's go for a walk," said Frank suddenly.

"Do you mind if I don't? I'm just going to chill out here," Zoe said.

Frank nodded, understanding on his face. "Yeah, of course. We won't be long." Frank and Joe strolled through the woodland that led to a fence on the edge of the property. Beyond it was a vast landscape, rolling fields and pockets of trees; it seemed to Joe they could see for miles.

"You should keep an eye on your sister. I'm a bit worried. She's never gone through anything like this before," said Frank.

"Oh yeah, yeah, of course I will. She's tough, though. A bit scatty but tough. She'll be OK."

As Joe admired the view, casting his eyes over the green

fields, taking in the vista of grazing cows and tree lines, he realised something.

"This is a really remote spot, Dad. I can only see one other house," said Joe.

Frank smiled. "That's why I moved here."

"You've set up a great place. I almost forgot how great it was," said Joe. "What's the water situation?"

They began to stroll again along the path and the wooden fence.

"There's a well that draws up water from an underground aquifer. The pump has to be powered by a generator, so I'm looking into getting something sorted out so it doesn't need it. I have been thinking about a solar-powered system using lithium battery packs."

Joe nodded. "I'll look while I'm here, Dad, and see what the running requirements are."

"So, have you heard anything?" Joe added.

Frank glanced at him quizzically.

"Their next move. The push towards starting World War Three seems to be intensifying. Have you been following what's happening in Iran? I get the feeling they are preparing for something. Just not sure what to expect yet. I've got my sources, but the more info, the better."

Frank nodded understandingly. "I hardly speak to Carl anymore—six months ago was the last time, I think." Frank referred to his old boss and once friend, Carl Paterson at Ghost 13. "Griff has disappeared as well." He paused, then added softly, "I'm retired now, Joe. Bear that in mind."

"Yeah, I know, Dad. Just need some info."

They came to a natural stop and sat on an old tree trunk that lay across the path.

"I've been meaning to get the chainsaw out and deal with this," Frank said, brushing his hand over the bark, "I certainly could use the firewood."

"I can help you with that, too, if you want?" Joe offered.

Frank shook his head. "I dunno, though. I'm actually getting used to it being here. It's a great seat for the view."

Frank sat down on his log seat and gazed out across the fields. Joe joined him.

"There could be any number of warnings. There have been so many red flag incidents over the last ten years it's hard to know what's real and not," said Frank.

"Yeah, like the conspiracy theories and fake news they spread to mask the real intentions," Joe affirmed, nodding.

"It could be that the ATMs just stop working. Some major financial collapses, engineered or otherwise, or triggered by a Black Swan event, something unexpected that crashes the markets and leads to panic and chaos. It's impossible to know how it might come, but what do we already know? The whole financial system is teetering on a bloody cliff. They tried a flu pandemic and are still pushing that; they'll always try to expand or start a war. Some trigger events, computer glitches, and the whole system crashes. They can use that to usher in martial law, and then the games really start—" Frank coughed and reached into his pocket, pulling out a pack of cigarettes. He continued. "The trick is to keep an eye on changes happening in plain sight. They like to do that. Put stuff out in the public domain, using symbolism or some messages."

Joe crouched down and picked up a small stone, rolling it over in his fingers. "Yeah, I know. I worry about us being too late," he said. "We know they're planning some shitstorm. We've seen the evidence with White Horse—Red Horse—"

Frank lit up and blew grey smoke into the air.

"Ahh, yes, the horses. Four of them. What's next? Black horse?"

Joe nodded. "Then Pale Horse. Yeah, we looked at them already. It doesn't give much—"

"Black Horse. Something to do with economics—grain?"

Joe fished out his phone, opened his browser, typed in a search, and then began reading the text."

"I looked and behold a black horse, and he who sat on it had a pair of scales in his hand. And I heard something like a voice in the centre of the four living creatures saying, "A quart of wheat for a denarius, and three quarts of barley for a denarius, but do not damage the oil and the wine." Joe clicked off his phone.

"There you are. Famine."

Joe nodded. "Right."

***

They were all sitting around the old oak dining table while Joe and Zak brought in the dishes piled with roasted vegetables and a jug of steaming hot gravy. Zoe had been ordered not to help with the cooking, but she was allowed to sneak some cutlery onto the table.

Maria, their mother, and Frank's ex-partner had arrived the evening before, and the family came together to celebrate Frank Bowen's birthday, the event of Ed's death casting a long shadow over the gathering.

For brief periods, Zoe seemed to be coming out of her emotional turmoil and even allowed herself to laugh occasionally.

"You forgot the bird," quipped Zak, raising an eyebrow

accompanied by the hint of a grin.

"Your bird's flying around out there, somewhere. A pigeon, I think," Joe quipped.

"Don't diss pigeon pie. It goes well with cranberry sauce," he poured more wine.

"So, what was Ed's state of mind when you last spoke to him?" Joe asked his sister.

Maria looked up and frowned at Joe.

"Joe! You don't have to bring this up now, do you?" she said sharply.

He began to apologise, but Zoe stopped him.

"It's alright. The whole thing is like a swarm of wasps inside my brain. Talking it through might help."

Maria still looked unhappy at the prospect of the birthday dinner being spoiled by the conversation and where it might lead, and she sipped at her wine with pursed lips.

"I spoke to him the night it happened. Everything was fine. I mean, there was no actual way he would be considering jumping off the balcony, you know?" Her features darkened as if the whole thing angered her to the bones.

"What we were doing; betting on rice crop failures in the Far East, mainly China, because of the famine."

Heads around the table nodded. They had all seen the news.

"So, these unprecedented weather anomalies are having a devastating effect. We're talking about the world food supply. Our whole commodities team has been involved. All focused on this one area. Billions of pounds are involved, from what I'm aware. It might be even more."

"So, is this the bank making these short trades or bets?" Joe asked.

"We make the trades for clients. Over recent months, well,

long before the crisis started, the trades grew larger and larger. The time of their positions closing has been extended. That means this is going to go on for a while."

"Zoe. You're just doing your job. That's the job of banks to make money, to find ways to create wealth," said Zak.

"For themselves," Joe chimed in. "Just like they scammed the world in 2008 into thinking they had fixed the system after the crash. Then, they just printed a shedload of dollars or created them on a screen to prop up the financial system. Everyone got hit except the banks, who lined their pockets with the flood of money. Just like back in 1929, the money didn't disappear. It just moved somewhere else. The biggest con in plain sight."

Zak stared at Joe, his fixed smirk disappearing. "You're a bundle of snakes for the conspiracies, aren't you, Joe?"

"A term created by your employers to discredit any question of the narrative, Zak."

Maria dabbed her mouth with a napkin and stood up, taking her empty plate while Joe turned to face his brother, jabbing his finger as he got on a roll.

"I know you advocate the system. That's your job, right Zak? Protect the system. Protect freedom. But isn't the West just a gilded cage filled with birds chirping about how free they are? It's a nice cage with plenty of Starbucks, megastores, and endless feeds of mindless entertainment to keep people off track of what is happening. Hollywood does its part to reinforce the 'bogeyman', the so-called enemies of the state."

Zak snorted, leaning back in his chair with a defiant gaze toward Joe.

"The US and their allies are defending a way of life, freedom, Joe. It's called democracy. Or do you want to live in some communist state or something? Oh, I forgot, you virtually are. Your band of comrades, digging bunkers, stocking up on bean cans and gold, ruling by committee."

Frank sighed and stood up. "Let's keep it civil, eh? It's my birthday for—" He stopped himself and headed into the kitchen.

"But what freedom, Zak?" Joe continued, ignoring his father. "Freedoms are being eroded faster than ever. There's no basic freedom to choose what we put in our bodies or how to educate our kids. And the list of rules keeps growing, don't they? Thousands of volumes of laws are so vast we can't breathe without breaking them. Isn't collecting your own rainwater illegal in some states, huh? Seizing people's property and assets at the drop of a hat. Closing down kids' lemonade stands because they didn't have the right permit. And don't get me started on the Patriot Act. There's a whole shed of unconstitutional powers right there."

"Fuck you, Joe. The Constitution is fine. You want to see the bad in everything. There are many threats that I can't go into, but you would not believe the hordes of bad guys or rogue states that would love nothing more than to spill dirty bombs on our cities or unleash viruses, killing thousands or more. They hate our way of life and freedom and want to destroy it. We need to protect ourselves, and your paranoid mindset isn't helping."

Joe sighed, his gaze fixed on Zak.

"This freedom, this democracy where fifty-one percent control the forty-nine per cent? Let me tell you about your adopted country, Zak. America was founded on a constitutional republic. Democracy is a con, enslavement for the forty-nine per cent. We already have it, by stealth, funded by the banks. And you think I'm a communist? You think we live in a capitalist society when we have central banks?"

"Hey, Zoe was talking. You just hijacked the room," Frank barked from the kitchen door.

There was silence as both brothers stopped clashing heads.

"Sorry, Zee," said Joe, holding up his hands. "Just telling the kid how it is."

Joe and Zak laughed, instantly dispelling the tension, and Frank disappeared into the kitchen.

Zoe sighed. "Circling back. I think there is something funny going on. There have been numerous suicides in the banking industry. I mean, a lot."

"It's a cut-throat business," Zak said.

Joe glared at him. "That was inappropriate," he snapped

Zoe ignored them both. "Top-ranking executives as well as common floor traders. Do you think there's something in it?" She looked at Joe as Zak got up and headed to the bathroom, leaving them alone.

Joe scrolled through his mobile. "There's certainly a list of them. There are very few listed on mainstream media, but yeah, that's a lot—fifty this year alone!" He put his phone down on the table and picked at the leftover chicken on his plate.

"If you really want to see what is going on, my advice would be to follow the money. See if you can find a connection. Just be careful. Taking the lid off things like this always unearths a nest of rats."

Zoe nodded, her features impassive.

"I owe it to Ed to do something," she said, meeting Joe's eyes.

Chapter 11

The figure silently moved in the shadows alongside the high wall, black fatigues helping him blend into the darkness. Slung over one shoulder was a small backpack, and he wore NV goggles over his eyes. The night was still as he headed to the main gate of the mansion at the heart of the vast three-thousand-acre estate. On either side of the metal gates, adjoining pillars topped with the carved black marble statues of the ancient Egyptian jackal god, Anubis, peered down at him. The half-moon cast an eerie light on the driveway and surrounding estate. A line of dark trees obscured the outlines of the well-lit four-story classical-style stone building, the operative's target destination.

He pulled out an electronic device and hooked it over the security panel before pressing a button that began a scanning sequence of numbers in rapid order. A line of six lights slowly turned from yellow to green, ending with the soft click of the bolt sliding back into the lock. Easing the gate open, he slipped through and moved into the shadows of bushes that skirted alongside the drive. This led to a circular lawn in front of the house. The intruder waited at the end of the bushes, watching for signs of activity. After a few moments, his eyes caught movement in the shadows across the well-lit wall of the main façade archways. An armed guard appeared carrying a Tavor assault rifle in a high port position as he watched from his hiding place. The guard's approach had been so quiet that had the intruder not known that the patrol would be there at this exact time, he would never have been aware of his presence. The guard continued his patrol outside the house before disappearing around the corner.

The intruder checked a wristwatch, tapped on the screen, and checked the external security cameras' positioning relative to his location. They should be down, but he didn't want to assume they were. A few seconds later, he ran over to the wall of the house. Edging along a line of windows, he reached the last one. He drew a small knife from his pocket, slid it into the crack between the frame and the sill, and gently began forcing it open. The old window protested, the age of the hinges making it reluctant to move. As arranged by his employer, the lock had been left open, so after a bit more encouragement, he got the windows wide enough to climb in.

He pulled himself through after quickly checking inside, dropping into a spacious drawing room. His NV goggles were still on. He saw an array of ornate, expensive furniture and wood-panelled walls filled with old oil paintings inside gilded frames. Shutting the window behind him, he paused, listening for any signs that someone had heard him. The dusty and aged smell of the room reminded him of a museum. He moved past tables that hailed from some long-forgotten era. It seemed to him to be cluttered with chairs, a chaise longue and other Edwardian-style furniture. Paintings of historical figures stared down from the walls as the intruder moved to the interior door.

He paused at the doorway, looking up at the spiral staircase that led from the large hall. The floor before it was marbled with a long, oblong Persian rug that met the foot of the stairs. Satisfied it was clear, he crept up the stairs with measured footfalls, the exterior light casting his shadow through the hall window. A quick check of his wrist device confirmed the target room—the first one on the left on the next floor.

There was a dull background hum that he had barely noticed until it stopped. He froze at the sound of movement coming somewhere from the floor below, listening hard, waiting with shallow breathing.

Just a boiler switching off.

He moved again, ascending the stairs to the next floor, pausing outside the first door. On the wall next to it was a steel access keypad, the numbers illuminated with a faint red dot on the bottom. He checked his wrist device and typed in a sequence of numbers, a frown appearing behind his mask when nothing happened and the red light remained.

He double-checked the numbers and retyped, much slower this time.

Again, no luck.

He glanced down the dark stairwell and inhaled. This didn't make sense. The intel was bang up to date, and it should have been the correct entry code.

He re-entered it again, refusing to panic. On depressing the last digit, an alarm kicked in, filling the house with low-pitched, repetitive beeps. The hallway suddenly flooded with light, and a Hispanic man in a black suit ran toward him. The intruder turned down the stairs only to find two more guards approaching him, armed with handguns, pointing directly at him.

"Don't move!" they shouted up the stairs.

The intruder turned on his heels and sprinted down the corridor away from the Hispanic guard. He had almost made the first corner when two bullets ripped through his chest, and his legs crumpled beneath him. A crack reverberated through his skull as he hit the marble floor, plunging his vision into an abyss of darkness.

The Hispanic guard got to him first and held up his hand to the other two to signal them to hold back. He kicked the still figure with his boot, then leaned down and felt for a carotid pulse before turning to the two subordinates, shaking his head slowly.

"Shut off the alarm and start sweeping the outside area with the rest of the security personnel. I'll handle this," he said. The two other men quickly returned back down the stairs.

He stood up, stepped over the body and walked to the door that the intruder had tried to enter and, pressing a button on it, spoke into a small communication grill embedded in the wall next to the door frame.

"Mr Runsehield, sir. This is tango alpha one. Code: red viper."

After a few seconds, there was movement behind the door, then a click of the lock. The door opened slightly, and the pale face of Leob Runeshield peered out, looking at his head security man with blurry eyes and grey hair tousled from sleep.

"What is it? What's happening? Did I hear gunshots? Was that the alarm?" he demanded.

The security man nodded, his slicked-back black hair catching the bright hall light.

"It's all under control, sir. We've had an intruder, but it's safe. Nothing to worry about. He was most likely looking for rare paintings or antiques. Our security teams are thoroughly

66

sweeping the grounds and house."

The old man's eyes darted from the half-burned face of the bodyguard to the body on the ground behind him.

"Alright. Thank you. Good work. Give me a full report when you have the all-clear. And get that body out of here," Runeshield said irritably with a sweeping gesture of his hand.

"Yes, sir. Apologies, but I need to sweep your rooms to make sure all is clear."

Leob Runeshield's frown deepened. "Make it quick then," he muttered as he stepped to one side, allowing his security man access to his quarters.

Chapter 12

London UK

Stark grey clouds, edges bleached by an unseen sun, moved behind the ultra-modern apartment blocks of Canary Wharf that stood towering overhead. Zoe stood in the entrance courtyard, looking up at his apartment on the thirty-eighth floor, the balcony from where he fell.

An obvious suicide.

It was ridiculous that Ed would choose that way to die. Even if he had suddenly decided to commit suicide—which Zoe knew he hadn't—there was no way Ed would want some poor sod clearing up the whole gruesome aftermath. He couldn't stand the thought of all the fuss that would create, not to mention the police and ambulance people, strangers all, seeing him sprawled out on the ground like that.

He was a considerate soul underneath the sharp suit. No, this 'suicidal action' was not in his nature, not by a mile.

With Ed's key card clutched in her hand, Zoe made her way up and approached his door. She took a breath. The instant she opened the door and stepped inside, her memories started flooding back. Her pulse intensified, and a jackhammering started in her chest. She took a couple more steps into the apartment, the familiar smell of Ed returning to her. A cold sweat started to cover her body, slowly sticking her undergarment to her body. 'Just close your eyes and breathe deeply,' a specialist told her.

Yes, that's it, more oxygen to the brain.

She couldn't believe he was gone. Never again would she cuddle up to his chest, the comforting feeling that made everything alright.

Sweet whispers, tender touches.

Never again.

I lost my man, and I'll never get him back.

As if it had only just become apparent, that realisation hit like a brutal punch in the stomach. Heavy tears welled up, and her whole body sagged as she gave into her overwhelming grief, her legs collapsing uselessly beneath her.

Her vision seemed to tunnel into a dark void as her chest jerked in sobbing gasps. Heart pumping too loud.

Fuck you, Eddy. Why did you leave me?

As the tears streamed down her cheeks, her shaking hands frantically searched her bag for her Buspirone pills.

She retrieved the meds and struggled to the kitchen to grab a glass of water, gulping them down two at a time. Just the act of taking them calmed her. She took several deep breaths, slowly walking around the lounge area with her water while the meds worked their calming magic. She finally sat down on the couch, staring at the sheepskin rug. They had brought it together. She had chosen it, of course, from the famous Camden market. It was one of those days you don't forget. After getting the rug, they walked around Kew Gardens in the sunshine and ate lunch. Nothing special. She just remembered the feeling; nothing else seemed to have mattered. All woes and baggage from work faded into vapour on days like that. Time just melted.

She wanted to keep those moments and place them in a jar to keep forever. She allowed herself a smile at the thought.

If only it were so simple.

Photos. Of them together. He must have loads.

Suddenly, she wanted to see them, relive their last few moments together.

She hauled herself up from the couch and walked into the bedroom. The framed Banksy images hung on the wall, a gym bag on the floor, packed ready to go. She sat on the bed, taking the digital photo frame off the nightstand. She looked down at the frame at the image of herself and Ed, beaming smiles when they had gone to Venice just a few years previously. Their first holiday together. She held the frame to her chest as she wept again in earnest, warm tears rolling down her cheeks.

She slowly returned to the present and returned the frame to its original position. Running the length of the far wall was a large six-door built-in wardrobe. She padded over to it, pulling the doors open. All his suits and shirts were lined up in perfect order. The shelves were stacked with folded T-shirts. Pigeonholed compartments reflected Ed's zero tolerance for chaos. He had always been so tidy and organised. Indeed, his life had been a series of neat boxes.

She began to go through the wardrobe, pulling out the white storage boxes and opening the lids.

Most of them held little keepsakes, souvenirs from their past holidays, not quite good enough to sit out on display but still too sentimental to throw away. One held essential documents: his apartment deeds, passport, and random bank statements. The final one she pulled down had a random assortment of cables and leads. As she sifted through, she spotted one of his old mobile phones, a Samsung with a cracked screen that he had not bothered to fix.

Zoe placed it back in the box.

So where was his new phone?

The police handed back all the things they had found on Ed. She took out her phone and gave his number a call and, without hearing it ring, was directed straightaway to his voicemail. She went to the kitchen and looked on the side near the charge where he often left it.

Nothing.

She returned to the bedroom and checked both bedside cabinets and the bed. Again, nothing. Moving back to the living room area, she studied the couch. As she slid her hand down one of the cracks in the couch, she felt it. Smooth, cold glass. She fished it out and hit the power button, but the battery must have died some time ago. She took it over to the kitchen and plugged it in to charge. Soon, the black screen came to life, and she stared at the passcode prompt.

Ed invariably used his date of birth backwards, so she tried that, but no dice.

She typed in his date of birth in the correct order. Still nothing. Then, she tried her own date of birth. A smile spread across her face as an animation danced across the screen, and the home screen appeared.

Swiping across the smooth screen with her thumb, she looked at the call history. A local number was tagged with the name of that Italian he liked: Abelli's. His last calls. The other call was received from Zoe a few minutes later. The last time they had spoken. She felt her stomach tighten at the thought.

She looked around the apartment for evidence of this take-away he had ordered. Nothing was left in the fridge, and the bin had a few screwed-up food wrappers. As far as she knew, apart from the police officers who had briefly looked around the flat, no one else had been in since.

Maybe the restaurant would have a record? Wouldn't the delivery person have seen him? She tapped the number and paced the apartment, stopping at the windows to gaze over the city.

"Abelli's?" came a gruff-sounding male voice.

"Oh, hi. I want to track a delivery order from a few weeks ago. Is there any way you can do that? It's really, really important."

"Orders are done through the Ultra Food app."

"This one was direct through to you. He, my boyfriend, phoned you directly. It was on the twenty-sixth of August. I want to know if he actually received it and whether the delivery man or whoever could remember anything about it?"

She could almost hear the man inwardly groan, but he remained polite.

"Ah, so then it was early evening, madam?"

"Yes, he ordered at 7:08 p.m. Order for Ed Flanagan."

There was a pause and a light tapping at the other end of the line.

"Ah, OK, I see the order."

"Great. Do you know who delivered it? Does it say?"

"No, I can't tell you who that was, but I can tell you that it was returned, undelivered. The note says there was no answer at the apartment, and the phone was not answered either. I'm sorry."

"OK, thank you." Zoe hung up and slumped back down onto the couch.

She sighed, glanced around the apartment as if a clue might present itself, and then idly began scanning through Ed's missed calls again.

He ordered a takeout Italian and then jumped off the balcony.

Zoe shook her head, closed the recent call window and tapped his phone browser into life to see what Ed may have been recently viewing.

She froze at the sight.

It was an article about a spate of banker suicides going all the way back to 2008, with the most recent having occurred just weeks before. The victims were hedge fund managers, investment bankers, CEOs, and vice presidents from banks worldwide. The article described the various suspicious circumstances of their 'deaths' from hanging, shooting, and various train, plane, and vehicle crashes that all had unanswered questions but had officially been declared accidents.

Zoe began to breathe heavily and felt her legs weaken. She sat down and gave herself a few moments to regain her composure.

She scrolled down the list. There were hundreds of them.

Zoe felt a sudden urge to leave and get back home. Being here didn't feel right. Her anxiety rose, pinpricks of heat welling up on her neck. She placed Ed's phone in her bag, looked around, and left the apartment.

Chapter 13

The Jeep Wrangler wound its way east from Santiago, the Chilean capital, along narrow roads dotted with shack-like cafes and stores. It was quiet, just the occasional vehicle passing by them on the road. Further along, they came across a row of residential properties, partially hidden behind foliage-covered walls that the casual eye could have easily missed.

"Another nice quiet spot you've found here," said Joe, staring out the passenger seat window.

In his familiar white shirt contrasting against his tanned skin, John Rhodes rapped his fingers on the steering wheel.

"We'll see how long it lasts this time. I'm getting tired of burning locations every few months, but sadly, it seems essential now."

"You're a true nomad, huh, John?" said Joe, ribbing him.

"True nomad, yes, that's right. A nomad trying to stay free." Rhodes laughed without humour, then turned his head towards the other passenger.

"And you, Hanna? Been to South America before?"

"Nope," she replied loudly from her seat in the back. "So glad to be here, though."

Rhodes steered the jeep off the long road onto a track with thick bushes on either side that scraped the sides of their vehicle. The route ascended, climbing higher, twisting and turning until it reached a plateau, and then followed another clifftop road that arched around into a section of trees and scrubland.

They parked on a patch of ground in front of what looked like bushes and nothing else, and Rhodes switched off the engine. As Joe stepped out of the vehicle and its air-conditioned interior, the humidity hit him like a blanket of dampness, accompanied by the sweet smell of the dense foliage and plant life.

"'Where the fuck's your house? We're in the middle of — nowhere," Joe asked as he looked around.

Rhodes slammed the Jeep door closed, then gestured to a gap in the foliage where two bushes overlapped a narrow path.

"Hidden in plain sight, dear boy," he replied in a mock upper-class English accent.

Joe nodded slowly as he shouldered his travel bag. "Right, you literally dug yourself a hole to live in behind some tree."

"Well, you two are sleeping in that hole. I've got the master suite. C'mon, Anna is fixing lunch."

They headed through the bushes, stooping to avoid a few low-lying branches and came onto a stone pathway leading to a single-storey building completely screened from their view.

Joe let out a whistle at the sight. "You certainly know how to find them," he muttered, clearly impressed.

"Cash rentals are the way to go."

They headed along the stone path leading to an expansive veranda overlooking a sloping garden, heavily populated with fruit trees and a lawned garden that curved away from sight. The house had two stories, and the light glinted off rows of solar panels on the roof. The setting was like a hidden paradise, walled off from the world and emanating a tranquillity emphasised by the bird song drifting over the garden.

Joe and Hanna dropped their bags and slumped down at a large round wooden table set on the veranda with wood-carved benches on either side while Rhodes disappeared inside and returned with a tray of cold beers.

The old man eased himself down across from Joe and Hanna before chinking his bottle's neck with theirs. Anna, John's wife, joined them, sporting a glass of tonic with ice and a twist of lemon. They chatted for ten minutes, mostly small talk before Hanna asked for the shower room. Anna led her into the house.

"Any messages?" Rhodes asked.

Joe sighed. "We're nowhere near ready. We have tons of work to finish on the Tennessee place. Andalucía is all good, but that's because I'm directly running things over there," Joe said, raising an eyebrow in Rhode's direction. "Gianna said she might like to go to the new hive in England, just as a change of scenery."

"Is she capable?"

"Yeah, I think she has what it takes, but it's hard to really know someone until you throw them in with the sharks. She's involved with Hugo now, and I want to keep him where he is."

Rhodes leaned back, shades covering his eyes, and peered across the gardens.

"Ah well, we'll need someone over there, but we must find the right person. I'll leave it to your discretion, Joe."

He nodded without a word and cast an eye down onto a list of items he wanted to cover.

"What's next?"

"I didn't tell you about Zoe. She's had a rough time—"

"So I heard. Sorry to hear that, Joe."

"Yeah, well. Anyway, Ed's death was suspicious. I mean, there was no way he would jump like that."

"Pushed?"

"Maybe. We checked the police reports. No sign of a break-in."

"Well, they wouldn't leave any sign at all – unless they wanted to send out a warning," he added darkly.

Joe nodded as if it confirmed his own thoughts.

"She thinks Ed's death is linked to some other suicides – forty bankers or traders have offed themselves in the last year, ten of them this month alone." Joe laughed humourlessly—a grim, staccato sound.

"Keep an eye on her, Joe. If she's fragile—" said John, his voice trailing off.

Joe sighed as if the subject troubled him, but his words were upbeat.

"She'll be okay, and, yeah, I'll certainly keep an eye on things. She's strong, though. Deep down, despite her problems, she'll come through."

"Good. Well, let me know if you need anything."

***

The following morning, Joe and John Rhodes entered the lounge, where a series of sofas were arranged around a wooden chest that acted as a coffee table. Rhodes poured out some steaming hot black coffee and handed Joe a cup.

"Thanks. Let me look at those." Joe nodded towards a collage of photos pinned to a corkboard on one of the walls and walked over. He spotted a picture that brought back an instant memory of years before. The image showed Joe standing next to John in a small courtyard.

"This was when I came to see you in Ecuador, wasn't it?"

Rhodes stood up and joined him, focusing on the same picture.

"Yes, that's it, back when you first got involved in Liberatus – when you saw the light." He chuckled.

Joe nodded, recalling the memory.

The old man smiled. His eyes were almost misty with the memory. "How old were you then? It was just after you left the army?"

Joe paused, his focus drifting over to the gardens framed by the French doors. "Yeah, that's right. I grabbed a rucksack and hit the road. Happy days. After travelling around Central America, I headed down and joined you in Ecuador – you were based in Colombia before, weren't you?"

Rhodes sucked in his breath and nodded. "Colombia? Yes." He looked up at the ceiling, recalling a memory, "2001? Or just before? Yes, it was before 9/11. That was around the time your dad was working with me." Rhodes paused as he continued to ruminate about the past before continuing. "Yes, I had to take the family and leave Colombia after that. Nasty run-in with the intelligence lot – CIA too."

Joe nodded, only vaguely aware of some of the story he was hearing – his father, Frank, had shepherded an asset to Colombia. It had been a messy assignment for him and had nearly made Joe fatherless on several occasions.

"Dad was the one who suggested I come and see you. Of course, initially, I didn't think it was a good idea, but when I finally rolled in, I was pretty glad I did," said Joe.

The visit had helped Joe focus, get his life back on track again, and given him a new purpose. His mentor, John Rhodes, had inspired the young prodigy.

Joe spotted a picture of John standing with his brother Michael, pale, his white hair falling about the shoulders, and rooted to his wheelchair. The eyes were dead-set, staring into the camera with fierce determination.

"That was the last time I saw Mike, a few years ago, in the flesh anyway," said John, with a tone of resignation.

"I don't think I ever met him. Is he still running Goya?"

"No, the board threw him out of his own company. The bastards."

Rhodes sighed. "It's a long story. Maybe I'll flesh it out when everyone arrives."

"By the way, he wants to come to visit you in Andalucía as soon as you're back there. Troy too. It's about this comms business. I'll fill you in."

"OK, sure," Joe replied.

The two men walked out onto the terrace, continuing to talk and standing beside an outdoor coffee table overlooking the secluded gardens.

"The whole thing blew up so fast," John said, letting out a laugh, "the development of his corporate and personal comms laid the groundwork for every type of VOIP technology we use today. The Silicon Valley VCs threw money at him, and over the last twenty years, it went from a simple garage start-up to the multi-billion dollar company it is today. You know the story.

"Now, I hear the place is a vast complex over hundreds of acres, filled with a science division, leisure facilities, parks, and living quarters for those employees pulling all-nighters. But an adult playgroup for those lucky enough to be recruited."

Joe nodded admiringly. "That's incredible. You didn't do

too badly yourself with the little media empire. You're both very driven."

Rhodes let out another laugh, almost bitter.

"But for how long? The three letter agencies are busy trying to hack into our servers and close us down." They both settled onto recliners as the sun drifted behind the trees on its daily wind down.

"You know what drove us, inspired us? Our grandfather, Felix. A great newspaperman." John dropped his head slightly. "I remember him fondly from when we were kids. Our mother would drop Michael and me around to stay with him and Grandma during the summer holidays. He never spoke much about his working life to us, but he did tell us the story once.

"During the twenties, he owned and ran *The Big Apple Herald* in New York. A genuine beacon for independent and free journalism – something that's a rarity nowadays.

"Things were looking good for our family, apparently. Right up to the '29 crash, when banks began to recall the loans that crushed countless businesses. Not to mention the ruinous impact on the population. Of course, it had a tidal effect on the world, fuelling Germany's destruction and the rise of Hitler— another story.

"Felix always had a theory, which became pretty obvious years later, in my lifetime, that the whole crash was engineered, like all the subsequent crashes. You can't have too many people getting comfortable or rich. If the population gets too affluent, they engineer a crash, pull the rug and destroy livelihoods. Then they'd see what's happening, wake up and revolt – take a seat, Joe." Rhodes gestured to the chairs around the coffee table.

"Of course, who controlled the banks? Well, the Runeshield

family mainly and some others. My grandfather always blamed them when our business collapsed. The paper closed, and our family had a rough time of it."

"They want to control the world, squeeze it dry till the bloody pips squeak, but no one cares or wants to know," Joe chimed in grimly.

"Except us. Look at what we've achieved. How we exposed their activities countless times."

Joe nodded. "I know. Some part of me thinks we haven't hit them hard enough."

Rhodes sipped his coffee and watched a macaw land on a nearby branch before flying off again.

"I wanted to continue what Felix had started, and after seeing the harsh reality of the political world when I was with the Secret Service, I just knew I had to do something. All the bloody false flags, the manipulation, psych. Ops—" Rhodes shook his head in disgust. "Knew I had to do something to fight back. So, that was the newspaper and then came the community. I talked in halls, meetings, and protests – to anyone who would listen. Of course, they labelled me a crank, but we wiped the smirks off their faces and exposed some seriously bad apples. Then, as Michael grew successful, he helped financially, in secret, of course – but it enabled us to become a serious thorn in the side of the establishment. Troy took us to another level with the Icarus app and got us online, giving those who wanted to expose the truth a secure system."

"Yeah, your son is a genius, that's for sure," Joe said.

Rhodes nodded and smiled. "He is, indeed. That's the key. Getting younger generations to help us to be the future freedom fighters. Like yourself, Joe. We'll need everyone we can get. We've grown fast, but we're running out of time."

Joe turned to the older man. "So, how many hives have we got now? six, seven?"

Rhodes took a deep breath. "Give or take. A couple in the UK, then the groups in Europe, your own Andalucía, Germany, Tennessee and Oregon."

"And any word on the ex-military groups we talked to?"

Joe and Rhodes had initiated talks with various groups for their military wing, but it had taken an age to organise.

"There's some interest. They're mostly on board with what we stand for and what we're fighting against, but they all have their own personal agendas and want to do things their way. As far as I can see, only a major catastrophe would unite us all."

Joe shook his head, "Jesus, after all the evidence we've shown them of the dark shit we're up against, they're still unconvinced?" Joe said, then added in an accusing tone, "You should have kept me in the loop."

Rhodes waved a hand and refilled their cups from the coffee jug. "I'll talk to them again soon."

They sat in silence for a while, and bird song drifted across the trees.

Chapter 14

Over the next few days, a trickle of new arrivals came to the house, and Rhodes gave each a brief tour. Marcus Brady was the first one, the man who ran the media operations of Liberatus News, once a regular hardcopy newspaper, but which then expanded rapidly online to generate a massive internet following in the hundreds of millions. This was an obvious threat to the status quo of the authorities and their controlled media outlets. As a consequence, the whole operation had come under increasing pressure through court actions, direct sabotage, and even anonymous threats. This was nothing new to the hardened, driven individuals flying the flag of press and freedom of information, yet there was only so much they could humanly take.

As Troy Rhodes, John's son, arrived, he received a particularly warm welcome. In his early twenties, still filled with energy and enthusiasm, which the older characters could only marvel at, Troy had built the network of an online encrypted chat system, Icarus, which was now the primary communications platform for Liberatus.

From Addington in South London came Raj Singh, who, together with his siblings, had quietly built a formidable power base of supporters. Another English contingent from Suffolk on the English East Coast was Danny and Bel Thorpe, who would join by video link due to the imminent birth of their first child. Then there was Bruno Scholz, a passionate visionary for the organisation's future direction, who came from a hive built up south of Munich in Germany.

From Oregon, California, a tall Japanese American woman, Magna Yoshida, headed a large, resourceful community out on the West Coast.

Sarah Edwards, one of the original whistleblowers code-named 'Pandora', was the last to turn up. She had exposed so much about the early Ghost 13 formation and collaboration between GCHQ and MI6 to bring mass surveillance to the United Kingdom under 'Operation Oculus' in the late nineties. She had been hiding out, mainly in Cuba, with the help of John Rhodes.

The group gathered in one of the upstairs rooms that Rhodes had turned into a sparse library.

"I lost half my books, moving around so much," he complained as they settled down around a large table. On a screen at one end were the faces of Danny and Bel who, on being acknowledged, gave a brief wave and smile to the table.

As the small talk of greeting and chatter ended, John Rhodes cleared his throat and called the meeting to order.

"First on the agenda. As most of you know, my brother Michael has partly funded our operations. Unfortunately, he has been ousted by the Goya board, but he assures me our financing will continue. For some time, we have been monitoring certain communications from the cabal. We managed to identify a few key individuals and slowly put the pieces together. We also have a key asset within one of their key bases for the first time."

Rhodes paused and sipped from a glass of water before continuing.

"From what we can gather, the cabal is getting ready to strike. There seems to be more activity and a certain sense of urgency in their communications. We are still working hard to determine exactly what will happen. Still, by looking at their current actions, we can say they are working hard to bring about a global catastrophe to wipe out a larger part of the population and create their own utopia. This is beyond a mere conspiracy theory – we've come across the evidence time and time again—"

"So what do we know so far? The global intelligence apparatus set a global surveillance network in motion – as far back as the nineties. Then they establish a new kind of agency, a top-secret operation – Ghost 13 with an elite military arm, we believe, solely to do the cabal's dirty work. We know a bit about that thanks partly to the help of Joe's father, Frank." Rhodes gave Joe a nod. "We managed to quash that, forcing them to put it on ice, but the hiatus didn't last long. 9/11 brought it back online without opposition, along with all the executive orders flooding through."

Rhodes sighed, almost looking relieved as he shared the burden of all his knowledge of that past event. The others around the table watched him closely.

"They initiated the avalanche of war in the Middle East, manipulated the populations of the West to justify their actions, as they always have – pushing their secret agenda. They targeted our organisation on several occasions – and we will probably become targets individually if that has not already happened.

"Then, we came to this decade, and what did we get? Operation White Horse. Their plan was to re-engineer the H1N1 virus

85

– the Spanish flu. Unfortunately, that release of information may have been a big mistake on our part."

There were glances around the room.

"I'm not blaming anyone. We must not only learn from the outcome of our mistakes, but any future twists of fate that allow them to achieve their objective might be fatal to millions, not just ourselves."

"Then came the push for total war in Iran," Rhodes continued, "We know that they backed and helped create ISIS, and then when they were beaten down, they helped create the UIS to unleash a deadlier vortex of destruction on the Middle-East. They even managed to let off that dirty bomb purely to stoke the conflict. We're still at risk from a global war with Iran, China, and Russia, all proxy players but edging dangerously closer to the abyss."

"The fact is we don't know what's coming, but we know something will come, and that's what all our years of preparation have been about – we have to forge an alternative to their plans. Otherwise, everything is lost—"

Rhodes paused and looked around at the faces at the table.

"Forgive me," he said, "I will get back to Michael and the Goya Tech. The secure communication technology they've created utilises a low-orbit satellite and quantum entanglement for their communication. It was initially created for space travel but would equally be an effective backup system—"

"That they can use for themselves?" interjected Joe.

Troy leaned forward. "Yes, developed for use by the US military, but we have inserted some useful backdoor code in their software that could potentially make it ours." Troy smiled.

"What does that mean, exactly?" Joe asked.

Troy brushed a hand through his floppy blonde hair and slumped back in the recliner, the most comfortable chair in the room that he had somehow managed to attain.

"You really want a physics lesson, Joe? We'll be here all day if you do," he said with a grin, "but I'll give you the broad strokes. All communication is essentially, physical. We communicate through particles – calls, texts, the internet, all ride flecks of light and electrons. Information is recorded and broadcast on actual objects, even those we cannot see. However, physicists discovered something called the quantum Zeno effect. It's like transferring a quantum state from one site to another with no quantum or classical particle being transmitted between them."

Troy stopped talking as he sensed he had already lost some of those in the room. He shuffled in his chair and sat upright.

"What we've got here is basically an unhackable method of communication. As I was saying, the tech heads at Goya were contracted to implement it for military and intelligence satellites, but it can also be used for any communication in the event of traditional comms being unusable for whatever reason."

"So we could use it ourselves?" Magna Yoshida asked.

"While I was involved in the project, I may have put in back-door access to the satellite operating system," Troy smirked. "The equipment has been tested and is ready to distribute. So, wherever our people are in the world, we can all communicate via the satellite system without fear of interception, even in the case of a major comms failure."

"Shipments are already on their way to all the main hives," Rhodes interjected. "There will be a learning curve on all this, so we should get that communicated as soon as possible."

Rhodes gestured to Joe.

Joe turned to Troy. "If you can give me as much information about this before you leave?"

"Yeah, sure."

"Great," Rhodes said, "What's next?"

Chapter 15

Haleema tapped her knuckle lightly on the oval-shaped door and waited. She wanted to see her father.

She heard a click after a few moments before the door slid open.

Her father, Karim, had visibly aged since they had been brought to 'the pit', as she now called the vast underground facility. His facial lines seemed more profound, the once-trimmed beard now scraggly and unkempt, the hair thinning and as white as ever, but his face visibly brightened up at seeing her.

"Haleema, what a pleasant surprise. We're not often off shift at the same time. You want coffee?" he asked.

He wore a dressing gown with pyjamas underneath and black slippers.

"I'm sorry I'm not dressed," he added quickly.

She hugged him and then walked into his compact but modern living quarters.

"No problem," she replied.

The default large media screen on the wall displayed a list of announcements related to shifts and work patterns, a constant reminder of their monotonous lives. A digital bank of approved movies and series could be accessed, but it was limited, and most of those C-class employees had worked their way through the decent ones.

"Coffee sounds good," Haleema mused aloud and continued, "How are you keeping, Dad?"

Karim prepped the coffee jug behind the kitchen bar, pulled two mugs from the cupboard, and mumbled in response.

"Sorry, Dad?"

"As well as can be," her father said more clearly.

The mood in the tiny room was sombre. The reality of their situation that they were imprisoned underground, the fact that they were being forced to work for their new masters had also quickly sunk in, and finally that there seemed no way out of their maze. And as that realisation grew, Karim's hopes that his wife and Haleema's mother would join them had wilted on the vine.

Haleema had argued that bringing her here would make her a prisoner too. She missed her mother terribly, but getting her to this place? It didn't make sense.

"But at least we would all be together," he repeatedly said. As it seemed the ruling council in the facility would not allow it, it was a moot argument anyway, as far as Haleema was concerned. But, if a significant global event happened, as all these nuclear fallout tests she was doing suggested, perhaps she should be here. She was completely torn as to what was the best thing to do.

Karim brought the coffee jug and mugs to the table on a tray as Haleema checked her watch.

"You have to be somewhere?"

Haleema helped pour the coffee. "Yes," she said.

Karim shuffled back to the kitchen area, returned with a round tin, and beamed at his daughter as he opened it. Inside were small light cakes – fragrant flavours such as rose, cardamom, saffron and almond. The release of their smell was instantaneous.

"Oh, how did you get these?" She took one and studied it with rapt pleasure before taking a small bite.

"Incredible."

"Ivan – my friend works in the stores. You know they are bringing more and more supplies, enough to feed a city! He took these as a sample. They have many luxury things like this. Dry fruits, fruit preserves, fine wines, coffee." Haleema nodded. That tied in with the supplies rumour her colleague, Laura, mentioned in the gym.

"But he also said there are whole aqua pod gardens for growing vegetables and fruit, laboratories for growing meat, bakeries," her father continued, "I mean a whole ecosystem set up somewhere down here."

Haleema sipped her black coffee and nodded thoughtfully.

"That's what your friend said he saw."

"Oh yes," her father confirmed.

"That'll be our masters in the council, living like emperors while we scrape by on the processed shit they produce. Don't get into trouble, Dad. I don't know what would happen if they found out. Tell your friend to be careful."

Karim held up one of the small cakes and winked at her. "It's just cake, Haleema." Then he popped it into his mouth and rolled his eyes in mock ecstasy. She laughed and took another. "And a very nice cake indeed."

It was amazing how small things could lighten the darkest of moods.

After ten minutes, Haleema glanced at her watch. It was an old Casio digital wristwatch she'd found in the IT stores. She still had time to check out this report on all the incoming supplies for herself.

"I have to go," she said reluctantly, standing up.

"You have a breakfast date or something?" her father said teasingly.

"I'll tell you sometime, but not now."

Karim looked at her, intrigued.

"Then, I hope you are careful, too," he concluded more seriously as his daughter exited the apartment.

***

From the section of the walkway that gave a partial view of a transport road below, Haleema could see a continuous line of automated electric trucks moving in the same direction deeper into the vast underground facility.

The silent trucks cast continuous flickering shadows across the curved walls arching overhead like an old movie reel.

She edged against the wall and glanced both ways before bringing out an old Android phone that she switched on and held down in the palm of her hand. As it booted up, she heard a noise further down the winding walkway like the creaking in a ship's hull – the distant echo of voices.

Haleema checked the phone, opened the camera app, pointed it at the trucks and took rapid photos. She then moved along the walkway, found a different position, and took a few more.

Then, she returned to her work section on the fifth level, passing several other 'station dwellers', workers, operatives, and security. After so many months here, she knew many familiar faces. However, the number of new faces had increased in the previous few weeks. This place was getting busy.

It was time to make a report to Joe.

She turned into one of the tunnel walkways, took an escalator back up to the fifth level, and headed to the service cupboard.

Haleema opened the door, slipped inside and closed it behind her. A thin strip of frosted windows near the ceiling provided enough light from the corridor for her to see what she was doing. She could not risk switching on the light for fear of being detected.

In the L-shaped cupboard, more like a storage room, she had access to the tools to communicate updates to Joe Bowen in relative privacy.

She rooted around in one of the plastic boxes filled with tech equipment, looking for the old laptop she had previously used, and fired it up. There were two parallel lines of ceiling-high industrial shelves, behind which she could clear a small hiding space in case she was disturbed. It would be tough to explain what she was doing there. Ideally, she would have worked between the shelving lines, but it was too cramped, so Haleema placed the laptop in a space on the front shelves furthest away from the door and fired it up.

Her communications with the outside world had to be carefully managed to avoid detection. Her first procedure involved using a VPN to cloak her IP address. She connected remotely to access the external internet. Once she connected, she opened Icarus, the encryption comms tool. She typed a message, attached photos of the trucks and sent the bundle via the external link she had hacked.

As the progress bar on the laptop edged along painfully slowly as the message was being sent, Haleema strained to listen for any noises from outside in case she was disturbed.

***

When Fagan first saw the aquarium display on the screen, it had been a mesmerising sight, and it had been easy for him to be fixated on the brightly illuminated images it displayed, but now he barely glanced up at it. The scene could be changed to anything, cityscapes of New York, Paris, London or even the dusty red dunes of Mars, but Fagan never bothered to change it. He sipped his noodle soup at the glass table, set in the circular apartment pod, one of the hundreds allotted to those who served the cabal, laughingly known as the 'penthouses'. Apart from the curved sofa, a couple of plastic plants, and a few personal items, there was nothing much there to speak of. The rules for bringing anything in of your own were strictly applied.

He had been pulled from a tech corp and recruited into Faber and Xael as an IT Security consultant. Then, he was IT lead before being drafted into the new order. Until a few weeks ago, Fagan had been on short contracts at Station 12, with most of his time in London working under Eva Villar, but now he had been transferred to the station full-time. That meant a long stint deep in this shithole.

Fagan finished his soup when the PDA he carried around with him beeped. This was nothing unusual. The internal comms system pumped out the alerts regularly. It would come over the radio or even the PA system if it were anything serious.

Nevertheless, Fagan couldn't help himself and picked up the device. It was an alert for a small spike in external web traffic. Most of the enormous underground facilities had an internal network. Any activity such as browsing or file transfer on the broader internet was only for the privileged and trusted few and heavily monitored. An alert meant larger data packets for that time of day or other unusual activity. The only locations in Station 12 that used an external network were the central comms room and a few workstations with only authorised access.

Fagan stood up, stepped over to his internal phone, and rang the comms room. No answer. Then, he tried the desks of a specific workstation. He could have located the IP address on his workstation, but doing it from his apartment would take too long, so he phoned them.

"Commissary Facilities Room?" came the reply, "Officer Kelly speaking."

"It's Fagan. I've just been alerted to external web traffic – are you hitting it with anything?"

"No, sir. I just came in from lunch, and there's no one else here."

Fagan slammed down the phone and immediately dialled the extension for the server rooms.

"Officer Jones?"

Fagan asked the same question.

"We have an internal test, so the external network has been switched off all day," came the reply.

"Ah yes, of course," Fagan replied. He already knew of this internal test but, at that moment, had forgotten.

So, who was accessing the internet?

He tried the comms room again – still, no answer.

He would walk there on the way back to his shift.

Fagan left for one of the walkway tunnels from his living quarters on the third level. Industrial lights buzzed overhead as he headed to a connection hub area that forked off in multiple directions. He passed other facility workers and various security patrols and, at the hub, walked down the east tunnel towards comms in the old part of the facility. Fagan had learned the central section was built between 1959 and 1968 with newer alterations and extensions in the 1990s under cover of the Denver airport development. And this was just one of many, all interconnected via an elaborate tunnel and transport system – all constructed in total secret.

As he approached the doorways of the comms room, a security guard held up his hand and asked for his ID.

"You still don't recognise me by now?" Fagan said, bristling.

"Sorry, Mr Fagan. We had a new order for making ID checks, no matter who it is."

Fagan complied with a scowl and headed into another vast circular room. Around the whole edge of the space, a bank of screens and distant tower blocks of computer machines interspersed with winking lights. Fagan's eyes narrowed, focusing on the few figures in the room, and then he spotted the comms room manager. She was a thin-faced woman with tied-back hair, leaning over a screen on the far side. He looked down at her screen: a blueprint 3D image of the comms system. A line of red error messages indicated a problem.

"I called, but no one answered," he growled.

The woman barely glanced round at him. "We've some issues with the internal phone lines. I'm just looking into it," she said evenly.

"Why wasn't I told?" Fagan went on, his irritation rising.

"It has only just occurred, and I'm telling you about it right now," she replied, matching his manner exactly.

Fagan didn't care for her tone, but he let it go. "I saw a bump in external traffic – anything to do with your department?" he continued, glancing around the lightly staffed room.

She stood up and faced him. "There's been a shutdown of all external communication today for testing. So no, there's no external web traffic from here."

Fagan nodded. "That's all I need to know. Just wanted to check." He gestured at the screen. "Keep me informed of the progress on this, will you? By radio, if that's still possible?"

"Yes, Mr Fagan."

He turned and headed back out, glancing down once again at his PDA, a nagging feeling tapping around the periphery of his mind that something wasn't right.

***

The last image had nearly been uploaded, and Haleema stood ready. When it was finally completed, and the whole package had been sent to Joe, Haleema sighed with relief, finally able to get out of there. With efficient speed, she packed the laptop back into the box, rearranged things as she had found, and headed for the cupboard door.

As was her habit, she peeked out along the corridor and was about to walk out when she heard the double doors further down the hall open, followed by the sound of footsteps moving towards her. She slowly closed the door, moved back into the L-shaped room, and slipped around the corner. The footsteps grew louder, then stopped outside the door.

She slid her petite frame between the two parallel lines of ceiling-high industrial shelves she had prepared earlier, just in case this happened and then crouched down just as the door opened and the light came on.

If the person came directly and stopped in front of her, there was a chance she would be seen through the gaps, but it was too late now.

Haleema sensed the shuffle of movement as someone moved along the side of the shelves. Slowly turning her head, she glimpsed the brown overalls of a male technician through a gap, standing but facing away from her. Then, a low murmuring of curses was under his breath as he pulled out a plastic box from the shelf in front of him and slammed it on the floor. He rifled through the computer parts and sighed out loud.

There was a whispered, "Aha!". The tech pulled something out that Haleema couldn't see and replaced the box in its place. Within a minute, he had gone, leaving Haleema crouched in the low-lit space, breathing heavily with her eyes closed.

A few minutes later, she slipped unseen out of the room.

Chapter 16

Back in her apartment, Zoe tossed her handbag down on the couch and slumped down next to it. She felt washed-out, empty, as if she had been running on autopilot. The surrounding high-rises cast dark shards against a grey, bleak sky, which seemed to dominate through the panoramic window. A light rain began to patter against the window, and Zoe dropped her face in her hands, breathing slowly to draw on any remaining courage she hoped to find.

"Would you like some soothing music?" came the voice of Goya, her intuitive monitoring system, intruding on Zoe's grief.

"Not now—" sighed Zoe.

"How about—"

"Just shut the fuck up."

Despite the grief, questions were scratching away just beneath the surface of her consciousness. Questions that she undoubtedly wanted to push away, to stifle with a pillow. In one way, it would be so easy for her to move on with her life; to ignore that Ed had jumped out of a window, apparently for no reason.

Finally, Zoe stood up, headed straight towards the open-plan kitchen, put on the kettle, and threw a herbal tea bag in her favourite mug decorated with a Manga-style cartoon cat.

Maybe Ed did have a reason? Perhaps he made some error at the bank, lost some clients millions, or more? But then she recalled her boss awarding Ed a bonus that morning and pushed that thought out of the equation. She finished making her tea, walked over to her handbag, fished out Ed's phone, and went straight to his email.

"Goya put me online," she commanded her monitoring system, which silently complied.

The large living room screen set into the main wall fizzed with aqua blue, and a Goya logo appeared.

"Trace a search on 'Banker Suicides in the UK'. Just in the last year or so."

On Ed's phone, she navigated to his emails again and began to go through them one by one. Various trade notifications and contract notes were connected to different client accounts. Each notice detailed the amount of the trades—all standard stuff, as far as Zoe could see.

A ping announced a list of results from the online search, which appeared on the big screen. As Zoe scanned them, her eyes fell on the very same story she had seen when she first found Ed's phone.

"Third story – open it up."

A Liberatus News article flashed up, and she stared at the headline momentarily, feeling that anxiety flutter inside her stomach.

"Send it to my tablet," she commanded and almost immediately heard the buzz of vibration from her iPad confirming the transfer.

She rose unsteadily from the sofa, tea clutched in her hand and went to the dining table that had become a makeshift desk with her work laptop, her iPad and a pile of reports left from when she was still working. She was still on extended leave and handed her remaining work chores to a colleague before heading to Ireland.

The same article was already on her browser tab, and she flicked her finger in upward strokes to scroll through. It was astonishing how many of these deaths there were, literally hundreds. She continued to scroll past a list of mainly middle-aged males in the fifty to seventy age range. According to the accompanying copy, there was a woman in her mid-twenties who was a mother of two who worked for an investment fund, Bayer and Harlow, as a VP Portfolio manager. Apparently, she loved trekking and travel, and her husband claimed that, as a couple, they had never been happier, just before she had slit her own throat in a hotel bathroom while on a business trip. Incidentally, the weapon was never found, yet it was still deemed a suicide by the local police.

"What the hell?"

She continued scrolling down the list with her fingertips, and the face of a young man, obviously in his twenties, fresh-faced, vibrant with a touch of arrogance, had recently thrown himself in front of a train. This was again deemed a suicide.

Then, with a jolt, she saw a face she recognised from her days at Cambridge University. It was of someone called Alan Walgrave, one of the students who had been on her Economics course. She hadn't been very close to him but remembered him as an intelligent, well-measured, self-assured person who always walked on the line. She read on; he had gone to work for London Capital Group as a futures trader. Then she took a deep breath as she read the following paragraph:

"Walgrave jumped off his twenty-second-floor balcony in

Manhattan."

Oh god.

On the surface, it seemed like a misadventure, as his death had been proclaimed, but from what Zoe could remember of him personally, Walgrave was a million miles away from being the type of person to take his own life.

Just like Ed was.

As she contemplated this, Zoe remembered that she knew someone in futures trading at London Capital. What was her name?

Tessa.

She switched over to her phone and flicked through the contacts.

Tessa Wilcox.

Zoe paused for a second and then tapped the green phone icon to make the call. After various failed attempts to connect, Zoe finally got through to the correct number only to find an answering service with Tessa's voice on the line asking callers to leave her a message.

Zoe started to speak when a female voice came on. "Hello?"

"Oh, hi, is that Tessa Wilcox?" asked Zoe.

"Speaking."

"This is Zoe Bowen – from ZEOS banking group. We've met a few times – most recently at the LBI Christmas party at Oxo Tower?"

The party, held almost a month before, had been a lavish affair. The London banking industry had begun to hold extravagant shindigs, inviting key players from different banking institutions. The most recent one was a Brazilian Samba theme, and the entertainment involved beach bars, troupes of dancing girls, and unlimited expensive booze.

"Oh yeah, Zoe? I remember our chat. What a night! How are you, and to what do I owe this pleasure?"

Tessa was well educated, her accent bordering on Etonian, like many of her fellow students in those days, and quite a few had followed through into the financial industry.

"I'll cut to the chase then, Tessa. This might seem slightly out of the blue, but I'll say it. Did you know Alan Walgrave very well?" adding, "I have only just found out that he has died."

There was a pause. "Oh, Alan. Such a tragedy. Yes, and you knew him from Cambridge, didn't you? I remember you saying that at the party." Tessa paused and continued, "God, what a waste of..." She trailed off.

"Yes. Horrible," Zoe replied. "I guess I just wanted to clarify the story that he... You don't mind talking about it, do you?"

"No, fine. When we heard of his death, it shocked us to the core. The guy was solid and happy. Had a great girlfriend. He seemed to be doing well. He had been given an exclusive client account. Going up in the world. Yes, yes, tragic—"

"So the report of how he died was true?"

"Yes, yes. As far as we know, anyway. Our manager pulled us all together the following day and told us. We were stunned." Tessa spoke with grim acceptance as if it was something everyone was getting used to.

"I see. Well, thanks for talking to me. I guess I just wanted to – talk it through," said Zoe uncertainly.

"No problem," Tessa replied, perhaps sensing Zoe's own shock about the loss of their mutual friend.

"You said he had an exclusive account? Can you remember who?"

"Yes, Bayer – Bayer and Harlow?" Tessa said.

"Yes, of course. I'm sorry. Well, thank you, Tessa. Bye."

Zoe ended the call, pulled up her Facebook account, and searched for Alan Walgrave. There were quite a few, but she managed to find the right man after a few minutes and clicked on his public photos. There were a series of usual holiday snaps with an attractive girl, presumably his girlfriend – more of the same in various expensive restaurants, with friends. Then, one came up of Alan, arms around another suited man his age, smiling at the camera at a conference.

She leaned back on the sofa and stared out the window at the bleak sky and a lone gull hanging aloft on the cold wind, its white feathers bright against the solemn grey clouds.

The 'mortality rate' of those within her industry was literally through the roof, yet outside this elite group, it was hardly known. It was certainly never mentioned by the mainstream media.

Zoe couldn't shake a feeling of increasing dread. Nothing tangible yet, but a growing sense that there was much more under the surface behind this awful mortality rate.

Chapter 17

Dressed for more relentless cold and rain, Zoe left her apartment and took her usual route through the narrow roads of the housing estate, around the new builds and walkways, and past the little café bars that spanned the dock and canal waterfronts. Apart from the odd person sipping a cappuccino, most of them were nearly empty, the baristas wiping down the tables, eager to leave.

As she headed through the winding estate towards Canada Water station, a gloom had descended, and building lights were coming on already, despite it not even being 4 o'clock.

She took a long way to her destination instead of taking the ferry but didn't mind the walk. It gave her time to tune out from the questions swirling around her head, if only for a while.

Arriving at Canada Water station, she stepped onto an almost empty carriage on the waiting underground train for the short trip to Canary Wharf.

Was she really doing this? She had the ominous feeling that once she started down this path of digging into what really happened to Ed, it would be hard to turn back.

As the train moved off, Zoe typed a text to her manager explaining she might go into the office to get a few things. Officially, she had taken leave for the rest of the month.

Minutes later, she was walking out from the steel arches of the Canary Wharf station and across the plaza towards her work building that loomed over her, a tower of dark glass.

She walked into the marble-floored lobby, went through the security barriers and headed up to the fortieth floor in the glass elevator. She scanned her pass and went through the open reception area, then onto the vast trading floor, a sea of desks with monitors. One line of desks had twelve screens stacked up in two rows – the control centres, as her colleagues called them. There was a low bluish light as some screens had been left on, and, at the very end, a line of larger dark monitors usually displayed the market trade data – on standby. The office was closed for the bank holiday, and Zoe didn't think she had ever seen it as empty.

In a few days, the place would be alive, noisy and filled with the hum of the relentless silent cycle of the money-go-round. The adrenaline and excitement had truly motivated Zoe in her first years, but now she felt glad she wouldn't be in this place to see it.

Zoe walked straight up to Ed's old desk and sat down. It had been cleared of all his personal belongings, wiped down and ready for the next trader coming up the ranks. She closed her eyes, then hit the power button and took out Ed's mobile phone.

She typed in the password she knew he normally used, his date of birth backwards, and then an empty field box appeared for the one-time access code. On clicking on the Send icon, Ed's phone buzzed with the list of numbers, and she typed them in.

His desktop image appeared, with a panoramic desktop picture looking out across the fields of Spain, showing the

Sierra Nevada mountains in the distance. Zoe recognised it immediately simply because she was there when he took the photo.

Memories flooded back instantly, and Zoe fought the sadness that threatened to engulf her again. At least they hadn't deactivated his computer yet. Otherwise, her journey to her workplace would have been a complete waste of time.

After a few clicks with the mouse, she opened his email inbox and trading records software records, which listed the trades in more detail.

She clicked on one of the trades and scanned the emails inside.

Bayer & Harlow trading through account 713. This was where all the financial transactions took place related to that client.

There was a flicker of recognition.

She read a few other trade notification emails from the last few months, hundreds of them not unusual in their line of work. Most were call options betting on the rise of Pithcore Gen for the same client: Bayer & Harlow. A quick search told Zoe Pithcore was a bio-science corporation that stood to gain from any global food supply disruption with their promotion of Pithcore's genetically modified food products.

Then there were reams of put options, betting on the rise of food commodity prices, especially grains. Other trade notes displayed put against the Chinese stock market average and dozens of other companies Zoe had never heard of. The figures were absolutely staggering, hundreds of millions in various currencies, from the dollar to the Chinese Yuan. All were pushed through by Bayer & Harlow and seemingly increasing in the last few months.

She picked up her phone and revisited the social media

profile of that woman who had slit her own throat in the hotel and wrote down her name on a notepad: Lexi Karl.

She pulled up the Goya search engine on the main screen and typed in "Bayer & Harlow Lexi Karl". Their website came up, and the unfortunate Lexi was listed as one of their traders. B & H were an investment group that had used Zoe's employers, ZEOS and their trading arm for a list of relentless deals.

She looked into the Corporation Status records online. B & H were owned by Faben & Xael Group, a multinational investment firm with hundreds of trillions in assets. She dug deeper and immediately saw they held majority stakes in Cryostone, Salbio Corp and Pithcore Gen, not to mention Bayer & Harlow.

Zoe could almost hear the pieces clicking together in her mind, and the enormity of it all was beginning to emerge. Scanning the information again, she focused on one name in particular.

Cryostone.

That name was especially familiar to her. Her brother Joe had talked about them once. Key directors, shareholders and other personnel of that organisation had gone missing on Flight 313. After a certain amount of time, the whole company and its military technology had gone to the Faben & Xael Group. A group, she noted, with one Jason Runeshield as a very significant shareholder.

All these pieces. How were they all interconnected? Her head was spinning with information overload, and a dull pain now ebbed in her head.

She needed to map all this out and talk it over with someone. She needed to talk to her brother, Joe.

Chapter 18

"I'm in the building. Can it wait?" Eva Villar said sharply into her mobile phone.

"Yes, probably. It's just some alerts that you'll want to look over. I wasn't sure if they were urgent," Kai Martins replied. Officially, he was Kacper Fagan's replacement as her deputy but had also been instrumental in the 'wet work' as part of recent operations.

Eva walked briskly, the sound of her heels on the marble floor echoing around her, phone held tight against her ear. Behind a huge, long desk that ran parallel to one wall, the faces of two security guards glanced up. Behind them, the mammoth chrome Faben & Xael logo glinted from the invading sunlight that flooded down from the arched glass roof of the lobby area.

"I'll look at them when I'm up. See you in five." She disconnected the call, swiped her access card at the security access, and then walked through the barrier towards the escalators that led up to a mezzanine area.

Suited employees could be seen through the silent glass elevators that ferried them up and down the multiple floors of the building.

She stepped into the elevator, tapped the button for the forty-seventh floor and scrutinised her face in the mirrored wall. Her sharp features seemed exaggerated, her usually vibrant auburn hair seeming duller than usual. Clearly, the increased workload was taking its toll.

Eva closed her eyes for a second.

No time for weakness or slowing down now. Her masters were watching closely. She would be judged, rewarded, or punished for how the operation fared in the coming weeks.

With a soft sigh, the doors opened before she knew it, and Eva stepped onto the forty-seventh level, where the corporation security offices spanned the whole floor.

She greeted a few of her colleagues with a thin smile and a perfunctory good morning nod. Pleasantries were not in her nature, and being friendly or getting too close to other employees was a chore she preferred to avoid.

Security was a serious business to Eva Villar. The security at Faber & Xael and her broader mission were a priority above even her own life.

Eva approached her private corner office, swiped her card across the access panel and, once inside, placed her handbag and laptop bag on one of the chairs surrounding a meeting table. Through the expansive windows, the hazy London skyline was a monotone grey. Stark and bleak.

There was a tap at her open door as she moved around behind her desk.

"Ms Villar?" A shaven-headed Kai Martins stood there with a tray holding a jug of coffee with two cups. He was a large and intimidating-looking man rugged face with the demeanour of an ex-military man, having run the gauntlet of security, assassination and mercenary gigs throughout his post-army life. He had snuffed out more than his fair share of lives.

Yet he was quietly spoken, polite and more intelligent than

his appearance suggested.

Perfect for the job Eva had chosen him for.

"Morning, Kai. Thank you for bringing coffee. Let's look at these alerts, shall we?"

After pouring out the coffee, Martins pulled up a chair to the desk, pulled out his tablet and swiped the screen as Eva accessed her security system on her desktop computer.

"What have we got?" Eva sipped on her coffee.

"An automated alert last night was triggered from an employee machine out of office hours," Martins said, glancing at his tablet.

Eva scrolled through her seemingly endless emails.

"Someone doing overtime? Not unusual," she mused out loud

She found the alert and clicked on it.

Martins shot her a glance. "It's unusual in the fact it's an ex-employee account."

Eva saw the name and immediately recognized it.

Ed Flanagan.

He had been on the list of key figures who had needed to be taken out of the picture.

"He's dead, right?" Eva asked.

"I know he is," Martins said.

"So, who was accessing his emails?" Eva asked casually.

She read through the report that his email had been accessed via Flanagan's desktop again after his death. Someone had obviously been snooping around.

"Thank you, Kai. Leave this with me. I'll look into it and let you know if I need anything."

Martins gave her a sideways glance, then stood up, retrieved his coffee mug from the desk and left the office.

When the door closed, Eva logged into the Faber & Xael security account, which gave her top-level access to a surveillance system developed by the company itself. A red icon next to Ed Flannagan's name confirmed that the alert script, which had been covertly installed on Ed Flanagan's main work machine, had been activated. The same script had been installed on countless other devices used by personnel to keep Eva in the loop with her army of assets in the banking and trade industry and used the information that she had accumulated to gradually take them out of the picture, one by one. Her 'zombie assets'.

Clicking on Ed's name brought up a list of file links linked to his devices: his work computer, laptop and phone. Eva clicked on the phone icon that revealed a list of files and actual audio recordings of all his calls.

That could wait and would take time to go through. The main proof was in the script of remote control malware on Ed's laptop, which had hijacked the camera, installed long before his death.

It would reveal the face of the snooper.

She clicked through on his work PC link that opened a new window and smiled as a series of images appeared.

A young woman, no older than thirty with shoulder-length blonde hair, stared at the screen with a concentrated frown. Her face dropped slightly as she read something, clearly unaware of the camera recording her.

Eva's mind began ticking over. Was she a fellow employee? Or there was the possibility she was British Intelligence, police or a private investigator.

Whoever she was, Eva was determined she would find out soon enough.

Sipping more coffee, she picked up her phone and spoke to her secretary.

"Jenny, clear my diary for this morning. I'm not to be disturbed either, thanks."

She replaced the phone and continued to stare at the image of the young woman frozen on the monitor screen.

Where to begin her search?

Whoever this woman was snooping around was obviously connected to Ed Flanagan. So she pulled up his file, which contained a vast information resource on the former trader. It included everything from his main life events, personal financial info, and logins for a few critical websites sourced from the malware. It had been necessary always to keep close tabs on their zombie assets. After giving this financial information a cursory glance, she scanned the phone records of Flanagan's mobile before focusing on his social media fingerprint. Most people hardly realise how much of their privacy could be broken just by viewing social media profiles.

She logged into his account on Facebook and began going through his photos. It wasn't long before she spotted the familiar face. She had been involved with the asset, cuddling up to him in a holiday snap. There were many others, and within a minute, Eva had a name.

Zoe Bowen.

It had taken time as meticulous research and cross-referencing of the information does, but by lunchtime, Eva found she had a comprehensive file on this snooper.

Bowen had been born and raised in London. Her parents were Frank Bowen and Maria Amerman Chapman.

Siblings: Zak and Joe.

She had graduated with honours at Cambridge in Economics

before taking a gap year in Asia. Then she snapped up an offer of a placement at ZEOS bank, where she met and became involved with Edward Flanagan, a co-worker.

That made sense to Eva. Leaning back in her chair and steepling her fingers, Eva could understand the logic if just for a fleeting moment. This young woman was trying to dig into her lover's death. Naturally, she was trying to find out what happened, but, on this occasion, seemed to be taking it a step further than the average person.

Nothing she could prove, Eva summarised, and she wasn't particularly worried. The emails this Bowen woman had accessed were perfectly legal trades. There was just a hell of a lot of them.

Still, who knows which dots she might start joining if she peeled the onion too much?

As Eva dug further into Bowen's family, alarm bells began to chime like those from a church across a valley on a foggy morning. The father, Frank, was nowhere to be seen on the internet. A few news stories from the nineties of an incident in Hong Kong had been deleted from several news sites. She kept looking until she found one story that had been missed on the way back machine: the helpful tool to see websites from the past. She read the scanned text from a Hong Kong news site dated September 1991, although it must have been uploaded many years later as the public internet did not exist then.

Eva zoomed in and read the text.

Hong Kong authorities are searching for UK citizen Frank Bowen in connection with the recent terrorist attacks where several explosions rocked the city. On the MTR underground train to Causeway Bay, the first bomb was quickly followed by a blast on the North Point-bound tram at Chun Yeung Street market. Police would not answer further questions in regards to the suspect.

That was it. There was no other mention online, apart from stories about the incident. Someone holding the strings must have cleaned it up and wiped it from history – a common intelligence tactic. Eva made a mental note to investigate further and moved on to the siblings.

Official records revealed her brother Joe was involved in Liberatus, an organisation on several watch lists, headed up by John Rhodes, of whom she was well aware. That would need a closer look.

Then she looked at Zak, the younger brother who had migrated to the US and was a chief intelligence officer in the CIA.

Eva leaned back in her chair and stared at the screen.

What was happening here? Was this all connected? Was she a CIA asset recruited by her brother?

A feeling of distinct uneasiness swept over her. She quickly drained her coffee, moved over to a wall safe, dialled in a combination, and opened it to reveal several leather briefcases and a military-grade laptop. She pulled out the computer, started it up, then logged into the Ghost 13 intelligence portal and began a more in-depth search.

Eva held her breath and read that Frank Bowen worked for MI6 during the nineties. After that, his file was classified, and even Eva's access was denied. She made another mental note that his handler had been Carl Paterson.

Interesting and worrying at the same time.

Next, Eva searched for Joe Bowen—service as a Sergeant in the K company of Royal Marines 42 Commando, British Army. Long travelling stint and currently working for Liberatus in the Spanish arena.

It felt like she had opened a can of worms, and her confidence that the whole operation was running smoothly now seemed to be evaporating fast.

Her mind began to race, and she had to move, to think. She paced, then stared out across the London cityscape. A glint of sun in the distance through the dark clouds blanketed the city.

Time to request an 'ECHELON package' on this one, Eva thought. The world's most powerful surveillance satellite network, the Five Eyes network, would have no problem tapping into Zoe Bowen's phones and email.

Chapter 19

In his VIP Bell 430 helicopter, Jason Runeshield let his gaze drift across the Denver skyline and the cluster of skyscrapers ahead. The breaking dawn sky, with its strips of pink and yellow clouds against the faded backdrop of the Rocky Mountains, made it particularly picturesque. He'd seen it hundreds of times from this altitude. It was one of his favourite places in the US.

As the helicopter positioned itself above the landing pad on the rooftop of the Faben & Xael building, Jason glanced down at the security guard dressed in a dark suit, wearing shades, waiting for his arrival. The chopper began its descent, buffeting the wind of its downdraft across the helipad, violently tugging at the suit of the waiting security guard until it had touched down. The pilot cut the engine, and as the rotors gradually began to wind down, the security guard bobbed under the slowing blades and yanked open the door. Jason climbed onto the pad and headed across to the walkway leading down to the building entrance.

Walking into his penthouse office suite, he tossed his briefcase onto one of the leather sofas arranged around a wide, circular coffee table with touchscreen technology.

"Open blinds," he muttered. Goya followed his command,

activating the slats that whirred into action, flooding the suite with sunlight and revealing ceiling-to-floor windows to display a spectacular view of downtown Denver. His polished mahogany desk, a curved semi-circle resembling a cake segment, was set in one corner of the suite, with a leather and chrome recliner parked behind it. Just then, a polite knock at the door. A sharp-suited young woman with dark hair tied back into a bun entered carrying a tray with an ornate silver coffee pot, cream jug and one cup. She placed it down on the low table, rattling the cutlery as Jason waited in uncomfortable silence, then straightened up and turned to her boss. She was about to speak when he raised a finger to his lips. She nodded with understanding and quickly left.

Jason sat down at his desk, swivelled the chair around to face the view of Colorado and waited. He looked at his Swiss gold watch—6:35 a.m.

The phone on the desk rang, and he turned back around and picked it up.

"Jason Runeshield."

"Mr Runeshield," came the voice from reception. "Your secretary is on the line. He says it's an urgent matter."

"Put him through."

The line emitted a series of clicks before Jason heard his secretary, Jim Linfield, speak.

"Mr Runeshield?" The tone of the voice on the line was grave.

"Jim?"

"I'm afraid I have some terrible news—" There was a pause. "Your father – he was found this morning. I'm afraid he's passed away, sir."

Jason exhaled a long, controlled breath.

"When was this discovered?" Jason asked, his tone remaining carefully neutral.

"About ten minutes ago, sir, he was found in his bedroom. One of the house servants received no answer and went in." The secretary paused briefly and then continued elaborating, "His doctor has just arrived, but there's no doubt—"

Jason let out a sigh. "He had numerous health problems. It could have been any number of things."

"Will you be coming over, sir? I can make arrangements—"

Jason let another pause hang. "I'm sorry, it's a bit of a shock."

"I understand, sir. Please accept my sincere condolences."

"Thank you, Jim. There could be many ramifications to this news. I need a tight lid on this getting out too soon. Please keep it to yourself, and I'll be back in touch as soon as possible."

"Certainly. You can count on me. I'll await your call."

Jason replaced the handset and leaned back in the recliner, allowing himself a thin smile.

***

Several hours later, Jason entered the main conference room set on the upper floors of the Faben & Xael building. He had arranged the emergency meeting for the council of thirteen, and due to the urgent development, he was determined to strike while the pieces were in flux. He tapped the GoyaMeta app on his phone and put on a pair of Augmented Reality (AR) smart glasses that appeared no different from regular sunglasses. The AR glasses overlaid a virtual reality onto the real one; as other council members logged in to their conference rooms, they appeared to Jason through the glasses in his meeting room. Laurent Wolf appeared as an animated avatar. He looked grave and uncertain, clearly caught off guard. Jason thought he must be logging in from a computer and viewing the meeting through a regular screen.

Kalb Runeshield, Jason's uncle, had risen from his bed, which may as well have been his deathbed. Jason observed him with hidden disdain. Dishevelled and particularly aged-looking this morning, the man was clearly knocking on Death's door, and Jason didn't consider him a threat to his plans of any kind. Natan Helms, the senator Jason knew was needed to play a vital role in the months ahead, clasped his hands together with a look of bemusement at the hastily arranged meeting. He knew something was up.

Henry Oberman, the CEO of ZEOS bank, looked immaculate – his white shirt and light suit in direct contrast with his dark skin. His vote would come to Jason, guaranteed. The others, Robert Heller, head of Cyrostone, the military technology corporation so vital in their plans, would also vote for Jason. Like Jason himself, they were the younger half of the council, mostly in their forties and fifties, and it was their time now, Jason thought, his fist tightening by his side.

Natan Helms, Laurent Wolf and Mendes Runeshield, his aunt, would definitely vote for his uncle. They were the old guard, near death yet clinging to the reins of power until the last breath and would not change their minds. Besides, Jason had picked the target of the blackmailing very carefully.

Jason shot Laurent Wolf a glance, acknowledged the table and took his seat. The absence of Leob, the driving force and head of the council, was evident to all. There were glances from some of the assembled toward his empty chair.

"Gentleman and Mendes," Jason intoned, acknowledging

the assembly before continuing. "Firstly, my apologies for this sudden calling of the eighty-ninth meeting of the Council of Thirteen. I have just heard the grave news concerning my father, Leob Runeshield." He paused for dramatic effect. "He passed away last night..." He paused again, letting the gravity of that news sink in. Faces that were confused earlier turned grave, followed by mutters of condolences.

Jason wiped his eyes, looking down onto the oval tabletop, then held up his hand as if to halt the murmuring.

"Thank you all for your concern. There will be a send-off befitting that of a great man who has contributed greatly to spreading our ideals, making our utopian vision a much closer reality."

"This is a sad occasion, but we must stay focused now. The rules are clear. A new ballot is required for the council leadership. To take place immediately."

There was a long pause before Jason's uncle spoke. He was the brother of his father but a mere shadow in terms of the power he wielded within the council. Yet even with this weak position that paled into relative insignificance in the Council of Thirteen, he held more power than most CEOs of major corporations.

"Jason. Who are the nominees?" he asked. More glances around the table. It was common knowledge that it could only be between the two remaining male Runeshield family members.

Jason smiled and held his hands out in a gesture of honesty. "Well, I would be lying if I didn't feel I was ready to take the council forward with the plans already in place, laid down by my father and his father before him. We're at a critical juncture right now. There can be no hesitation – not at this stage.

My father's—" Jason leaned on the table, as if for support as he paused, "—my father's death must not cause a single destruction – nothing will change, we go on toward 'Pale Horse' and the world beyond it."

All eyes turned to Kalb Runeshield. He tapped his finger on the table as if he were in the room itself, not just a virtual augmentation and leaned forward.

"I think we all agree on our responsibilities that need to remain intact," he glanced over at Natan Helms and then back around the table. "As Leob's brother and elder of the family, I believe I have first rights to the accession—"

Jason shook his head in disappointment. "Uncle. Of course, you have that right – no one is contesting that at all. I am just staking my claim here. The time is right to have...younger blood leading the council."

He looked around in defiance. "So, we take the vote?"

Everyone nodded in agreement except Kalb, who sat stony-faced, staring hard at the digital manifestation of his nephew.

Chapter 20

The golden liquid splashed against the bottom of the bowl-shaped crystal glass. After savouring its rich aroma, Jason sipped the vintage Napoleon brandy.

His efforts had finally paid off. That one vote which had assured his assuming leadership of the Council. Ordering his own father's death didn't even raise an iota of regret inside him. The sweeping aside of the old blood with their old ways was long overdue as far as Jason was concerned.

The death of his father was simply a means to an end.

Now, at last, the next chapter, the finale, could be opened, the planning of which had taken place over many decades and even centuries could finally move forward.

He looked up at the finely rendered portrait of his father, Leob, in its brass veneer ornate frame and held up his brandy tumbler in the form of a silent salute.

Farewell, Father.

A father who had been cold, indifferent and sometimes cruel.

Despite that, he respected the strength Leob had possessed. His duty was not to any of his children but to the order of the Baphomet. Their bloodline would continue, and the world would ultimately kneel before them. The awakening was coming, and that must be the priority.

Jason casually strolled along the gallery, past each painting of his descendants – the bloodline who had planted such vital milestones over the previous decades and centuries.

From his father to his grandfather, Leob II, all the way back to the five brothers who, in the 1800s, had established banks and money-lending companies in London, Paris, New York and Rome. Sent by their father, Mayer Runeshield, the brothers had set about with their plan. They stood together – young, poised and determined – in their long black coats, waistcoats and starched collars as befitted their stature in the era, standing together against a sepia-washed background.

Their concept was simple. Attain power and forge the world according to their vision.

And they knew how to go about it.

Dominate the financial systems and make much more money than their counterparts, lending to governments at every opportunity because taxes would always guarantee the debt. It was simple but brilliant.

The opportunity to extend this manner of thinking came with the war between England, its allies and France, especially the conflict that resulted in the Battle of Waterloo. As both armies approached the flashpoint, the stakes for the winner were huge. If Napoleon's army claimed victory, France would dominate Europe, and if they lost, England would hold the undisputed balance of power in Europe with an opportunity to expand its influence, and the power of France would surely recede.

The regular news updates from the war were brought home to England by horse-riding agents employed by the Runeshields. They understood perfectly that controlling the flow of information would be vital to their plans. A way of thinking that would inspire the take-over of newspapers and media in the decades to come.

The news they brought back to London, ahead of any other sources, was that Napoleon had won, defeating the combined troops of Britain and Prussia.

Fake news at its finest.

With carefully accumulated funds pooled across the banks they owned, Jason's ancestors funded both sides of the conflict. Jacob Runeshield's banks in Paris lent money to Napoleon, while Maurice Runeshield in London funded the British. It was a hedging strategy that they would continue to use to the current day, financing both sides of major conflicts across the world.

Sowing the seeds of destruction while getting rich from it.

And they continued to do so.

In 1916, while the first great war raged in Europe, a certain Leon Trotsky and a gang of Bolsheviks arrived in New York. They received guerrilla training by secret elements and, with $20 million worth of gold supplied by the Runeshields, they boarded the ship S.S. *Kristianiafjord* bound for Russia to start the Bolshevik revolution.

Soon after, when the revolution had succeeded, Russia's ruler, Tsar Nicholas II and his family were murdered on orders from the Runeshield-run cabal.

The tsar's opposition to their League of Nations charter, blocking their world government plan in 1815 at the Congress Of Vienna, and Tsar Alexander II siding with President Abraham Lincoln in 1864, had sealed that president's fate.

The Great War and new wars had been outlined in a letter by Albert Pike to Italian politician and fellow Freemason Giuseppe Mazzini, an associate of Jason's great-grandfather.

The planned wars.

The first Great War, Pike wrote, was to 'permit the cabal to overthrow the czars' power in Russia and make that country a fortress of atheistic Communism'.

From there, the great communist machine would rise, and a Second World War would be fomented by taking advantage of the differences between the Fascists and the political Zionists.

The cabal banks ensured this vision was realised by funding Hitler's Nazis' rise to power.

The cabal-engineered crash of 1929 also helped that rise, causing hyperinflation and chaos in Germany, from which the Nazis rose to power.

Since the Battle of Waterloo, The Runeshields had wasted no time increasing their influence and power base wherever they could, especially in America.

Jason smirked at the memory as he stepped onto the patio. The distant sprinklers hissed with the spray as they watered the vast lawns.

According to Jason's father, their master stroke had been to assassinate the leading bankers and wealthiest Americans of the time who were opposed to the Runeshield plans to create the Federal Reserve banking system.

The place of their 'assassination' would become one of the twenty-first century's most famous disasters: the sinking of the *Titanic*. All their enemies had been on board, and like the 9/11 attack that occurred eighty-nine years later, it had apparently taken an incredible amount of detailed planning by the dark agents of the cabal to pull it off. The brainwashing of the captain ensures his suicide mission. The switching of the *Titanic* with its near-identical sister ship, the *Olympic*, which had fundamental problems with its hull due to an extensive coal fire that had softened the metal on a previous voyage.

Or so his father had told him.

Jason finished his brandy and chuckled out loud. He had never been entirely convinced the *Titanic* story was true, but he had no doubt his family could have put all the parts in place and made it happen.

Either way, a year after the sinking, the cabal had virtual unopposed control of the central banking system in America and Europe.

A congressman at the time, Charles A. Lindberg Sr., had proclaimed: 'From now on, depressions will be scientifically created.'

He was right.

With complete control of the central banks, periods of inflation and deflation could be manipulated, and vast profits made. By inflating the money supply by sixty per cent, most of which poured into the stock market, the world's true rulers could manufacture booms. The process, of course, could just as easily be reversed with busts. When the lines of credit were suddenly snapped shut, traders had no choice but to sell, and the downward spiral of the stock market began.

Jason's thoughts wandered back to the Pike letters and the planning of a third world war. The predicted clash between the political zionists and the Islamic leaders had ebbed and flowed for decades. The funding of terrorists, the manipulation of the public view via mass media, the catalyst event of 9/11, and the turmoil in the Islamic states that followed. The rise of ISIS, its inevitable destruction and then, with the cabal's powerful influence, the resurrection in the guise of the new United Islamic State to light new fires of hell in the Middle East.

All were planned and shaped by the hidden hands of those elite controllers.

"All the world's a stage." Jason reflected on Shakespeare's ubiquitous genius in speaking to global truths

Some events, of course, happened outside the cabal's control. It was never smooth sailing, and there would always be unforeseen setbacks, but the stoking of the Middle Eastern fires had succeeded in general terms. The dirty bomb incident in Iran, the accusations of Turkey's involvement, and pulling in Russia had created a world on the brink.

The governments of the West seemed to be set for the inevitable hot war with China and Russia. Tensions were rising fast, and navy fleets and armies were positioned on the global playing board.

Jason smiled. None of that would matter in the end. It was all smoke and mirrors, for the actual event was now very clearly on the horizon.

The one event he had personally helped nurture and grow for decades, like so many seeds in the garden.

Now though, there was no one to stop them.

Chapter 21

White Butterfly.

It was a painting on the wall of the spacious corridor in the vast country house where he waited to be given details of his next assignment.

There were many other pictures in the house, mostly of century-old figures or battles from some different era that he did not understand.

But it was the butterfly that captured his attention.

He could see it, clear as if it were there now. It took him back to when he was a boy, seeing the butterfly settle on the wire lattice of his cage before it disappeared into the darkness. He had hoped it would come back, but it never did.

Not until the flames had burned him. Then, he saw it again, a vision in his mind. But it was as real to him as if it had been there, right in front of him.

He had been outwitted, well and truly. Would he meet his adversary, who was responsible for his defeat again? That Hugo Reese? He certainly hoped so. He would never forget him.

Jamall Salazar unconsciously lifted his hand to his face and felt the ridges on his skin as his memory returned to that night in Spain when a wall of flame had engulfed his whole body, and he had heard his screams for the first time.

He had bolted back into the grove of trees, dived and rolled his body repeatedly. Jamall was still aware of where he was, and some part of his training must have kicked in despite the searing pain from his burning clothes and skin.

His memory of what happened next was foggy, but somehow, he had found himself in an aqueduct ditch, cold water flowing all around him but which failed to soothe the fiery burns that ate at every inch of his body.

He had passed in and out of consciousness and sensed rather than saw the morning light of the dawn. Even with all the white noise that penetrated his skull, he caught the sound of distant sirens before finally passing out.

There had been voices, and Jamall had sensed himself being examined, injected, and then moved carefully onto a stretcher, all the while intense pain, like a swarm of hot ants under his skin, tormented and tortured his body. Hands attached an oxygen mask over his face, and Jamall felt himself being carried before passing out once again.

There were then further flashes of memory.

Jamall was in a private hospital room when he next awoke, hooked up to an IV drip.

Numb. Dehydrated.

How much time had passed? His memory of what happened came back in sporadic bursts.

His mission was—incomplete.

He tried to move and grunted with the effort. A nurse came over and spoke softly, but he couldn't make out the words at first. She leaned over with a pill tray.

"This will help with the pain," she said.

He slowly moved his right arm, which didn't seem so painful, took the tablet and put it into his dry mouth. The nurse then moved a glass of water closer to his mouth, and Jamall took sips.

"There is someone to see you," she said before heading to the room.

Through puffy eyes, Jamall saw a figure stand up from a chair at the end of the room. His body flinched, and his muscles tensed. He was exposed: they would kill him.

The tall figure, a man dressed in a light grey cotton shirt, moved closer. Jamall recognised the familiar, steel-rimmed spectacles and thin, blond hair.

It was his padre, Dr Red. His controller.

The doctor looked down at him and his bandaged limbs and torso.

"You did well. When you are well enough, I will be getting you moved back to the US for specialist treatment. I am getting a private jet converted, so you'll be comfortable."

"Thank you, Padre. Where am I now?" Jamall sighed through his cracked lips.

"You're in the burn correction unit at Quirónsalud University Hospital – Madrid. The best place right now. You'll need to stay here for a few weeks."

The doctor turned away and went to the window.

"You're one of the best. I need you back on your feet."

"Yes, Padre," Jamall mumbled.

The following months, based in a military medical facility in Colorado, it had been a painful rehabilitation and recovery process for Jamall. He received the best treatment globally, and the successive skin graft operations patched up the worst of the burns.

He was then transferred to a secretive training camp overseen by the Project 114 team headed by Doctor Red, who had 'nurtured' Jamall since he was a child in the Project Monarch programme, along with many other children. All were reared to be the perfect agents and killers.

Jamall regained his strength over a year of brutal training until he was ready to do the cabal's bidding once again.

A voice snapped Jamall back into the present, where he sat waiting in the grand hallway. A bodyguard Jamall had not seen before had come out of the Georgian doors and gestured to him.

"Mr Runeshield will see you now."

Jamall entered the vast living room. A crystal chandelier hung over a velvet corner sofa, and chairs arranged around a French Baroque-style coffee table. A series of French doors overlooked a sprawling estate.

Jason Runeshield stood by the fireplace, a brandy snifter in his hand. Behind him was a large portrait of an older man, and Jamall immediately recognised the similar features, the same thin lips and jawline.

It was Jason's father, who Jamall had been ordered to kill.

This man must have ordered his own father's death. Where else would the order have come from? He made no further assumption as to why.

The burglar diversion had accomplished the goal of accessing Leob Runeshield's private quarters, where they could surreptitiously poison the jug of water on his side table.

As Runeshield walked across to greet him, Jamall felt unsure why he had been ushered to see someone who was way above his Padre, Doctor Red, in the food chain.

It must be important. Very important.

"Mr Salazar. Can I call you Jamall?"

Jamall nodded, and they shook hands.

"Yes, of course, Mr Runeshield."

Runeshield grinned with a wolfish leer and gestured to the ornate silk-covered sofas.

"Take a seat. Drink?"

Jamall declined, and both men sat down opposite each other.

"The doctor tells me you have recovered well. He briefed me on the details. I'm sorry to hear about your ordeal."

"It was unfortunate," Jamall responded with just a hint of bitterness.

"Indeed. I'm sure the doctor will arrange to deal with those responsible."

"With respect, Mr Runeshield, I would like that to be my remit."

Runsehield nodded thoughtfully and sipped his brandy. "Of course."

He purposefully put his crystal glass on the coffee table with an emphatic chink.

"Bear in mind we have other work for you that needs to take priority," he said icily.

"Following my orders always takes priority, sir."

"Good. Because I have a very, very special project for you."

Chapter 22

"Hi, you OK, Zee?" The sound of her brother's familiar voice brought a smile to Zoe's face

"Yeah, I'm good," she replied.

"Just need to sound out some things with you."

There was a pause at the other end of the call, and then Joe cleared his throat and continued, "Let's switch to Icarus."

"Alright."

Five minutes later, Zoe and Joe re-connected their conversation using the encrypted phone chat app on the video channel. She had her earphones in and sat on a bench by the Thames, holding the phone in landscape mode. It was a rare, bright, but chilly January morning. Overhead, contrails formed streaks across a deep blue sky, and upriver, opposite her spot, the houses of Parliament were bathed in the yellow morning light.

"Everything going OK in SA?" she asked.

Joe had been vague about his exact location or even which country he was in, but it was par for the course with him nowadays. All she knew was he had flown to South America a few weeks earlier and, judging by the video screen, seemed to be sitting on a balcony with a screen of thick trees behind him, with the distant sound of exotic-sounding birds.

"Always loved this part of the world. Lots of rainfall recently, so it's nice and fresh at the moment," Joe responded in a convivial tone.

"Sounds idyllic. So, I have some things I want to run by you. Some stuff I found out after our last talk," Zoe said.

"You went ahead and started digging?" Joe's face looked sceptical.

"Yeah. I did," Zoe replied, aware of her brother's concerned look from her phone screen.

"I hope you were careful?"

"As much as I could be. Why do you think I wasn't?" Zoe was a little annoyed at what she felt was Joe's critical comments. Her brother had the occasional habit of making her feel small, like a little sister again.

"Just wanted to make sure. When the stakes are so high," he paused as if finding the right words, "people can do some crazy things to win."

"Yes, I know," Zoe responded, holding back her increasing irritation, knowing Joe really wanted the best outcome for her.

"And where are you now? In public? Can anyone hear you?" Joe queried.

"No, it's fine. Can anyone hear you, Joe?" Then, with her emotions getting the better of her, she tersely asked, "Do you want to hear this or not?"

A jogger passed by, and Zoe stood up. She felt a need to move anyway and headed in the direction of the South Bank.

Joe sighed, knowing too well what the tone of his sister's voice meant.

"Go on then, Zee, talk me through it."

"Alan Walgrave, someone from my Cambridge days, apparently took his own life recently by jumping out of a window in Manhattan. A woman from an investment firm over here

135

confirmed he ran an exclusive client account with Bayer and Harlow."

"Ed had also been working on trades for B & H through an account, betting on the rise of Pithcore Gen, the bio-science corporation that is gaining hugely from the current disruption in the food supply."

"There have been billions in put options on basic food commodity prices. The bets are that they would skyrocket, which apparently they have been, due to the ongoing drought."

"Bayer and Harlow are owned by Faben and Xael, who have big investments in Pithcore Gen...' Zoe paused for dramatic emphasis. "...including, get this, Joe – Cryostone."

"Impressive!" her brother replied with genuine approval. "You're starting to sound like a true conspiracy theorist," Joe said with a faint smile.

Zoe sighed.

"Did you know Jason Runeshield was on the board of Faber?" Zoe stated.

Joe's smile instantly changed to a grimace.

"I didn't know that. That bastard and his family are probably the world's real rulers, so no surprise."

"I'm at a dead-end, Joe. All I know is there must be answers inside the vaults at Faben and Xael."

"Well, it seems like the usual suspects are involved. Runeshield, Helms and Oberman. They're all involved in a lot of dark things. But if you're looking to connect them to these suicides in some way or the trading, you have to go to the next level." Joe said by way of summary

"What do you mean?" said Zoe, "What is the 'next level'?"

Joe paused and sipped from a mug.

"We need something more to connect them, something that

ties them to the events," Joe explained before elaborating. "So far, what you've found is suspicious but could be seen as just clever trading. You need some real dirt, like OJ's missing glove, to bring it all together. We need to get inside their servers, find some internal communication or directive – perhaps an old friend of yours might be able to help, someone you went to uni with..." His voice trailed off.

Zoe immediately remembered her closest friends. There were only a few, as work had been her priority in those days. Zoe smiled at the memory of her bestie from that time. Haleema Sheraz.

"Yes, there is one," she mused, "God, I haven't seen her for so long."

Zoe tried to remember. It was an alumni reunion in Cambridge, and then Haleema had returned to Iran, and their contact had dwindled over the following years.

"So, you're still in contact with her?" Joe asked.

"Let's just say she helps us out – the less said, the better."

Zoe had been going along the river walkways leading to the Golden Jubilee Bridges and Queen's Walk along the South Bank. The vintage cafe van parked up ahead on the promenade that sold her favourite coffee glinted in the sunlight as if beckoning to her.

"Let's see what she says then," as she headed towards the outside tables.

Chapter 23

George Bush Center for Intelligence (CIA), Langley, Virginia

A uniformed guard stood at the end of the long corridor in front of the secure doorway that looked like a submarine hatch. Zak Bowen flashed his badge before facing a panel next to the door and activating it. A retinal scanner confirmed Zak was indeed allowed to enter, and the door clicked. Zak opened it and stepped into a small room where another, more senior-looking guard waited.

"We'll need to store your personal items here," the older man said, holding out a plastic tray.

Zak tossed in his keys, mobile phone and wallet. The guard then inserted the tray into a metal drawer and locked it. Then, he handed Zak a ticket with a number on it and gave him a curt nod.

Zak proceeded to walk up a steel ramp with handrails that led to a metal- and glass-sided room, isolated in a large space, like a floating box supported by steel rods resembling scaffolding poles. It was a secure space called the SCIF (Sensitive Compartmented Information Facility), specifically designed so electronic ears could not penetrate.

Once again, at the entrance, Zak had his retina scanned and, on the opening of yet another security door, finally stepped inside the meeting room, where ten men and no more than a few women were sitting around a round glass table. Zak recognised the new secretary of state, Natan Helms, from an operation in the Middle East barely a year before. Opposite him was Kate Foster, the new head of Ghost 13 Intelligence and Zak's new superior. She had long been part of the CIA hierarchy as deputy director and was once very much opposed to the creation of G13COMM, as Ghost 13 was named. She had been at the zenith of her career, near retirement, and Zak wondered what made her switch.

It was an inevitable merge, Zak surmised. You couldn't fight against what the overarching new world order wanted while remaining in isolated agencies. And they wanted a global agency, all dancing to their tune.

Another familiar face was Major General Dean Wexhall, the long-time head of Ghost 13 military arm, whom Zak had also met several times during operations in the Middle East.

The other people in the room were unfamiliar to Zak, and he politely nodded to the few faces he knew.

He had been on secondment to Ghost 13 Intelligence for some months and had been told days earlier he was to be permanently relocated to Denver, where most of the alphabet agencies, CIA, NSA and FBI, were in the process of joining G13COMM in Station 12 in Denver, the notorious and vast underground facility under the airport.

Zak would be joined by his wife, Rhoda, too. It seemed whole families of critical assets in the intelligence community were being moved there.

Something was definitely up; Zak was in no doubt about that.

There had been colossal upheavals and re-organisation for

months, and it all seemed to accelerate with increasing speed.

When everyone was settled in their places, Helms kicked off the meeting.

"Thank you all for coming in. This will be short and brief. As some of you know, the main intelligence agencies for the United States have been relocating to Station 12 over the last year, and we're approaching the final phase of this resettlement." Helms glanced over at Foster. "Ghost 13, I believe, is fully embedded, but Major General Wexhall and Director Kate Foster can fill you in on that."

"'Operation Hallows' is a nationwide drill that tests our responses in an emergency for the entire underground network across the US. Full details will be handed down through the relevant channels so everyone knows where they need to be. Similar drills will be taking place in both Canada and Europe."

It is of paramount importance that we have the process of getting our key people, from government figures, Intelligence people and everyone in between, safe in an emergency."

Helms then stood up.

"I'm afraid I need to leave right now, but Dean and Kate will take it from here. Best of luck, everyone." With that, he exited the 'security bubble', and Kate Foster cleared her throat to redirect the attention of those remaining.

"Everyone, I'd like to welcome Zak Bowen, the new chief intelligence officer. He will be coordinating G13COMM intelligence assets in the field, based at Station 12, where the headquarters for 'Operation Hallows' will be located."

All eyes turned to Zak, and he gave the assembled faces an unsure, quizzical smile in return.

Foster gave him a reassuring nod and continued. "Zak worked in CIA operations in the Middle East AO with Major

General Wexhall and did outstanding work. Like many of our intelligence colleagues, Zak is now permanently assigned to Ghost 13. Welcome to G13COMM, Zak."

"Thank you," Zak replied evenly with a slight nod of his head. It was hard to know whether this huge step up the ladder was good for him, but time would tell.

Foster turned to address the room again. "October 31st is the date for the drill, only weeks away now, so it's all hands on deck. Perhaps you can go through some of the operational aspects, Major General?"

Wexhall looked as though he had been impatiently waiting to get on with it and waved a remote at the main screen on the wall.

"Yep, glad to, thanks, Kate."

He looked around the room. "What we have here, ladies and gentlemen, is a very delicate and important drill that has to, I repeat, has to run smoothly without any mistakes."

Chapter 24

Zoe jogged from her apartment in Surrey Quays along the river's familiar walkways and roads. She knew a number of different routes around the area well, making it a mission to get to know all the nooks and crannies of the locality and also to mix up her routine. Breaking routine was the key, and Zoe tried that as much as possible.

Opposite the skyscrapers of Millwall and further upriver, Canary Wharf appeared as a collection of grey monolithic shapes in the morning mist.

The day before, the conversation with Joe had brought up one main question against all the others: was she ready for this? The plan had formed when he called back after eventually getting in touch with Haleema.

Her friend was holed up somewhere with limited resources and time to help them get past Faben's firewall. As Zoe saw it, the only option was to physically get one of Haleema's scripts to do its work.

That would mean access to the server room in the building, plugging in a USB to upload the script and logging into the network to 'make a few things happen' as Joe had described. This would set up a way to search for the files and hopefully find the secrets they kept.

Of course, Zoe mused, having done that, there may well be password-protected files and other hurdles to overcome.

"I've got no one available who could help. I could ask Dad," Joe had said, "or see if he knows anyone, but not sure I want to get him involved in this—"

"I'll do it," Zoe had replied.

"No chance!" had come Joe's quick and terse response.

They argued back and forth, but Joe dug in on this.

"I need to do this for Ed – and for me."

"And you're still my little sister, always will be—"

"I'm an adult now, Joe – with my own decision mechanism," she quipped, and with that, she had terminated their conversation.

Now, as Zoe reflected on that decision and jogged towards the building in question, she wondered what she had actually got herself into. It was dangerous, as Joe had continually mentioned. She knew that. She also knew that the death of Ed, the man she was sure she would have married, had uncovered a global conspiracy that was affecting the entire food chain of the world.

She arrived at the Docklands pier, where passengers were boarding a small ferry and glanced down at her watch, just after 10 a.m.

Once on board, she stared out across the water as the boat set off, crossing the Thames for the short trip to the Canary Wharf side. Once across, she strolled up the walkway from the pier and continued jogging across the promenade, Westferry Circus, and West India Avenue towards Canada Square.

Ten minutes later, she arrived outside the metallic Faber building at the West edge of the Wharf and stopped at a bike rack on the plaza. She began stretching while taking furtive

143

glances towards the main entrance.

She watched two smartly suited employees, young men, exit the rotating doors, laughing as they trotted down the adjacent steps. She could glimpse a main reception desk through the doors, with a man and woman sitting behind it and both on their phones. Zoe moved across the plaza to the bottom of the building steps, rotating her hips and swinging her arms left to right as she went, then stretched one leg out, resting the foot on the step and began calf exercises. Zoe saw a better picture as a set of doors on the main entrance side slid open. Beyond the reception, a woman scanned her entrance card, walked through a metal turnstile, and checked again at the elevators.

All standard security stuff.

A security guard suddenly walked into her field of vision, surprising Zoe, so she looked away and switched the stretches to her other leg. Then she moved away a few steps and pretended to be absorbed in her phone. By coming here, she was hoping to get some inspiration on how the hell she was going to do this. She recalled her dad's often-quoted adage: 'time spent in reconnaissance is never wasted'.

A fit-looking young man on a bicycle with a food delivery box on the back pulled up. She found herself checking him out and approving of his physique.

Come on, Zoe, now's not the time!

He locked his bike and headed up the steps with his detached box.

Was that a way in? she wondered. Getting the work gear and looking at the part wouldn't be too hard. She watched to see how far he was allowed into the building. He went up to reception, pulled out his phone and waited. A few minutes later, a young man appeared through the turnstile and collected his food. The cute biker left, closely followed by a UPS delivery driver who wheeled a trolley across the plaza from the nearest road where he had double-parked. He went through a similar security checking process, not even clearing the reception area.

So, she concluded, dressing up as a delivery woman wouldn't work. So, what were her other options? Steal someone's ID? These people are at work every day, so it wouldn't give her much of a window to get it and use it, as they'd report their loss pretty sharply. Unless she could copy it and get the original back?

Everyone's movement would surely be followed and recorded as soon as she entered the building. Even how long they spent in the toilet was probably recorded. Not that this information was supposed to be used for anything.

So what was she supposed to do? Kidnap someone, take their ID and break in? She might get away with it, but her face would be easily pulled from the security footage as soon as that person reported it. She looked up at the tall metallic building.

Am I going to have to actually scale the outside in the cover of darkness, like something out of Mission Impossible?

She shook her head and continued her jogging around the wharf and back towards Jubilee Park. Up ahead, a digital billboard came into view with the image of a beautiful turquoise sea. The angle of the video panned back to reveal a tanned, immaculate woman in a swimsuit looking out from her sun lounger, a cocktail perched on a side table next to her, underneath the words: 'Visit Barbados' accompanied with a travel company logo faded in underneath.

Perhaps she did need a break from it all. Maybe this was all futile. Go away somewhere and take it easy for six months – but then she remembered that feeling before. Travelling somewhere when you had worries or were running from something didn't help. The environment changed, but your worries did not.

The advert switched to men and women in suits sitting around a board table, looking happy, looking like their careers were heading for the stars – a recruitment ad.

Zoe stopped jogging and stared at the screen.

An idea formed.

This was her way in.

***

Zoe woke up Goya and commanded an online search as soon as she got home.

"Start my shower and get me the recruitment posts from Faben and Xael in London, then send them to my main computer."

"No problem, Zoe, I'm on it," came the response.

She made the shower a quick one and padded back to her computer set-up in her dressing gown. As requested, the screen had already been switched on, and the recruitment section waited.

The usual roles were being advertised in all departments, as expected for a large corporation, but as Zoe scanned, she couldn't see any openings to apply for and get an interview with her skillset.

Another problem: The turnaround time for applying and getting an interview so she could get inside the building could take weeks or months.

She leaned back in her chair, her motivation evaporating.

There must be someone working there, I know, she thought.

She clicked over to LinkedIn and began scanning through

the London-based employees. There were hundreds, and as she painstakingly scrolled through, it became clear she had no direct connections.

Zoe gave a long sigh and idly clicked around, her mind wandering.

Need coffee. That was clear why she wasn't getting anywhere.

Then she found herself on the Faben New York Division page. The list of employees came up.

And one connection she did know was Mark Digham. She had dated him a few years before meeting Ed. The split was amicable and mutual as it hadn't been going anywhere – just a bit of fun. Mark had moved job roles a few times, judging by his profile and ended up at Faben as a regional manager. Perhaps he could arrange an interview?

"Do I really want to go there?" she said out loud with a sigh.

"Go where?" Goya asked.

"Nothing. Deactivate for a while, Goya."

Zoe also spotted another name from her past: Bea Lawson, who worked in the marketing department at the London building. A meeting with her would be the perfect reason to stay in the building after an interview.

She leaned forward and began typing a series of emails.

***

Zoe paused at the bottom of the building steps and inhaled. She had chosen a dark-navy trouser suit with flat shoes. Stylish enough for the interview, yet easy enough for her to move around in. She had everything that should be needed in her shoulder bag: gloves, the flash drive with the malware and a small flashlight.

147

With a pair of AirPods in place, Zoe walked up the steps and through the revolving doors into the spacious reception. At the long desk, she gave her details and took a seat on the L-shaped couch, as requested. A business magazine gave some cover as she flicked through the pages while surreptitiously taking in her surroundings. A single visible camera pointed to the front entrance doors on the wall behind the oblong reception desk. If there were any others, which Zoe thought there must be, they were well hidden.

Mark had responded quickly. In fact, he was delighted to hear from her and more than happy to help. Almost like an excited puppy, Zoe sensed between the lines that he was angling for more than being asked for a career reference.

It seemed he had a lot of connections in the company, and one of his London-based associate managers had agreed to an informal meeting.

Now, she was in. She had to focus.

Her head was abuzz with Haleema and Joe's detailed instructions. For the past three hours, she had been searing the map of the building into her brain.

Was she really doing this?

Until now, Zoe had just been remotely investigating, staking out possibilities, and immensely enjoying the process if she was honest with herself. But now, she was about to delve into industrial espionage that could probably land her in a police cell – so many unknowns.

An approaching clip-clop of heels on the marble floor made Zoe raise her head. A young blonde woman in her twenties walked toward her and flashed a smile.

"Hi, Zoe Bowen?"

"Yes, hi," said Zoe, flashing a smile of her own in return.

"I'm Emily, personal assistant to Miss Surrage."

"Pleased to meet you."

"If you follow me, we'll get you a guest card."

They headed to the reception desk, flanked by several staff members who handed Zoe the card and asked her to sign in for it. Then, the young PA led Zoe to the elevator, and Zoe observed which floor they were headed to. She had managed to pry information out of Mark, the old acquaintance who had set this all up, about where it might take place in the building, and he assumed it would be in the Faber & Xael suite of meeting rooms on the fifteenth floor.

Zoe grimaced as the PA tapped the button for seventeen.

When the doors opened, a throng of staff was waiting to access the elevators in a spacious lobby. The two women headed past the crowd and through frosted-glass doors where an expansive view of the city of London and the Thames opened up before them. Zoe followed the PA through the open-plan office suite filled with staff at their desks and screens. The space was shaped like a doughnut, and they stepped into one of the many meeting rooms behind more frosted glass.

Zoe declined coffee but asked for water, and the PA disappeared.

Zoe took her access card, flipped it over, photographed the barcode on the back, and then sent it via Icarus.

After a few minutes, Emily returned with a tray, a water jug, and several glasses. As she placed them on the round table, another woman in her mid-fifties entered.

"Zoe, nice to meet you. I'm Melinda."

Zoe stood up, and they shook hands. The PA soon left, and the casual interview began.

Zoe had impressive skills, Melinda told her, and although

149

there was no specific role available currently, they had wanted to meet her. They talked about the role Zoe had been doing at ZEOS and the potential upcoming roles at Faber, and then after twenty minutes, Melinda began to wrap it up.

"We'll keep you posted," she said again as they both headed back out to the elevator lobby.

"Oh, one thing, I have a meeting with a friend, Ms Lawson from Marketing, at the cafeteria now. Will I be able to get down there with my card?" Zoe asked.

Melinda gave her a quick, puzzled look. "Oh, right. No, you should be able to take the lift. Ms Lawson will have to show you through some of the access points to get out."

"Oh yes, she mentioned that wouldn't be a problem. Well, it was lovely to meet you. Thank you," Zoe said, holding out her hand to shake goodbye.

At the cafeteria, Zoe grabbed a bottle of sparkling elder-flower, took out her phone, switched it to silent mode, and pretended to converse. She spotted her friend at the far end, who, luckily, had not seen her.

She casually wandered back to the doors with her drink, slipped out as someone else came in, and headed back to the elevators. A few other staff lingered, waiting. She continued the imaginary conversation, making it sound like she was helping resolve a serious work problem. She joined another group of office workers in the spacious elevator and pressed the button for the fifteenth floor while still speaking into her phone.

A man got out ahead of her, and she followed him closely as he headed through the office doors, flashing him a sweet smile as he held open the door. He walked off, and she strolled around a similar space to the one she had seen several floors previously up. She kept her eyes out for a remote computer, but from the layout of the workstations, she would easily be seen at most of them.

In one of the work areas a few metres ahead, cut off with wall dividers, two men stood up, grabbed their jackets, and turned to face the door.

They were about to leave an area of work machines empty.

That will do.

She loitered for a moment as they left and headed to the elevators. Her heartbeat sped up as she pretended to finish her call before walking towards the vacant workstations.

The login details were memorised and ready to go. Under a minute, if that. Zoe reached into her pocket and clutched at the tiny USB drive.

Just as Zoe walked towards the empty workstations, a woman in a dark suit stepped out of a meeting room. Her red auburn hair was tied back into a ponytail. She appraised Zoe with a sharp face and thin smile.

"Can I help you?" The woman made a point of staring at the access card lanyard hanging from Zoe's neck.

Zoe stumbled for a second, then found composure. "I'm here to see a friend who works here."

"Name?"

"Bea Lawson from Marketing. We're meeting in the cafeteria on the second floor, right?" Zoe did her best to act brazen, nonchalant even.

The woman assessed Zoe with suspicion, then nodded curtly.

"Yes, I'll show you the way."

Zoe glanced down at her name badge: Eva Villar.

They walked to the elevator and waited with a handful of other workers.

"So, what is the purpose of your visit today?" Villar asked.

Zoe held her breath.

"Oh, a meeting, well, interview with Melinda Surrage," Zoe almost stuttered. Should she be giving away this information?

"Oh, with Commercial Banking? On seventeen? You've got a bit lost, haven't you?"

Zoe felt her pulse racing as they stepped back into the elevator.

"Trying to find a toilet – they were all busy down there—"

"Right," Villar replied.

There was an awkward silence.

The doors couldn't open quickly enough, and when they did, Zoe headed out first and towards the cafeteria, where she had just been fifteen minutes earlier. Her new escort was sticking to her like a leech and walked close behind. It was clear she did not buy Zoe's story and wanted to see this 'friend' of Zoe's for herself.

You better still be there, Bea!

She scanned the busy canteen and couldn't see any sight of her friend. She checked her watch. Fifteen minutes late, but still.

Then, she saw the familiar tall figure walking towards them, holding a tray with lunch.

"I'm so sorry I'm late, Bea. The interview went on a bit."

Her friend smiled and shook her head. "That's no problem. Did it go well?"

Zoe turned and glanced at the Villar woman.

"Well, I'm glad you found each other. Best of luck," Villar said.

"Thank you," Zoe managed to say, staying civil.

With that, Villar finally walked off and Zoe and her lunch

date headed to an empty table. Bea spoke, but Zoe barely took in the words as she churned inside.

She had screwed it up.

Not only had she failed to plant the programme in the network, but she had also almost been rumbled in the process of trying.

When they sat down, Zoe glanced again to the exit doors and spotted the Villar woman glancing back at her as she left as if to confirm her fears.

Chapter 25

Station 12, Denver
12:05 PM

Haleema's old Casio watch beeped, and she immediately logged out and pushed her swivel chair back from the desk.

It was time. This was the riskiest job that she had undertaken since arriving.

She picked up her small gym bag, left her cubicle work area, and headed to the door. A few of the other worker drones were also logging off for their designated lunch period. As Haleema headed along the metal walkways, she casually glanced across the sea of monitors of the dim operations room for Fagan but, thankfully, couldn't see him.

As she approached the doors, her supervisor, Leone Kaine, came through towards her.

"Ah, Haleema, before you go to lunch, I need to have a word. Won't take long." He gestured with a hand back the way she had just come.

Shit. It better not, thought Haleema, conscious of the task she was about to undertake.

She followed Kaine back along the walkway that split off, one leading back to her work floor, the other to a suite of meeting rooms. They took a seat around a large round table with power points in the middle and flat screens embedded into the surface of each seat.

What the hell was this about? Had they found out about her little side activities? No, it wouldn't be Kaine talking to her now if it was, surely?

Stay calm.

Haleema gave Kaine a thin smile as he opened a bottle of water.

He leaned marginally towards her, saying, "You've done well on forecasts and the data modelling. You also have infiltration skills, which could be put to better use. Nothing has been confirmed yet, but you might well be transferred. I'll be sorry to lose you, Haleema, but the powers above and all—" He thumbed upwards to the ceiling.

"Transferred where?" For a moment, Haleema forgot the mission she was supposed to be doing with Zoe. Was she being transferred out of here? She felt a flurry of hope.

"Cyber Intelligence unit – G13COMM. You'll be going up in the world – well, at least up a few floors." Again, he jabbed a thumb upwards as Haleema's heart sank. She was still stuck in this underground sweatbox.

Kaine stood up. "That's it. I think you deserve to know."

"Thanks," Haleema managed to whisper.

"Enjoy lunch."

Haleema headed back out and made her way to the service cupboard, looking at her watch. Running late.

G13COMM. She knew the name in another form.

Ghost 13.

The global agency was supposedly going to replace the Western world's alphabet agencies as the new world order fell into place. For a brief time, they and the NSA were her direct opponents when she worked for the Iranian cyber army in Tehran.

The prospect of being continually cooped up in this place was a terrible prospect. Haleema felt that her mental state was fragmenting as the months went by, but the transfer opportunity might shake things up. It offered a change of scene, different work and possibly increased access to their online systems, not to mention different parts of the facility. That made her feel better, at least a little.

Would she still be able to see her father? She forgot to ask that.

One thing was sure: Haleema would be closer to the heart of the beast.

She passed a security guard, who, recognising her, exchanged a nod. He was used to seeing her head to the gym around this time, but Haleema continued past the frosted doors and headed down the stairwell to the level below.

She looked up and down the corridor and stepped inside the storage room, leaving the light off as routine, with just the exterior corridor light to guide her.

A glance at her watch told her she was running late.

Shit! This was not good. Sorry, Zoe.

Haleema took the laptop she had used before from a storage box and a power supply. She quickly went through her routine, checking her hiding place behind the industrial shelving was clear before placing the laptop in a space on the shelving. She was positioned around the corner in the L-shaped room and away from the door.

She fired up the laptop, connected the VPN and then opened the network settings to connect to the external internet as usual.

Using the encrypted Icarus desktop app, she called Zoe's ID number.

***

Meanwhile, Zoe nursed a cappuccino in the coffee shop near the Faber and Xael building and glanced anxiously at her watch. Where the hell was Hal's call?

Along with the frustration of failing to plant the USB came a growing sense of grit and determination. Her brother, Joe, had always inspired her, although she had never previously understood his drive when it came to Liberatus. Now, however, she was beginning to see the evil monster of tyranny and oppression that humanity faced. She suddenly understood why he spoke in terms of war: it was indeed an information war, a secret war raging on the people who barely knew they were being used, manipulated and funnelled down the road to hell.

The initial plan to get into the building using a job interview as cover to get to a work terminal had failed, so a new, bolder plan was required. Joe and Haleema had hatched it. This would not be possible without her old university friend's hacking skills. Then, the thought of what she was about to do made Zoe feel nauseous.

Why the hell had she agreed to this?

Zoe caught a glimpse of her reflection in the ceiling-high café window; her blonde hair was now dyed darker, with minimal makeup. A girl who wouldn't get a second glance. She couldn't decide if it suited her, but at least she would blend in more. She wore jeans, a zip-up hoodie and plain trainers.

A beep came through her earpiece. Zoe checked her phone and immediately spotted a blue dot next to the name Sirus on the Icarus app. Haleema had come online and was calling her. Finally, she thought.

Zoe put in her earplugs to take the call.

"Hello. Ha—" Zoe just stopped herself from saying Haleema's real name. Encrypted or not, Joe had drilled this rule into her repeatedly, and she had nearly broken it right off the bat.

"Hi, Sirus."

"Hello, Nova. I hope you're good. I'm sorry I'm late."

Zoe smiled at hearing her new codename.

"No problem. I'm good, thanks. It's great to hear from you."

Once again, Zoe stopped herself from saying her friend's real name. Their friendship at Cambridge University had been brief, but they had been close while it lasted.

"Listen carefully," Haleema continued. "My location is not stable at the moment, so I'll keep much of our comms via text."

Haleema spoke evenly and clearly, but Zoe sensed something on the edge of her voice, like nervousness. Zoe just hoped it wasn't for any particular reason.

"So, everything is set up okay? You're confident this will work?" Zoe asked, double-checking.

"Yes, It's been my side project for a while now, but you have to understand that I'm in a service cupboard working through one of the very few external internet ports."

"Right? What are you saying, exactly?"

"I'm saying there's a small chance we could get cut off. It's unlikely, but..."

"Great." Zoe felt resigned, and the pit of her stomach churned.

"I'll try to guide you through voice, but that won't always be possible. I've texted you basic instructions as a backup. You've studied the map of the server room I sent over?"

"Yep."

"You printed the card and got everything you needed?"

Zoe pulled out an ID card and ran her thumb over the embossed name of an employee Haleema had found.

"Yes. I have the card and everything else."

"Good, that will get us through most doors, but don't let anyone see it. When you scan it, try to keep it concealed in your palm. You can get away with it at a glance but won't if they look at the photo closely."

"Want to go over it all again?"

Zoe shook her head. "God, no."

"Alright. Well, the night shift should be starting now. So, let's go."

***

Kacper Fagan's features were tense yet concentrated, sharpened by the illumination from the line of monitor screens. The data graphs displayed the traffic of internal base communications, a relatively steady and predictable sequence. An alert had just pinged on his PDA and main workstation screen simultaneously. The same signal, one of many that had started since he began closely monitoring the network traffic.

The entire system restricted outside internet access for 'category C' operatives who had been brought in or 'taken' for their expertise.

And here it was again.

This time, he could pinpoint the location after upgrading

the network performance monitor. He tapped the screen of his primary monitor and scanned the diagram of the facility area network. The culprit IP appeared to be a communal workstation in the security area.

Unfortunately, that meant he couldn't access it remotely.

He tapped it to bring up the traffic logs and soon established that the traffic source was going to the workstation from somewhere else.

The intruder was making an effort to hide their tracks, and the possibility this was some security breach couldn't be ruled out.

Fagan logged off, picked up his PDA and headed for the doors—time to look around.

***

As she trotted up the steps to the main doors, Zoe inhaled deeply and whispered to herself repeatedly. "Stay calm."

She could feel the sweat on her palms and wiped them on the front of her black jeans.

Inside, groups of employees descended towards her, and when she headed inside, there was a hum of conversation. Blending in with the crowd reassured Zoe. Hopefully, she would blend in. That was the idea, anyway.

Striding as naturally as she could, the ID card in the palm of her hand, Zoe nodded and smiled at the security guy as she swiped the face of the card over the scanner. The gate barrier held firm.

Oh shit. Here we go.

Zoe glanced over at the guard, who was glued to his phone.

She tried again and inwardly sighed with relief as it swung

open. She strolled through to the elevator lobby. A short, red-headed man, in deep conversation, headed past her on the way out. Another group, two men and a woman in their twenties, talked and laughed as they exited the elevator. They ignored Zoe as she stepped inside.

As the doors closed and Zoe found herself alone, she whispered into the mic of her earpods.

"Inside, heading to floor fourteen."

"Follow my instruction," came the distant reply from Haleema, thousands of miles away. "When the doors open, turn left."

The doors parted, and Zoe stepped out and turned the corner as instructed.

"That's good. Now, stop and turn around. Get back in the lift and go up one floor."

Zoe inwardly shrugged and walked back into the elevator.

"What was that about?" she whispered into her mic as the doors closed again.

"It's just to show you on the cam loop. I'm disrupting the security system now, so get up there!"

Zoe jabbed the secure server level button on the next floor and took in slow, deep breaths.

***

With occasional glances at his PDA device, Fagan could see that the traffic spike had evened out. It was hardly a trickle, and he wondered if he was being too cautious.

He walked from his workstation along the winding tunnels and corridors until he reached the security section silo. This enclave set over three levels housed those responsible for the security of the entire facility of Station 12. It consisted of a cadre of security guards, highly trained militia, and their intelligence unit, all of whom were supposed to share intel with Fagan in his role as head of IT Security. He snorted with derision.

Like that ever had happened, he thought with a pang of bitterness. The overlap of responsibility, power politics and confusion caused a cesspit of resentment all around.

Fagan reached a hub that split into different tunnelled walkways resembling an underground train station. Signs on the walls pointed in different directions down the walkways. One pointed to a transport hub where authorised personnel could get vac pods to the furthest reaches of the facility. Another pointed to the military barracks, which Fagan had heard was soon to be occupied by an elite division currently based at Buckley Air Force Base. Fagan followed the tunnel to 'Area Security' and inhaled deeply, ready for confrontation.

The space opened up with double steel doors fixed with small windows. Above the doors, a small glowing red dot on a wall-mounted security camera hinted at the surveillance homing in on Fagan as he approached. He pressed a buzzer below a grid and identified himself before the doors parted, revealing a screening area like an airport screening point. An armed security woman in the familiar khaki jumpsuit gestured him over and checked his ID card before ushering him down the oblong space to another set of doors.

They opened, and a familiar face peered through. Private Jenson. "You did not think to call ahead, Fagan?"

Fagan glared. He didn't care for the tone of this: private.

"I couldn't get through," he lied. "Besides, I need to look at one of your workstations in person. I believe it's being used to send private data packets to the external web." He said 'private' in the most condescending tone he could muster.

Jenson looked confused for a second, then reluctantly let Fagan through. They walked into the first section of the circular silo space, another hub of activity with multiple screens displaying various parts of the vast facility in real-time. This was truly the surveillance state, within a subterranean state, thought Fagan with a grimace.

"Which computer?"

Fagan checked his PDA and looked around before spotting that the culprit machine was tucked away in an alcove. He gestured to it and walked over.

"Is this one used a lot?"

"Very rarely. It's just used for enhancing surveillance images of interest."

"Can we log on?"

"Alright. But I need to stay with you – protocol rules."

Fagan nodded impatiently.

Jenson logged on, then stood aside as Fagan pulled over a nearby chair and sat down in front of it. He opened up the network settings and clicked through, looking for clues.

"So this is about internet access? We access the external all the time," Jenson said.

"Yes, I know. I'm just investigating suspicious activity," he replied. He clicked on data usage and connection properties. That traffic was still going through the machine but from another location.

He'd soon find them. He was sure of it.

The rows and columns of numbers displayed data flow times, the protocols used and source and destination IPs. This was the key: find the IP and cross-reference it with his monitoring system. He had captured the suspect IP back at his desk and quickly searched for it. There were numerous matches, all corresponding with the times he had ring-fenced as suspicious.

This was it. The confirmation he was looking for.

An IP match meant he could find the physical location of the original source. It's all he needed.

He logged off the machine and stood up.

"Thanks. That's all the info I needed. I'll continue the investigation from my own office," Fagan said. As he left the security area, he accessed a list of hardware assets in the facility and searched for the IP address. It was linked to a spare laptop that was not in formal use, but its location was not listed either, frustratingly, just a blank cell on the spreadsheet.

However, he knew roughly where it might be. A service cupboard or a storeroom. There were plenty of those, probably five on each level. It would mean physically checking each one.

Fagan quickened his pace back along the pedestrian tunnels the way he had come.

***

Zoe forced herself to walk as if she belonged there. No one should be watching if Haleema had fixed the cams, but if some casual observer saw her, somehow, she thought she might get away with it.

Who was she kidding?

A shrill alarm would burst into life any second. She was almost convinced of it. Still, she swiped the card alongside the double doors that led to the server room. A resounding click released a lock, and she pushed it open and stepped into the temperature-cooled room that spanned the entire floor.

Rows of server racks were arranged like city blocks in the dim hue. Hundreds of lights flashed and winked like Christmas on steroids, and a large air-con unit set into the wall lightly hummed. Overhead, reams of cables were tied into a metal raceway that ran across the ceiling.

She checked her device for the next message from Haleema, who had sent them through in case they lost contact.

Row C, rack 4 was what she needed to find.

She silently moved along the edge of the room, past the switch points and sporadic monitors set on some of the rack shelves. She found the correct row and rack on which a laptop was resting. She opened it up, pressed the boot-up button, and took out a USB stick from her inside jacket pocket.

From what Zoe understood, she was to install a rogue operating system that would enable them to pull what they needed. Even so, something could definitely go wrong.

Forcing herself to concentrate, Zoe checked the text messages from Hal for reference. She slipped the USB drive into the laptop slot and forced another reboot while holding the shift key. When the screen turned back on, it displayed the boot screen options, and she chose the external rogue file on the USB and clicked 'restart'. As the laptop rebooted, the installation kicked in, and now all Zoe could do was wait.

A dull creak from the far side of the room spiked her with dread.

Just one of the machines? Was it another door opening at the far end she had not seen?

She listened intently but could hear nothing apart from the whirring fan of the air conditioning and her own beating heart.

***

In the storage room, Haleema stood in front of the screen, holding her arms. It was cold in the cupboard, and it didn't help her concentrate at all. Then, a message popped up. Zoe had done it and installed her rogue OS.

As they had lost contact through voice, Haleema typed a message. "We're in – hold fire."

She connected remotely to see the terminal screen Zoe had connected to.

There was something she had not mentioned to Zoe. Although she had worked on this malicious OS since she arrived in the facility, she could not test this latest version in a live environment. Whether it would be able to retrieve the files they needed from the Faben and Xael servers was still far from certain.

After a minute, to Haleema's palatable relief, the function worked. A ream of code appeared on her terminal window.

Her programme was now searching for the correct files to copy to the USB.

She messaged Zoe again.

"Let it run. I don't know how long. Ten to fifteen mins? Get all you can and get out of there."

Just then, Haleema heard a noise at the door.

Shit!

She shut the laptop with lightning speed and shifted into her hiding space behind the shelves.

The door opened, followed by the flickering of the lights coming on.

Measured steps protruded further into the room, pausing occasionally. Haleema slowly turned her head in time to see a dark suit and then recognised the pale figure of Kacper Fagan from IT Security, shaven head and hawkish nose as if he were smelling her out. She heard rummaging as he went through the boxes as if looking for something.

Just hold tight. He'll find what he wants, then leave.

He moved closer, turning the corner onto the line of shelves, where at the end, she was hiding, trying not to breathe for fear of giving away her position in the deadly quiet room. Haleema sensed he was scanning but not knowing what he was looking for instead of just getting a piece of equipment. Otherwise, he'd know where to go.

Fagan moved, and Haleema could not see him.

Then he leaned down, pulled out a container box a few feet away from her and began pulling items out, taking his time with each object as if revealing a puzzle.

A keyboard.

An internal drive.

A card-cloning machine.

The one that Haleema had used months ago to clone Leon Caine's access card. She had almost forgotten about it.

He looked at it closely, turning it over in his hand. Then he tossed it back, replaced the box and stood up before moving closer to her position.

Haleema had to force herself to hold her breath. She dared not breathe.

His eyes focused on something on the shelf just above where she crouched.

Her laptop!

Then, with horror, she realised it would still be warm.

If he touched it—

Even worse if he opened it?

This was it, thought Haleema. He would find her for sure. The game was up.

At least she had done what she needed to do for Zoe. She was on her own, which was not good, but at least there was a chance.

Fagan took another step towards it.

His radio came to life with a hiss of static.

Haleema, her eyes now closed, heard a voice at the other end of his radio.

"Come in, Fagan."

Fagan sighed.

"Yep, Fagan here."

"Are you at this conference or not? It starts in five!"

Fagan hesitated as if he had forgotten.

"On my way," he replied. There was a click, and he swore under his breath.

Haleema opened her eyes and caught sight of his torso moving toward the door.

It opened, letting in a brief shard of light before it faded, and the door clicked shut. Haleema realised she had been holding her breath and allowed herself to breathe again.

She stood up slowly and stepped out of her hiding place. Her legs were numb from crouching, and she bent each one back and forth to get her blood flowing again as she opened the laptop lid.

The screen kicked back into life, and for a split second, she saw the Icarus chat window appear and the remote terminal window displaying the downloaded code that hopefully Zoe had managed to get.

Then, with a cold rush of horror that ran down her neck, Haleema realised the VPN had crashed or not kicked in properly.

Fuck!

She closed the Icarus application, deleted it, shut down the remote viewer, and then shut the lid. Haleema swore again, incensed at her own mistake. Those seconds without the VPN meant her connection would pop up on the network like a beacon. And worse, they would know which machine, and probably where, if you had the logs.

Zoe was definitely on her own now. Haleema had her own problems.

She stashed the laptop back in the box where she kept it and moved to the door. Peeking outside and down the corridor and seeing it was clear, she slipped out and closed the door. She needed to get as much distance between her and that laptop as quickly as possible. Only then could she assess the damage and seriously think about how the hell to continue with this mission of helping Joe and his Liberatus friends.

That was too close to call, she thought, heading to the end of the corridor.

When she turned the corner, a sick feeling overwhelmed her at the sight of Fagan, who stood waiting for her.

Next to him was a security guard, armed.

Fagan smiled and nodded and gestured with a PDA in his palm.

He had seen. He must have known I was in there.

"Hello, Ms Sheraz."

Haleema stood there, frozen with fear.

"I knew it was you," he said. "I knew it was you," he repeated, almost in a whisper.

169

Chapter 26

Zoe could feel the panic rising from the pit of her stomach. She typed again:

Are you there?

No response.

On the screen, Haleema's software was ploughing through the server, hunting down the files they needed. The lines of code on the screen made no sense to Zoe. It was doing what it was supposed to, which was great, but Zoe was feeling the opposite of great.

She just hoped it was apparent when it had finished. And worse, there was no indication of how long this would take.

Her legs felt heavy. She needed to pee, and the room seemed to be getting colder by the second. She desperately wanted to get out of there.

Haleema was gone. She knew it. Whatever Haleema had previously warned about getting cut off had just played out.

Zoe's unease began to escalate to sheer panic. She was on her own, and that realisation soon triggered her anxiety with rapid heart movement and a deep desire to vomit.

Deep breaths, she said to herself.

She took three of them, which eased her agitated state a little, and then she fished out her Buspirone pills and swallowed one.

It stuck in her throat for a moment without water, and she nearly went into a coughing fit.

Were the cameras still down? Or would she need to just run for it and hope for the best?

There was a beep and a popup message on the laptop screen. The message read: scan and download complete. Time to go!

Yes!

Hal was a genius, no doubt about that.

She hit the 'Esc' button to close the programme and then navigated to the power shutdown on the screen.

As the screen darkened, she pulled out the USB and slipped it into her jeans' front pocket.

Finally, time to go.

Now, she worried about the next step. Getting out of the building.

Don't fuck it up now, Zoe. You're nearly there.

At the exit doors, Zoe peered out through the frosted glass. It seemed quiet. The elevator lobby was empty. She swiped her card and pushed open the doors, striding forward as if she had every right to be there. She lingered at the elevators, pushed the button, then changed her mind at the last second and headed for the emergency stairwell.

Once through the fire door, she leaned over the railing.

Distant voices, probably near the bottom of the building. She could not see anyone. Then, a door closed, and voices disappeared.

She moved down the stairwell and had only descended a few floors when the sound of another fire door opening stopped her in her tracks,

Voices. Closer this time. Just a few levels down.

She crept to the edge and caught glimpses of a man and

woman moving up the steps towards her.

Echoes of conversation.

Zoe caught the odd words: 'server room' and 'check the exits'.

Shit! Had she unknowingly set up some silent alarm or been seen on some hidden camera?

As Zoe reversed direction and headed back up the steps, she thought about how familiar the woman's voice was. She continued past the server room floor, then stopped and listened. Zoe half crouched and peered through the railings, ready to keep moving if needed, but she wanted to check.

They arrived at the server floor and saw the back of them exiting through the door.

Auburn hair in a ponytail!

It was that woman, Eva Villar, who she had encountered at the interview. The one who eyed her with suspicion then escorted her to the canteen.

When the door slammed shut, Zoe waited a few seconds, then descended two steps at a time, soon falling into a rhythm, jumping the last three or four steps on each floor. Occasionally, she stopped and listened before going down another level.

By the time Zoe had reached the ground floor, she had worked up quite a sweat and took a few moments before peering through the square window on the door. Directly opposite were wall mirrors that gave her a view of the main reception area and her route out of there.

Don't screw up now.

She inhaled sharply, brushed down her jacket and opened the door. At the exit gate, she scanned the card and moved through it, heading towards the main exit doors. The lobby area was quiet. Just one security guard sitting behind the long counter.

A crackle from a radio made her jump. He glanced over and caught her eye. She smiled back and went to open the door.

Locked!

She rattled the glass door again, but it was stuck in place.

She turned back to face the guard, waiting for him to come over and grab her, shout or demand a body search. She had failed at the last hurdle.

Instead, he gave her a wave.

"Have to buzz you out at this hour."

There was a hum from the door, and she pushed it open.

"Good night," he said.

"Night," she replied, flashing the guard a quick smile, quickly stumbling out, relief seemingly ebbing from every pore in her body. She drew a deep breath and kept walking along the immaculate paved streets towards Canary Wharf station. The cool air felt like a breath from heaven on her face.

Chapter 27

Set on the slopes of Beverly Hills, the luxury villa belonging to Ryan Byson, the son of a prominent British politician and CEO of a private bank in LA, was beginning to get lively.

Eva, dressed in a short black skirt that showed off her long legs, heels, a white shirt under a waistcoat, and her red hair tied back into a ponytail, moved with smooth elegance through the crowd, her tray of canapes held aloft. Her outfit was both glamorous and provocative, making her look even younger than her eighteen years and also fitted in perfectly with the other waitresses. Their efforts kept the party fuelled with champagne against a backdrop of indie rock music.

Byson held court in one of the elegant dining rooms, surrounded by some of the wealthiest people in that part of the country. A small group of guests bayed at his crude jokes. The tall brunette girl, Anne, the bait, stood outside the circle, laughing along.

Eva caught her eye and couldn't stop glaring, silently urging her to get on with it.

On a sofa in the corner, a woman in a cocktail dress sat leaning over a metal tray on a coffee table with lines of cocaine. She snorted one off the tray and lifted her head, pressing down on her nostril.

Eva moved through to the back of the house, where double doors opened up to the garden and swimming pool. In the fading evening light, other guests had gathered in small casual groups there, laughing and chatting. She headed for the spacious kitchen at the back, where a small group of catering staff kept busy uncorking champagne, filling crystal flute glasses and preparing a variety of canapes. Her cohort colleague Mahaska passed her holding a tray, and they gave each other a knowing glance.

It was their first live mission as a team. Their first major test.

Blackmail was a prevalent tactic the cabal used to control the lower ranks. Doctor Black and Mother had been specific about this. The target, Ryan Byson, was to be 'honey trapped' by his own penchant for younger girls. A camera had been set up in his bedroom upstairs. The plan was a simple one. Lure him in with the bait, film him with an underage girl, and then he would belong to Doctor Black.

Eva took another tray of snacks and returned to the main party, where Byson was finally talking to Anne. He was tall, tanned with silver-cropped hair, the whole square jaw look and, in Eva's opinion, a good-looking man.

Eva watched as the girl tilted her head slightly, working her charms before leaning over, touching his arm and whispering in his ear. Byson chuckled but seemed distracted. He turned to another man standing nearby, and they both laughed. Cruelly, it seemed.

Eva could see straight away he wasn't interested in Anne. Shit!

At that moment, Byson looked directly at her as she passed by, and she gave him a demure smile.

She walked into a hallway, closed the door and headed to a cloak nook away from the party. She moved inside and spoke discreetly into the mic inside her shirt.

"Sunrise. We have a problem. Bait is ineffective. He's not going for it."

Eva thought for a moment before undoing the top button of her shirt. She spoke into the mic once again.

"Sunrise. Acknowledge."

There was a pause before Mahska's voice came over the line.

"Got it. What are we going to do?"

"I will try. Keep on standby and be ready."

Further down the corridor, a door opened, and from her spot, Eva could see Byson coming through it, heading to the stairs.

She deliberately stepped out and caught his eye with a wide smile.

"Oh, hi, Mr Byson. I was looking for some cigarettes."

He paused and checked his pockets while she walked toward him.

"I rarely smoke, but—" he began.

Eva used all the training Mother had given on seduction. Her lips were slightly open, her eyes wide, searching his face and lips as she approached him.

"—perhaps in my bedroom," he finished, as his eyes searched her face before dropping to her cleavage.

"Sounds good," she replied seductively.

The signals were unsaid but unmistakable. Boldly, Eva moved a hand down the front of his shirt towards his crotch.

"Hmmm, keen as mustard, aren't you?" Byson said, hardening under the feel of her hand.

"This way." Byson led the way up the spiral staircase as Eva superstitiously removed her small hidden earpiece and placed it in her pocket. They headed along the hallway towards the master bedroom. Byson walked in, leaving the door ajar, and Eva followed him into the elaborate suite. A four-poster bed formed the central focus, surrounded by ornate furniture. A dressing table adorned with feminine paraphernalia, clearly his wife's domain. She knew the camera was hidden where it had a clear view of the grand bed.

He fished around on a bedside table and turned with a wry smile, holding a pack of Marlboro Lights as if they were newly discovered treasure.

"I don't really smoke," she said coyly. Then she moved to the bed. "That was my 'in'."

He laughed. "Impressive. What's your name?"

"Clara," she replied. It was the same cover name she had used to infiltrate the catering company.

She was about to drape herself onto the bed when he held up his hand.

"On second thoughts, maybe not here. It's where my wife sleeps. However, there's a lovely little private garden at the back. Let's take a look, baby."

Eva hesitated, then smiled.

This was not going to plan. She knew the hidden camera that had been covertly placed in a face cream jar on the dressing table the day before would be filming them right now, but it would be all for nothing if it didn't proceed to sex.

However, there was a backup plan. She needed to get word to Mahaska. She turned away from him, ambled around to the dressing table, moved her hand up to the hidden mic inside her shirt, and pressed the button so Mahaska would hopefully hear.

"Under the stars in your little garden sounds great," Eva

said slowly.

Byson led her into the hallway and back in the opposite direction. They came to a narrow staircase that led down to a series of back rooms, well away from the main party. Byson opened a set of French doors into a secluded garden surrounded by tall hedges, and decorative lights hung around the boundaries, giving the space a Christmas feel. Set near the top of the garden was a rattan garden sofa outside a pavilion.

They both took a seat, and Byson didn't waste any time. His rough hands squeezed her breast as he moved his lips to hers, taking her by surprise. He pushed her down onto the sofa and began to kiss her neck. Eva looked around to see any sign of Mahaska in place to film, but there was no sign. Byson began to force himself on her.

"What's the hurry?" she gasped, attempting to slow him down to buy time.

"I am," he whispered with a grunt and ripped her shirt wide open, tearing the top buttons and exposing her lacy bra.

Then, he hesitated and moved his head to see better.

"What's this?"

She followed his gaze to the inside of her shirt, and her heart nearly stopped. It was the mic.

Byson straightened up and pulled at it, revealing a long wire.

"Just comms for the catering team," she said quickly.

"Bollocks."

His large hands grabbed her head, and he looked into her ear, jerked her head, and peered into the other one.

Eva was panicked. Frozen.

Byson grabbed her by her arms and hauled her to her feet.

"Who the hell are you?" he hissed. His smooth demeanour had long gone.

Eva was silent and stared back at him wide-eyed.

He brought his arm back in one swift movement and gave her a hard slap across her face that jerked her head.

"Tell me, you bitch."

As he brought back his hand to hit her again, Eva finally snapped out of her shocked state and wriggled free of his grasp.

"No one sent me, you crazy bastard. I told you it's for staff comms."

He stood back with a momentary look of confusion as he considered that possibility.

Eva began to move away from the house towards an iron gate set in the high hedge.

"Wait a minute. Where are you going?"

He sprinted after her, grabbed her lengthy ponytail, and pulled her back towards him. Eva twisted her body, turning to face him, dropped to one knee and, with one violent action, swung her forearm into his groin. Her hand-to-hand fight training was finally kicking in.

Byson grunted and staggered back a few steps before doubling up, his hands holding his crotch.

Eva leapt up from her crouch and grabbed the back of his head, pulling it down and jerking her knee into his face. There was a crack, followed by a low, guttural growl of deep pain as Byson fell sideways. His head caught the side of a large concrete plant pot, and his body lay still, slumped on its side, his eyes dilating in death.

Without hesitation, Eva disappeared into the darkness, through the gate and away from the house.

***

In her office at Faber and Xael, Eva had often reflected on that failure occurring on her first live mission. She had been lucky that, although Byson had died, it had also gotten rid of a thorn in the shoe. Not that Doctor Black was happy about it, but he seemed to believe in Eva and apparently saw enough real potential in her that he was willing to move on from it.

Her ascent over the following years to the status of a cabal doctor was rapid and without any further hindrances. Eva had learned valuable lessons and had vowed never to lose control again.

Eva let out a long sigh. She had been relocated to England and had never seen Mother again. However, somewhere deep down inside, she hoped that perhaps one day she would.

Her thoughts returned to Zoe Bowen. She had been alerted to that job interview and had decided to get in her face. Without a doubt, she had rattled Zoe, but there had been no evidence of any foul play.

A rapid knock on Eva Villar's office door interrupted her thoughts.

"Come."

Kai Martins came in, holding up his phone.

"One of the engineers says there's something we should look at – in the server room."

"He wants us to come up there? Ask him what it is. I'm busy," Villar replied in a low, deadly tone.

Martins held the phone to his ear.

"What is the problem, exactly?"

After a few seconds, Martins looked up at Villar.

"There's been a security breach. A rogue OS was installed on one of the workstations. He's shut it down, but it may have been used to—"

Villar immediately got to her feet and headed towards Martins and the door, waving her hand at him.

"Alright, tell him we're coming."

When they reached the elevators, the lights indicated that one was on the ground and above at the top. Villar sighed impatiently and then gestured to the stairwell doors.

"Take the stairs," she snapped, demanding, "What else did he say?"

They went through the doors and began to ascend upwards, their shoes clattering on the metal steps.

"Just that they got an alert of the network dropping but not coming back online, probably due to this rogue OS."

"Fuck," Villar muttered. Her mind raced—a deliberate breach of security. Someone was trying to access their servers. But who? And why?

They climbed the rest of the way in silence and exited the stairwell on the server floor.

Inside, the engineer that had alerted Martins stood over one of the laptops next to the server racks. He was young, no older than twenty-five, with a hipster beard and baggy shorts.

"What have we got?" Villar demanded, immediately dispensing with the niceties.

The engineer didn't take his eyes off the screen, taking his time as he spoke in a West Coast American accent.

"Some kind of rogue operating system, a nice piece of work. Really nice. I managed to isolate it, so it's no threat now, but I have no idea what it did yet. That'll take time."

Finally, he looked up at Martins and Villar with a deadpan expression.

"There's no way this was planted remotely. I'd guess someone came up here and physically plugged in a drive."

"When?"

"Within the last hour."

Villar shot a glare at Martins. "Go pull up the cams. Get spooling, now!" Martins hurried out of the room.

"For what purpose? A hack? Have they planted anything on our system," asked Villar.

"I've got a trace looking, but it could take a long time to be certain. It could be they just copied files," the engineer replied.

"Keep me informed directly—" she looked down at his lanyard ID card, "—Josh."

Villar headed down to the security office on the tenth floor, in the elevator this time, where Kai Martins stood over one of the security officers. On one of the many screens that blanketed the wall, they stared at a fast-forwarding video from the elevator lobby on the server floor.

"Anything?" Villar demanded.

Martins shook his head and said nothing.

They all watched the spooling footage of an empty corridor for a few minutes before Villar spoke again. "Get the main lobby footage up as well. From the last two hours."

The security guard, a grey-haired man clearly weeks from retirement, clicked around on his keyboard before pulling up the requested footage.

"From around four pm?" he asked.

"Try around the shift change at five."

Villar paced, arms crossed, around the room as they continued studying the screens.

"What are we looking for?" Martins asked.

"How the fuck would I know?" Villar retorted. "Anything that doesn't look right – someone who doesn't—" She moved closer to the screen.

A woman dressed in a hoodie and jeans with black shoulder-length hair walked across the reception lobby. Something about her, the gait of the walk, seemed familiar.

"Can you get any closer to that woman going through the gate?"

The video stopped and zoomed in.

Villar narrowed her eyes and tried to find something to work with on the pixellated image. It was still unclear, and there was no way of identifying the woman.

"Keep it running."

The video displayed the woman swiping her ID card and moving through the barrier gate towards the elevator.

"OK, freeze it. Get me the logs for that gate access. I want to know who that is."

The security guard obliged, swinging his chair around to face a computer where he began typing in a password. Within a few minutes, the screen displayed employee details for Martha Matthews, aged thirty-four, and the photo appeared to be the same woman at first glance.

"Looks like her," Martins said.

Villar pointed to the employee information on the form alongside the photograph.

"Not if she's eight months pregnant and off on maternity leave."

Villar turned back to the CCTV frame of the woman and realised where the familiarity came from. It was the same woman she had seen a few days earlier in the building, which had initially aroused her suspicion.

Zoe Bowen.

Chapter 28

After leaving the Faber and Xeon building, Zoe headed to the Canary Wharf underground station and took the tube to the next stop at Canada Water. The rush-hour crowds of a few hours before had long since dispersed, and it was easier to keep an eye on her 'six', as Joe called it, to make sure she wasn't being followed.

She had not been trained in the art of counter-surveillance, but there was a plan, and Joe had briefed her in. A small part of her had found it hard to believe she would get this far. The looming prospect of what she had to do had not exactly helped her concentrate when Joe talked about the plan afterwards.

However, she remembered the basics: keep invisible, anonymous and watch the exits of the trains and any transport when you jump off. Use window reflections and corners to check behind you.

She had wiped the phone used to communicate with Haleema, taken out the sim card and battery and discarded them in different locations.

At Canada Water, she switched to the overland train to New Cross and then waited at the station, checking for the presence of anyone potentially tailing her, before boarding the return train back to her local station at Surrey Quays.

Fully confident no one had tracked her, Zoe slipped back through the streets and waterways and into her building and apartment and leaned heavily against the door, breathing slowly. She felt her legs weaken as she ventured inside and needed to use the wall as support for a moment.

Her success had lit some fire inside her. The old Zoe might have crumpled to the floor in tears, tried to hide and taken something to numb the pain. Now, determination and rage welled in her stomach, and she pushed herself off the wall and walked into the open-plan apartment.

She gulped down a glass of water, then started up her laptop and inserted the USB. There was a simple file manager app with a search bar. The first words she typed were 'Ed Flannigan'.

That drew a blank, so Zoe retyped his full name.

No results.

Zoe dropped her head into her hands.

"Fuck!" she shouted out loud.

If all that running around was for nothing.

Every hope had been pinned on finding something out.

Anything! Any fucking clue on why the hell Ed had thrown himself off the balcony.

Zoe stood up and stopped herself from throwing the laptop to the floor. Instead, she paced, pausing in front of the living room window that looked over at the winking nightlights on the Isle of Dogs.

In the quiet apartment, she heard her stomach rumble. Realising she hadn't eaten since breakfast, Zoe headed to the fridge after feeling too nervous leading up to the whole day's events. Soup, salad – it was pretty much bare. She heated the soup and made some toast.

Feeling calmer, Zoe sat back down by the computer and

spooned soup into her mouth. Her brother had requested copies of what she had taken from Faber & Xael as soon as possible, so she opened up Icarus to send the data and information via the decentralised blockchain that would be impossible to see or trace. When the upload began, Zoe continued clicking on random folders that caught her eye and scrolled through more subfolders inside. There were vast lists of documents, too many to go through individually. If Joe and his Liberatus friends wanted to sift through all this, they were welcome, as far as Zoe was concerned. It would probably take months.

She finished her food and tried another search, shortening Ed's surname, letter by letter: Flannig, Flanni, Flann—

Probably clutching at straws, she thought.

Then, a result.

A reference to the phrase: FLANN-E083. The document was buried in a folder named Op Hightop. She opened it up and found a list of names with images. She immediately recognised some of the faces. They were the same bankers who had died in accidents or committed suicide that she had read about weeks before.

With trembling fingers, she opened up the search bar and typed FLANN again to search the document – she clicked on the result again, and it jumped to an image of her former partner, Ed Flannigan.

She felt tears well up at the sight of him. It was his company photo. She scanned the accompanying text: his full name wasn't mentioned, but it listed his address, occupation, health records, personal banking details and a host of other private information. Then, the words 'Cessation' followed by the date of Ed's death a few months before.

186

Zoe gaped at the text, her hands now holding the side of her face.

"Cessation?"

She realised with what felt like a sickening punch in the stomach that she was staring at a hit list. Zoe stood up, nausea rising and rushed to the kitchen sink before vomiting up the food she had just eaten. She turned on the tap, rinsed out her mouth, and washed away the rest of the vomit.

"Ed," she whispered. "What the hell is going on?"

Her mind spun as much as her stomach. The reality and confirmation that Ed had not killed himself swirled around in her head. But was this enough evidence? Should she go to the police? Get a lawyer? What would she say when they asked how she obtained this information? She remembered Joe's words of warning that she was flying in the face of authorities. They would not protect her or dig too deeply into any case she gave them. In fact, he had said, 'They will come after you with everything they've got.'

Those words lingered for a moment, and she slowly walked back to the computer.

"They..." She mused on that thought. The faceless elite, the ones pulling strings. Murderers.

Her anger returned, and she brought herself to look once again at the list of dead bankers, including Ed. She went back to the top of the document to look closer at the text and began reading more carefully this time.

Mission Prog: OP HIGHHAT

Subject: Asset Cessations Batch 017

Facilitator: Dr White (Eva Villar), Henry Oberman.

Eva Villar. The redhead from Faben!

Zoe began to dig deeper into the files, searching for 'Villar' and 'Doctor White'.

An old case file popped up.

She began to scan through the text: "...series of control experiments. Eva's family terminated to cause maximum trauma to the subject who was taken away to the Colorado facility."

"Jesus. These people are sick," Zoe whispered under her breath.

Zoe mentally noted Henry Oberman's name and then messaged Joe on Icarus: "We need to talk urgently."

Chapter 29

It was several hours before they could get online and have a virtual meeting. Zoe's brother, Joe, was still somewhere in South America. He appeared in a small window on the screen with a slight tan, nodded an acknowledgement and grinned. It was the first time she had seen his face since Ireland, and his beard seemed to be getting out of control.

"Well done, Sis. Very well done," Joe said.

"On connecting to the call," she answered sarcastically.

"Well, I guess it's technical too – no, well done on the job." His facial expression changed from a smirk to concern. "Are you still in your flat?"

"Yes, I know, but finding somewhere is—"

"Any friends you can trust? Better still, I have some contacts I can give you but please, just as a precaution, disappear for a while if you can."

Zoe nodded. "Sure."

"It's important," Joe added.

"Yes, big brother, I'll get on it after this call."

An older man with a craggy face and combed-back grey hair appeared. He gave Zoe a warm smile. For a moment, she had the feeling of being star-struck and nervous. She knew he was John Rhodes, the founder of Liberatus and trailblazer for freedom since the 1990s and a thorn in the side of successive governments and the whole establishment. She had also read about his brother, the famous tech billionaire Michael Rhodes, who built the Goya Tech Corporation.

"Good to meet you virtually, Zoe. Joe's told me a lot about you." John said.

Zoe managed a thin smile. "All bad things, I expect?"

Joe cut in, "Oh c'mon, there were good things mentioned, occasionally."

They all laughed, instantly dispelling the tension.

"Actually, John may have met you when you were a baby, way back when Mum and Dad were in London. If that counts?" Joe continued.

"Oh, right. I don't think I remembered that," Zoe answered with a grin

"Anyway, we should get down to it," Joe said. "We've got some serious discoveries from our little raid on Faber and Xael. Zoe, we fished through what you sent over, but you go with what you've got first."

Zoe cleared her throat and spoke slowly.

"Thanks. Well, there is clearly a hit list that Ed was on. This list also had names of other individuals from the banking industry who had died under mysterious circumstances. There were names marked as Facilitators. A certain Henry Oberman and Eva Villar, also known as Doctor White."

There was a moment of silence before Joe spoke.

"I'm sorry to see that confirmed, Zoe. I guess the mystery is solved. So, it looks likely Ed's death was brought about by these people. We already know the cabal has these high-level so-called 'Doctors', Doctor Black, Doctor Red, and now this Doctor White, who we've found out about thanks to our friend,

Sirus."

"She went offline unexpectedly, by the way. Is she OK?" Zoe asked.

Joe paused for thought. "I'm sure she is, but I haven't heard from her since you came out of Faber and Xael. I'll keep trying."

"Right. I'm really worried about her. Where is she anyway? Can you tell me that at least?"

Joe shook his head. "She's in deep. Let's say that. Working for them while helping us. We put her in there."

Zoe pinched her fingers around the bridge of her nose.

"Oh god. Is she their prisoner effectively? I didn't realise that."

"It was her choice, ultimately," Joe said solemnly.

Zoe wondered whether Joe was being economical with the truth but decided to let it go.

Zoe nodded and said, "OK, let's move on. I also just came across this. The shock of losing Ed made me forget the big picture for a while, but you can see that there has been a shit ton of market manipulation. I've been out of the loop but looking at the markets. Well, the stock in Pithcore Gen, who are looking to be the biggest world food supplier with their GM crops, is skyrocketing due to the droughts in the East for months now devastating large parts of China and Asia."

"Which, believe it or not, we consider an engineered crisis," John chimed in.

"From what we've seen, it definitely is engineered," Joe added.

"What are you both talking about?" Zoe looked up and looked from Rhodes to Joe, confusion etched on her face, adding, "How can droughts be engineered?"

"So, up until 2015, there was a weather research facility

called HAARP, that's with a double 'A'," said Joe, checking his notes, "it stands for High-Frequency Active Auroral Research Program." Seeing the quizzical look on his sister's face, he continued. "What that did, in basic terms, was an experiment with the weather on a large scale. A high-level US Government file report published in 1966 called 'A Recommended National Program in Weather Modification' outlined the existence of this project, coordinated with multiple government agencies. I found this from an ex-researcher from HAARP who had a massive online resource on the blockchain about all this, a bloke called Dave Hoffington. He also exposed a lot of other stuff, including this paper, but he was labelled a crank conspiracy theorist and has since disappeared."

Joe leaned back and sipped from a mug.

"It does sound a bit crazy," Zoe chipped in, still sceptical.

"The cabal has played God with our biosphere for over sixty years," Rhodes said grimly. "Another one of their weapons added to everything else we've unearthed. See how the dots connect? I never imagined it was this bad." He shook his head.

"Well, Zoe, from the documents you've unearthed, it seems they never really closed down. It just changed its name to the Geo Weather Project and moved it to another location in Alaska. So, this drought in Asia looks to be linked."

"How the hell can they do that?" Zoe asked.

"Just think what bad weather can do to a foreign enemy: hurricanes, floods, droughts – no need for tanks or troops on the ground. You can control the populace from the comfort of your own home. If you have no water and cannot grow food, you can't exactly stand up and fight the fuckers."

"Oh, I understand they'd have the devious motivation. I mean, technically, how the hell can they physically change the weather?" Zoe asked.

"I'll zap over some background info, but there's a lot to it. All the data and evidence is there. The climate engineers at this facility have been experimenting with the weather patterns for decades, promoting extreme weather conditions like the droughts in California in 2013 and the freeze-fry events across America since are just a few examples I could fish out, and it's all blamed on climate change. From what I can make out, they use a combination of 'cloud seeding' from aircraft and fire-pulsed energy beams that modify the ionosphere. Using this, they can also block any inflow of storms and moisture to specific regions. You can only imagine the damage this is doing to the biosphere and life support systems."

"So, how are they modifying the weather in China if the facility is in Alaska?" Zoe asked.

"The main control hub for all this is indeed in Alaska, but I read that there are GWP ships, more like floating oil platforms, that can target specific countries or areas. There are three ships positioned around the North Pacific Ocean."

"Jesus – and the governments of Asia aren't aware of this?"

Joe shrugged. "I've no idea."

"So, is this all connected?"

"We've got this Geo Weather Project, the Asian drought, a supply chain crash, massive turmoil in the markets. I see they're crashing as we speak, except for Pithcore Gen and a few other cabal-controlled corporations.

"How can we expose Oberman?"

"Liberatus News might do something on Oberman or this whole GWP thing, but remember. I don't run things over there anymore. That's Marcus Brady's department," said John. "However, I'll put you in touch with one of our best journalists,

Matt Fulford."

"Does that make a difference anymore?" Joe cut in. "If mainstream media don't pick it up, they won't. Then there's no impact. We need to get in their faces now, get up close and rattle them."

Zoe sensed that underlying anger rising in Joe.

"Liberatus Media has a huge audience, Joe. We're still relevant. Very much so."

Joe looked unconvinced. "What we need is action."

"I can help," Zoe said. "Confronting Oberman..." Her eyes moved across the screen. "I found a meeting schedule from the Faber files. He's coming to London in the next few days. You have good journalists here, John? Can they set up an interview?"

"Someone like Oberman would never agree to it. He wouldn't even acknowledge you," Joe said sharply.

"No, I don't mean Liberatus. I mean posing as hacks from somewhere else – another paper or magazine."

John smiled. "Ah, I see where you're coming from, Zoe."

Joe, however, shook his head.

"Complete waste of time. I say we bundle him into a truck and throw him in the river."

"I'm not sure what that will achieve," Zoe said in a clipped tone.

"We have to do something about him, and this GWP facility based in Alaska is causing all this shit," Joe spoke more calmly this time, but the anger had not dissipated.

"Look, let me put a plan together with Zoe. I think she is right. The legit angle works better, and getting it out there into the public domain should ruffle feathers," John said.

Joe remained stony-faced.

"OK, Zoe, stay on the line. Joe, we'll discuss this shortly."

***

Joe cut the connection to the meeting and threw down his headphones. In John Rhode's library, the tranquil scene through the open French doors to the gardens did not reflect Joe's mood. He had spent three weeks as John's guest, and together, they had done a lot of work on building up the organisation. On the political wing, many more recruits were joining and waking up to the threat of the cabal.

On the militia side, Joe had helped build up more hives across the US, UK and Europe, and his power base was building fast. They had hundreds of recruits: ex-military, mercenaries, and other good people who could keep the wheels turning in such an operation. That was Joe's skill set. He could pull together a team and helped turn Liberatus into a force to be reckoned with. At least, he hoped he had.

However, Joe was hankering for more direct action and wasn't convinced that the gentle approach that John and Zoe suggested would work. Sure, they had exposed previous plans, but things were changing fast. Joe almost felt they were running out of time. He couldn't shake the feeling that something would switch up very soon, that the end game was coming.

Yeah, the fucking cabal needs to get a real good bloody nose, and I know just how to do it, he thought.

Rhodes had taken the video call in the dining room at the back of the old Spanish colonial house and entered the study through the interior doors. He purposely turned, gently closed the doors behind him, and then moved into the room.

195

"What are you planning, Joe? You're not thinking of hitting that facility?"

"Why not? It's clearly a threat to humanity. According to those files, they've been doing this for decades. This drought in Asia is killing tens of thousands or more and pushing the world to the edge of starvation. We need to take it out, show them we know what they're doing."

"And poke a wasp's nest? What is that going to achieve – especially for our project? The whole thing could be torn down! Destroyed!"

Joe stared the old man down and then rasped, "It's my decision."

"For the record, I don't agree with it, Joe. You'd better think it through. Make sure it's planned down to a 'tee' and make it seriously covert. Dress your teams up as eco-warriors or something. Lay the blame elsewhere, for God's sake!"

Joe shook his head with a flat smile. "Don't worry, any op will be tight, but they have to know who hit them."

Rhodes looked concerned but decided not to push it.

"Matt Fulford has agreed to work with Zoe on this Oberman case. I've set her up in a flat that belongs to a trusted friend who's out of the country. She's leaving her apartment to go there right now."

Joe felt himself relaxing. "Ah, good, thanks. If she's on their radar, she shouldn't be anywhere near her home address."

"Clearly not. She seems stronger. More focused."

"Yeah, she's resilient, alright."

Rhodes gave a throaty grunt in agreement.

"We'll need to talk again before you leave. Make sure we're both singing from the same hymn sheet, Joe."

Rhodes left and closed the doors behind him without another

word.

At least Zoe would be safer, he thought. There were good people around her. Matt Fulford and Marcus Brady had worked with his father, Frank, and could be trusted at least. His thoughts turned to the Alaska op.

Was it time to test Hugo Reese? See what he could do. The facility just had a couple of engineers based there. It shouldn't be too high risk. Just go in, get inside and blow it sky-high.

"You OK, hon?"

Joe turned around in surprise, coming back from his thoughts. Hanna stood in the exterior terrace doorway behind him. He hadn't realised she was even there.

"Oh, hi, baby. Yeah, all good. I should be all done now."

"Anything I can do? You look pissed off," she asked, stepping inside the study room.

Joe shook his head as she walked over.

"Oh no, just work shit."

She gave him a long hug and then kissed him on the cheek. Joe tilted his head, forcing himself to smother his frustrations, but he couldn't.

"When are we leaving?" she asked, glancing briefly at the laptop he had been using.

"Soon, a few days. But—" Joe hesitated. "I may have to go away for a while."

"Oh, where?" Hanna stepped back, looking up at him with a frown.

"I'm sorry. Duty calls."

Hanna nodded slowly. "I understand. You have to do what you have to do. Is it dangerous?"

Joe reached out and hugged her.

"Naw. It's all good, all good."

Joe's eyes focused on a world map framed on the wall, and already his thoughts turned to Alaska. He wouldn't be going, but some of him wished he could join the crew and lead them in.

No, Hugo would lead this one. He needed the live mission under his belt.

Chapter 30

The team's position was well hidden, overlooking a vast field dotted with mounds of excavated dirt interspersed with sprawling items of rubbish, including rusty oil drums that poked out of the earth. An old wheelless tractor acted as a focal point in the middle. Behind it, at around three hundred metres, stood a derelict farmhouse close to a row of cattle sheds. Behind the field was the backdrop of Tennessee's lush green hills and forests.

Hugo Reese slipped out the water bottle from his side belt and took a long pull. He glanced at Marty Faulkner and Josh Pierce, dressed in forest military fatigues, lying prone, watching through binoculars towards the cattle sheds.

Those two vatos were like two fucking beans in a taco, Reese thought. Whenever Faulkner grunted, Pierce echoed in response. Whatever history they had, Hugo wasn't sure, but they had served in the same unit, no doubt.

It was a tight team that had operated well in their little Iranian foray, despite Faulkner's constant bitching about almost anything. Next to them was one of their many latest recruits, Kate Copeland, with her rifle aimed towards the farmhouse with an aura of deadly competence.

Hugo scanned the wasteland through his Fujinon M22 7 x 50

Binoculars, military-issue field glasses, from the tractor and then across again to the farmhouse for himself. Their enemy, the Blue team, was surely holed up inside. He moved his sight to his extreme right side and caught a glimpse of his Alpha squad stealthily moving around the mounds of dumped soil, now overgrown with weeds and moss. They were executing a flanking movement on the enemy team while another smaller unit did the same on the far left side.

Faulkner, who was hunkered down alongside Hugo, leaned over and whispered in a low growl, "I still don't think they're in there. Too obvious."

Hugo removed the binoculars, still staring ahead.

"What makes you think that?"

Faulkner shrugged. "It's what I'd do."

"Well, if they ain't in there, where are they?"

Just then, Hugo's radio hissed.

"Alpha 1 to Delta five. Message."

It was Gianna calling from the homestead operations room.

"Your girlfriend callin'," Faulkner muttered with a smirk.

Hugo glared at him as he answered.

"Delta five. Send."

"Sorry, I know you're on a training thing, but it's urgent. Call received from Nightowl. He needs to speak to you directly."

"Right now?" said Hugo, his eyebrows furrowing.

"Yep."

"Alright, on my way. Good Copy. Delta five Out."

Hugo glanced over at Faulkner, who raised his eyebrows.

"Hope ya ain't in too much trouble," he said, still smirking.

"Jus' keep your focus on the Blue team. I hate to say it, but you're now in charge, vato."

Hugo crawled away, rolled down a dip in the hill and stood

up, heading back to the makeshift parking lot, another area of wasteland. He got into his truck and drove along a rutted track, through the forest and towards the main road.

It was hard not to try and second-guess what Joe wanted to talk about so urgently. Hugo had no doubt it was serious, for Gianna would not have told him while he was out on an important training exercise. Was their time as a military division coming? Was the resistance war that Joe and others always talked about to explode?

Since Hugo had been given more of a military role in the setup, he was much happier than messing around with all the organising, and everything worked smoothly in the Tennessee camp.

Ten minutes later, Hugo pulled up outside one of the Command houses just in time to see Gianna coming towards him. Her dreadlocks were tied back in a bun, and she was in a dark jumpsuit, splattered with paint with the leg ends rolled up. Even in her work attire, she still looked hot, thought Hugo.

He nodded, "Hey." Gianna kissed him full on the lips, then stepping back from that embrace, she handed him his mobile phone, which, along with the others, had to be left behind when out on training exercises.

"You'd better get calling," Gianna said, adopting a more official tone.

"Right. Any idea what it's about, mi sol?"

"Nope. For your ears only." She had an expression of intrigue and sarcasm.

"By the way," she added, gesturing to a stack of crates dumped on the ground behind her, "I think the Quantum tech equipment just arrived.

"Alright. We set it up after the call."

He walked inside, heading to the ops room in the basement. He dialled Joe again, ensuring the VPN encryption was active.

Within seconds, Joe's voice came on the line. "How're you doing?"

"I'm good, vato, good."

"Sorry to pull you off the exercise, but I wouldn't have done it unless it was a priority," said Joe in a conciliatory tone

"Well, I figured it must be something hot, vato," Hugo replied

"I'm sending you some files. Study them closely, then delete them. It'll be better if you look them up on a laptop at Operations."

Hugo found an open laptop amongst the various computer desks, then logged on with his unique ID and opened the encrypted file Joe had sent. There, Hugo found himself staring at an operational plan for a demolition job at some place in Alaska.

Hugo called Joe back on the encrypted line as he was examining the laptop screen, plugging in his earbuds to allow him to manipulate the images more easily.

"Okay, Joe, what am I looking at here," Hugo asked.

"It should be a piece of piss, mate. Very lightly guarded. In and out of job. I was going to lead it myself, but it's complicated for me at my end right now. I'm sure you can handle it with a small team."

Hugo leaned back in his chair and rubbed his chin stubble.

"What are we doing exactly?" he said, casting his eyes over images of the terrain around a group of buildings set in a remote wooded location.

"Everything you need to know is on the report. It ain't there if you don't need to know it."

"Yeah, right, got it."

"Get your team ready—no more than five operators. I'm making all the arrangements. You've got seventy-two hours before wheels up," Joe said with a voice of absolute command.

"Got it, boss," Hugo replied, acknowledging.

***

"This looks like it might be dangerous," Gianna said, her voice low with concern.

Hugo shrugged his shoulders. "There's gonna be a lot more like this comin'—no doubt."

Gianna frowned and dipped her head.

They were walking along the winding pathway across the grounds towards one of the houses that served as a barracks and storage area for the growing militia side of the Liberatus Tennessee operation.

Hugo stopped walking.

"Hey, I'm sorry, G," he said, pulling her a little closer. "It's gonna be OK. Just a routine thing. We're gonna be in and out without even waking the birds."

He gave her a reassuring rub on the shoulders, but Gianna still looked unconvinced.

Hugo hadn't been permitted to share the exact details due to her level of security clearance, but Gianna knew it was a live op and one outside the country.

Gianna leaned into him and slipped her arm around his waist.

"Will you be able to say goodbye before you go?"

"Yeah, sure, Cariña," Hugo replied softly.

"OK, baby," she sighed.

They kissed again and separated, Gianna heading through

the gardens to the machine workshop where she had been using her skills to provide modifications to the team's equipment, enhancing its performance. Hugo watched her go for a few moments, then continued to the barracks.

Their relationship had developed in Spain when Hugo had gone back to the Andalusia base for a meeting with Joe. Their crazy adventure in Spain and the aftermath seemed to have sparked something, and Gianna decided to move to the Tennessee base to be with him.

Hugo smiled at the thought of how life had changed since his days in the Florencia 13 gang on the streets of South Central LA.

At the house, he walked in and entered the main front room. Once a living room in an old farmhouse, it was now an ops meeting room with a large table in the centre, whiteboards on one wall, and fixed screens on another.

Inside, most of the team who had just returned from their exercise were still dressed in combat fatigues and were called straight into the ops room on arrival. Marty Faulkner, Josh Pierce in his trademark baseball cap, Hodge Balfour, Billy Pitman and their most recent recruit, Kate Copeland. She had been one of the first female marines out of the recruit depot at Parris Island. She had served with the 'Thundering Third' better known as the 3rd Battalion, 4th Marines, for seven years before dropping out—just one of many new recruits coming through who had shown serious potential. The old guys, as Hugo called Faulkner and Pierce, were well experienced, that was for sure, but he wasn't exactly seeing eye to eye with them.

Hugo glanced at Faulkner and leaned both palms on the table.

"This is a live op. We're leaving in the next twenty-four hours."

"Before I start, let me just lay it out," Hugo added, looking again at Faulkner. "How y' doing with that wound, Marty?"

"What the hell are you talking about?" Faulkner snapped back

"You know full well. The shot you took in Iran," Hugo said, his voice becoming steely hard.

Everyone in the room knew Faulkner hadn't been as sharp since recovering from the bullet in the shoulder when they had gone on that mission to help Haleema Sheraz and her family.

Faulkner looked around at everyone defensively and rolled his shoulder, patting it with a gnarly hand.

"It's fine, I'm good." he looked insulted.

Hugo nodded. "Great. Cos, we need your expertise with explosives." Looking up at the rest of the team, he said with that same steely emphasis, "We jus' all need to be on it, one hundred percent."

A silence hung in the room for a few moments, and then Hugo proceeded to open a drawer from one of the cabinets, take and roll out a map onto a desk. He jerked his head towards the screen on the wall.

"Take it that's still busted?"

"Yep," Billy said. "I'll look at it later today."

The team moved closer to check out the map. It was an area of forest.

"What this public map don't say—" And pausing, Hugo proceeded to overlay a transparent sheet with a schematic diagram of a large group of buildings and what looked like a field of cross shapes deep in the forest. "Is what they got hidden in this area. This facility has been the cause of the big-time weather plays over in Asia. Our mission is to take it out – destroy it."

205

Hugo defined the mission as the team gathered closer, moving around the map and overlay. "Our two main objectives are first to find their server room and destroy their computer network. Second, place two charges in the building." Hugo pointed to sections on the main building. "Here and here. On bugging out, we'll hit the fire alarm, getting everyone out of the building before we detonate."

"The intel we got on the facility tells us there will be under ten non-military personnel on-site. If we trip the alarm, we will have around a forty-mike window before any security arrives. Should be in and out in under an hour."

The assembled team nodded one by one as they saw the mission's flow.

Addressing the unspoken question that was gathering, Hugo said, in summary.

"We exfil the way we go in, via Tok Junction airport, about 100 klicks from the Canadian border. If it all goes south and we separate, head back to the town."

Hugo stood up straight and looked around at the rest of the team, who looked back expectantly.

"Team going in will be me, Marty, Billy and Kate. The rest sit it out here. Any questions?"

"What's the route into Tok and timings?" Kate asked.

"Civvie flights from Atlanta to Fairbanks International is a nine-hour flight. Then we charter a private plane to Tok. Takes about an hour and forty-five mikes. There, a contact will meet us with all the gear we need. You'll get more details of the mission when we get there."

Hugo slapped a briefcase onto the table and opened it. Part of the earlier delivery along with the Quantum radio equipment. He took out manilla envelopes stuffed with documents.

"Here's our travel documents. We leave here in the morning."

"Do you happen to have the inflight menu?" Marty asked with a straight face. "My stomach is awful dicky nowadays, so I only eat a la carte – did no one mention this? I want peeled grapes."

A collective groan went around the room, and even Hugo himself couldn't help a wry smile.

"Alright, dis-fucking-missed."

Chapter 31

In one of the hotel conference rooms, tucked away towards the back of the hotel, Zoe, Matt Fulford, the journalist and Phil, their cameraman, waited in silence. A tripod camera in the corner faced the table where they had arranged the interview.

They had reviewed the details several times, and all they could do was hope that Oberman actually showed up. In the lingering wait, Zoe began to think this was all a mistake.

What would this actually achieve? Even if Oberman showed up, wouldn't he deny everything?

But then John Rhodes was smart. Without some plan, he wouldn't have given them the go-ahead for this mission.

Matt looked up from his laptop, from which he had been entirely focused and gave her a reassuring smile as if he had been reading her mind. He looked the epitome of a techy hack; unshaven, greying hair tied back in a ponytail, and rumpled clothes added to his dishevelled attire. Appearances were just an illusion, as Zoe had been told. Fulford was a well-respected journalist with a solid reputation for relentless investigative work. He had remained loyal to John Rhodes and Liberatus News for decades, whereas many others in his field had become simply mouthpieces for the state propaganda narrative. Zoe took comfort from his smile, knowing her colleague was no shrinking violet.

There was a chime on Fulford's mobile.

"He's here. You're up, Zoe," he said, turning back to his laptop.

Zoe looked the part she was playing in her smartest pinstripe suit and matching high heels; hair pulled back tightly to a tight bun highlighting her immaculate make-up and made-up to the proverbial 'nines'. They were posing as an interview team for a significant mainstream channel, and she had to look authentic. She walked out along the corridor, a lanyard swinging over her chest, towards the lobby area. There she saw Oberman, dressed in a black turtle neck top, jeans and suit jacket, talking to a stressed-looking receptionist. Next to him was a tall, suited, bulky man who was his bodyguard. Hearing the click of her heels, Oberman turned to Zoe as she approached.

"Zara Fields, *Time* Magazine. Great to meet you, Mr Oberman," Zoe said, flashing him one of her dazzling smiles, voice pitched to emulate that of an upper-class country girl.

"This way, please." She turned on her heel and led the group to the conference room.

Oberman peered inside the room and, turning to his bodyguard, instructed him to wait outside the doorway. Then he stepped inside, closed the door and took the seat that Zoe gestured to. He waved a large hand, refusing an offer of a glass of water to drink, and glanced at his watch.

"You've got fifteen minutes, max," he said curtly.

Fulford nodded at Phil, who proceeded to film the interview.

Zoe cleared her throat. "Mr Oberman, you've been a major player with corporations associated with the Runeshield family group for many years. It's no secret that the family wield incredible power in the world. How do you see their role-playing out?"

Oberman leaned back in his chair and began with what sounded like a well-rehearsed press release. The words came out fluently enough, but there was little substance within them.

When he paused, Zoe asked, "Can you explain the connection between Bayer & Harlow, the private equity group and ZEOS bank, of which you are CEO?" Zoe glanced down at her notepad, "Particularly regarding the call options betting on the huge rise of Pithcore Gen, the GM Foods group?"

Oberman snorted derisively. "I'm the CEO. I won't delve into the everyday financial transactions of a few managers. Bayer & Harlow are a valued client of ZEOS, certainly, but—"

Zoe abruptly cut him off mid-sentence. "In light of the global food supply and major droughts in Asia, doesn't Pithcore Gen stand to gain massively, putting them in the position to control the world's food?" she stated, fixing her gaze on Oberman's face.

Oberman stared at Zoe, and then Matt returned his own stare at Zoe.

"Probably. Sounds like a smart trade. It's the way of the financial world, love. We have thousands of investments. What is your point?"

As rehearsed, at that question, Fulford opened a manilla folder and handed Zoe a sheet of paper, which she pushed towards Oberman on the table between them.

"A trading account at Bayer, named 714, lists all the trades, reaching nearly 800 million and still counting as we speak," she continued.

Oberman leaned forward slightly to look at the sheet but didn't pick it up.

"Where did you get this?" his tone became darker as he

spoke.

Zoe ignored him and continued, "Bayer's parent corporation, Faber & Xael, also has majority stakes in Pithcore Gen and other corporations with controversial reputations. Cryostone, for example, the military tech corporation. Following that missing flight 313 several years ago, the missing key directors paved the way for its takeover." Zoe could feel her heart pumping harder in her chest, but she forced herself to remain calm in the face of the enemy.

"I'm not aware of that. Again, I don't follow the point of your questions," Oberman spat back.

"Which brings us to the HAARP project," Fulford chimed in for the first time, "and its successor, a covert weather manipulation programme run by Cryostone called the Geo Weather Modification Project – claimed by many to be the cause of the horrific droughts and over 100,000 deaths in Asia." Pausing for effect, he continued, "As a CEO in a bank with ties to all this, what do you say?"

Zoe pushed over a printout of an email.

"This email is from you to one of the trading managers, ordering the continuation of the trades, despite knowing the suffering and chaos—"

Oberman seemed to snap.

"Crackpot conspiracies! This line of questioning wasn't in the agreement. Are you even from *Time* magazine?"

He stood up suddenly with a face full of fury.

"How do you explain the suspicious suicides of over one hundred bankers working for your bank and many others?" Zoe said, raising her voice a level.

Oberman headed to the conference room door.

A mobile phone beeped, unheard, as Fulford fired another

211

question: "What did they know, Mr Oberman?" then gestured to Phil, who took the video camera off the tripod. Zoe and Matt stood up and hurried after Oberman, who was now speedily walking towards the lobby. The bodyguard stepped in front of them, arms outstretched as he tried to hold them off.

"You don't own this hotel. Get outta the way!" Zoe shouted in his face, the upper-class accent gone. Her sudden outburst put him off guard, and the trio pushed past him.

Then, alarm bells like those of a fire alarm inside sounded throughout the hotel.

Distant shouting was heard, and the few people present in the lobby froze in place, unsure of what was happening.

A doorman in a uniform who had been standing outside earlier was now inside, holding his hands up. He shouted as loud as he could above the increasing clamour.

"Everybody, please stay put. We have a situation outside. I repeat, please stay put in the lobby. A request by the police to—"

His voice was cut short as Zoe saw Oberman had walked straight up to the doorman and began gesturing, clearly demanding to be let out. Oberman's security shoved past them, knocking Zoe against the lobby wall as he joined his boss.

Zoe turned back to Phil with the camera.

"Are you getting this? Keep rolling!" she yelled as Phil moved forward gingerly, training it towards Oberman."

"Closer!" Zoe hissed, but he didn't move. She grabbed the camera off him and walked towards the commotion with it still recording.

"Get out of my way now! Let me out of here!" Oberman shouted as the doorman was physically preventing him from leaving the hotel. Oberman then pulled something from inside the jacket of his security guard. As Zoe got closer, she realised the object in his hand was a gun.

"Get out of my way!" Oberman demanded menacingly, waving the weapon

At the sight of the weapon, the doorman finally stepped aside.

"Sir!" the security guard pleaded with his boss. "I don't think—"

Gun in hand, Oberman went through the rotating doors onto the central London street. The guard followed. Meanwhile, behind him, Zoe continued to film.

The doorman had edged back into the lobby and was speaking to the few guests still standing, gaping at where Oberman had caused a scene.

"It's OK, everyone. Please stay put," the doorman said, pleading with them to move back into the lobby.

With the doorman momentarily distracted, Zoe slipped past the doorman and moved through the rotating doors, looking for the ZEOS CEO. In a split second, she caught sight of black vans at one end of the street and the black military-style uniforms of the British police's Armed Response Unit, rifles in hand, snaking down the road towards the hotel.

"Oh shit!" she muttered.

She hunched low next to a postbox while keeping the camera trained on Oberman. In all the chaos, a sense of calm came across Zoe as she watched the scene unfold. Oberman was crossing the road towards a line of parked cars, his gun still in hand. Beyond him, flashes of more ARU personnel were coming in from the other end of the street.

There was a shout through a bullhorn.

"Put down your weapon, sir!" came the voice of the lead

ARU officer ringing with absolute authority.

With the pistol clearly visible in his hand and still enraged by the recent confrontation, Oberman turned and pointed it towards the speaker. Immediately a double tap of rifle fire rang out.

Zoe caught her breath as Oberman fell back under the impact of the shots, then slumped down, crashing against a parked car. He grabbed his chest, then crumpled slowly to his knees and finally kneeled face down on the tarmac, blood slowly pooling onto the road.

There was a pause, almost as if time had stopped, and Zoe, breathing heavily to calm her pounding chest, lowered the camera and slowly moved back into the hotel lobby.

Chapter 32

Clouds of dust billowed out from the old shutters as they were slammed shut and then bolted into their closed position. All the windows in what had been Jason Runeshield's father's estate, nestled in the Rocky Mountains of Aspen, Colorado, were being secured.

Workman hurried to and fro to get the house secured. The precious items owned by his father – the paintings, antiques, rugs and mirrors that decorated the home – were all being carefully removed and packed. Crates lined the hallways, and removal men carried them out to several large removal trucks parked in the front concourse to be driven off to a safer location.

Jason looked out across the estate. The view was breathtaking. It was why his mother had first fallen in love with the place, probably why his father had bought it.

Happier times back then, he mused.

Taking a deep breath and locking that memory away again, he returned to focus on the task at hand.

Jason had wanted to personally visit the estate and take what he thought may be a last look over the old house. He was unsure when he would see it again. He could imagine similar scenes happening at the houses and estates owned by the cabal across the United States and Europe. Families were saying goodbye to homes that had been in their lineage for generations—one of the many sacrifices they were making for the greater good.

His mobile began vibrating in his inside jacket pocket, and Jason glanced at the screen. It was Doctor Black.

"Mr Runeshield, sir... I..." the voice began trembling with emotion.

"Yes?" Jason said sharply.

"It's Mr Oberman, sir. He's been killed in England," Black said with obvious fear, his voice still trembling.

"What?"

"There was an incident," Black's voice had dropped to a whisper.

"Killed?" Runeshield stared at the floor, dumbfounded. After a moment's pause, he spoke again. "Tell me exactly what happened?" Then, the shock quickly turned to rising anger as Doctor Black explained that Oberman had been duped into some media interview at the Savoy hotel, which seemed to have provoked him to a fit of rage.

"There was an incident; Oberman walked out of the hotel brandishing a handgun when a British police Armed Response Unit team that apparently had been anonymously called to the scene and an accident happened. There was a shooting—" Then his voice fell silent.

Runeshield was stunned into silence too. Oberman, his friend, his ally...was dead.

He breathed in slowly through his nostrils, releasing his breath with pent-up rage as he struggled with the emotions swirling like a hurricane within him.

"Listen very carefully", Runeshield hissed into the phone's mouthpiece, thin lips curling with rage. "I want whoever killed my friend, whoever actually pulled the trigger, whoever orchestrated this killing to be taken out of the picture. Do you understand? And, of course, I want a full report sent directly to me. I want to know who the hell is responsible! Every detail of what happened!"

Without waiting for further response, Runeshield cut the call and gripped the phone in his palm, staring at the floor for a moment. He then walked quickly over to an Edwardian oak cabinet, grabbed the Qing Dynasty vase placed on top, ready for packing, and threw it hard onto the floor, releasing a howl of anger towards the ceiling of the old building. There was a sharp crack as the vase shattered into hundreds of broken shards. Some workmen nervously glanced over but continued with their packing, knowing better than to get involved.

Jason stared down at the shards, his hands shaking.

"Fuck!" he screamed. The curse echoed through the vast room.

He cared not one iota that the vase was valued at close to eighteen million dollars and turned to the window, away from the room and hushed whispers and looked across the grounds as his eyes glistened with tears.

After a few minutes, he heard a low whisper behind him.

"Sir." It was his personal secretary. "We need to go now."

Jason sniffed and wiped an eye.

Yes, the evacuation needed to roll on. There were things to do. So much to do to get ready.

As he walked towards the door, he vowed that he would now take a personal interest and avenge the loss of his friend.

Chapter 33

Glancing down into the dark abyss from the footbridge that led to the G13 silo, Zak felt a sense of rushing vertigo and forced himself to focus on the doorway ahead. A rush of air from deep in the belly of the base had a metallic tinge to it, and Zak felt, as he had done since his transfer here, wholly disconnected from the outside world. He may as well be on some distant space station hurtling through the galaxy.

Zak swiped his access card and stepped into the first room, where a guard checked his ID and waved him into the inner sanctum of the Ghost 13 intelligence comms centre. Some of the other teams were already at their desks. Another colleague stood in front of a bank of screens covering the curved walls that provided a stream of data worldwide. Zak glanced up and saw Kate Foster gesturing to him through the glass window of her mezzanine office.

Not even time to get a coffee, it seems.

Zak climbed the metal steps and stepped into Foster's office.

"Morning, Zak. Sorry to jump you, but an asset, one of yours, has sent in some worrying intel." Foster gestured for him to pull up a chair next to her.

"One of mine?" Zak asked. He couldn't help feeling annoyed that Foster had hijacked his comms, but she was the boss.

"Who?" he asked, his curiosity piqued.

"Agent Darklight – embedded in one of the Liberatus factions, close to the top."

Zak remembered some of the details. Darklight had spent years infiltrating the organisation and had barely sent in any reports for nearly eighteen months. They had considered the possibility Darklight had turned and gone rogue, but it appeared not. As Zak had inherited a list of assets in the field, including Darklight, he didn't have a handle on the history or much else.

"Do we know who this asset's controller was originally?" Zak asked

"Classified. I can say it was handled by elements of the early Ghost 13 set up in London along with an undisclosed European intel service."

"Sounds messy," Zak grunted.

"Anyway, they sent this." Foster waved a hand at the screen.

Zak began reading the highly classified and decrypted short message:

'Agent Darklight to Dark Hive – suspected raid on secret Gov facility imminent. Co-ords are not known except somewhere in Alaska. Will send more intelligence if attained.'

"That's it?" Zak commented, somewhat bemused by the brevity of the message.

"Yes. Can you look into it? What facilities are there in Alaska that could be a possible target? I know there are dozens of Government, military and intelligence stations and bases, so this isn't that helpful."

"OK, I'm on it." Zak stood up and headed out of her office. At the door, pausing momentarily, he turned to his boss and said, "There's always the real possibility this asset is now a double agent," he said.

Foster nodded. "Yes, an excellent point. Maybe just giving us 'chicken feed'," she replied, referring to the possibility it was bogus or false information.

"Keep me in the loop," she added, looking away at a side monitor on her desk.

Zak closed the door and headed back down to his desk on the lower level. He headed straight to the coffee machine, poured one, made small talk with a colleague, and fired up his workstation.

As he began to look into the intel's possible targets, he couldn't shake off that there was a remote possibility that his brother, Joe, might be involved in this.

It took several hours to compile a list of possible targets. What the message said was a 'secret facility', so Zak had discounted the obvious military bases and focused on the more covert Government and military facilities.

Among the list of possible targets were CIA stations as well as military bases. There was also a research programme called HAARP or 'High-frequency Active Auroral Research Program' funded by the U.S. Air Force, the U.S. Navy, and the Defense Advanced Research Projects Agency (DARPA). The facility and vast antenna array were located in Gakona, on the southeast side of Alaska.

According to the report that Zak scanned through, the project had been officially closed down in 2014 but 'unofficially' had been replaced by the Geo Weather Project (GWP), which continued the work of HAARP with experiments on the ionosphere and other weather manipulation.

Zak shook his head with disapproval. He knew very little about it, but it was one thing for the government to keep the enemies from the gates and take down terrorist networks but quite another to mess around with the global weather systems. As instructed, Zak compiled a list of the most likely targets in order of probability as well as their ability to respond and repel any incursions that may happen.

Zak was finishing up the report when his internal phone rang. He picked up.

It was Foster.

"You might have wasted your time. We have an updated OTP from Darklight – it looks like we have the location details." Let's review the options we have to respond to this threat."

Back in Foster's office, they both read the decrypted message. It pointed to the GWP facility that Zak had just pulled onto his report.

"A continuation of the HAARP project, from what I could see," Zak offered.

"I'm sure if this intel were gold, it would be a great opportunity to give this militia a bloody nose," said Foster.

Zak shifted uncomfortably in his chair but said nothing, steepling his fingers and hiding his inner disquiet.

"However," she went on, "We do get a lot of these, and with so many resources tied up with Operation Hallows, I doubt whether we can spare many resources. You could check if there's a unit available in the AO." Turning to Zak and looking him fully in the face, she said with added finality, "I'll leave that to you."

Zak thought about Joe again. He wondered whether to try to contact him and warn him about this, but that would be treason. Besides, it would be near impossible to communicate with anyone in this place covertly. No, Joe was on his own, and if he was involved in this, well, he was clearly in over his head

221

and should know better.

Chapter 34

Southern Alaska. 3:01 AM.

Two large half-track snowmobiles, with two teams, powered along just below a ridgeline before descending towards a dark, thick forest that lined the bottom of a valley. It was a cold but clear night, and Hugo wasn't sure if this was good or bad. The snow fields and the moonlight illuminated the surroundings with a glowing hue. The snowmobiles slowed as they arrived at the valley's tree line, then looped around in a circle to face back the way they had come before finally cutting the engines. The smell of damp wood greeted Hugo as he whipped off his helmet and took a deep breath of sharp night air.

This was it. Finally, Hugo was leading his own live op. Not that there was any expected opposition. It was a sparsely manned science outpost. All they had to do was secure any misfortunate persons who happened to be there and then destroy the facility.

All dressed in white alpine camo, Faulkner, Copeland, and Pitman dismounted and quietly gathered their gear. They had minimal weapons: handguns and a few stun grenades. Hugo checked his watch.

"OK, let's move," he whispered.

The four figures trudged into the thickness and relative cover of the forest, heading north to their target.

So far, since leaving their base in Tennessee, everything had gone more or less to plan despite it being a long haul to the target. They had taken flights to Fairbanks International Airport, then took second private hires to get to the Tok airport, where they met the contact to pick up their gear and mobiles.

The only problem was half the automatic weapons they were expecting were not with the delivery. The contact, a tall, bearded guy who was apparently some sleeper agent for the Liberatus cause, just shrugged at the exasperation he got from Hugo. It was 'all he could get', apparently. However, he had been reasonably helpful in providing info on their target. He explained to Hugo that the original building plans had given him a good idea of where the server rooms were located as they would need an efficient cooling system. They were most likely found on sub-level one.

A jagged pattern from the moonlight spread across the snow-covered woodland ground. Apart from their footfall crunching into the snow, the surroundings were deathly quiet.

Gradually, dim artificial lights came into view through the thick pines as they arrived at the forest's edge. Beyond a wire fence stood a field of antennas, nearly eighty feet high, with spiked crosses near the top of each one, forming what appeared in the eerie moonlight as a vast spider's web high off the ground.

"Jesus, look at that shit," Marty whispered.

"One way to cook the planet," Hugo replied.

"We need to move along, nearer the buildings." He pointed over to the distant lights of the buildings they could make out. Just past the antenna array, a quiet fenced road led to the facility from a public highway about a mile away.

"Everyone, get your Night Viz on."

The rest of the squad pulled down their night vision goggles and checked their comms and equipment for a few moments.

Hugo signalled with a wave, and they all moved off in a staggered line, walking parallel to the fence and heading towards the building.

When they were alongside the building, Hugo gestured with an upraised fist to stop and crouched down. The others behind relayed the action and did the same.

On the far side of the fence stood the main three-storey building with the external lights they had spotted earlier. It was a nondescript grey block with darkened windows and two sections that created an L shape. It looked like no one was home, but Hugo knew this couldn't be the case.

A few places behind Hugo, Billy Pitman crawled to the fence with wire cutters and started to cut a hole in it. They all crawled through one by one, quickly jogging over to the exterior wall.

With Hugo leading, they proceeded around the building. Hugo stopped at a ground-floor window, turned and gestured to Pitman. Pitman shuffled up, checked the window and reached into his bag of tricks for his glass cutter. He attached the device and cut circular holes through the double-glazed window panes. Within a minute, Pitman removed a section of the window, large enough for him to reach his arm in and unlock it. When no alarm sounded, cautiously, he climbed inside.

Hugo turned and nodded to Faulkner and Copeland before climbing inside. Through the green hue of his NVGs, Hugo saw Pitman aiming his weapon down a circular stairwell before slowly descending.

Behind him, Faulkner and Copeland climbed inside, moving down the metallic steps as quietly as they could to the first subterranean level. The building was silent, just the hum of the forced air regulating the temperature. They came to an intersection, two corridors splitting off in different directions. Pausing briefly, Hugo looked around, trying to get his bearings. Their contact thought the server rooms would most likely be in the central section of that floor.

Hugo didn't much care for the vague info he had received. All they could do was start looking. He gestured to Faulkner and Copeland with two fingers and pointed down the East corridor where they were to begin planting T4 explosives. Then he nodded to Pitman, and they moved into the darkness.

Through his NVGs, Hugo could make out a series of closed doors on either side of the long corridor. They weren't numbered, so Hugo counted off in his head before reaching what he thought might be the server room. They both took positions on either side of it, and Pitman reached down and tried the handle. The door was locked but didn't look like it would offer much resistance. Hugo gestured with a nod and stepped back in front of the door. With all his force, he slammed his boot under the handle. There was a cracking sound, and the door gave way a little. He followed up with another aggressive kick, and the lock gave, sending the door swinging inwards. They moved cautiously inside and closed the door behind them, although it wouldn't lock now. A vast space opened up, packed with the multicoloured winking lights of multiple server machines on towering racks.

They kept the room lights off and immediately got to work, searching out the correct server. Pitman, the most tech-savvy of the group, had been briefed. Essentially they were planting a network virus into the system to cripple the whole control grid – from the command centre in which they stood to the mobile platforms dotted around the seas of Asia that were causing severe damage to those countries.

It took a few minutes for them to find the right server, then their USB drive was slotted in, and Pitman, crouching down, opened a laptop on one of the lower stacks, lifted his NVGs and then began typing in commands to run the programme.

After a few minutes, Pitman whispered, "Alright, it's running. We need to wait for a few minutes while it uploads, and then we're good."

There was nothing they could do but wait. Hugo checked his watch and exhaled slowly. Hopefully, Marty and Copeland had planted a decent batch of explosives. The last thing they wanted to do was underestimate what was needed to cripple this place permanently.

Then, a loud crack yanked him out of his thoughts.

He could barely react as the door was smashed open behind them, and a grenade tumbled onto the floor.

"Down!" he shouted. Both men rolled onto the ground.

Even with his eyes closed and ears covered, the shock wave from the stun grenade tore through Hugo's senses. He had a vague notion of people rushing into the room but felt the weight drive the air from his lungs as someone knelt on his back. Before he knew it, he was searched and stripped of all his weapons. Then, he was hauled up into a kneeling position.

A weapon barrel pressed against his head. He could make out movement behind the balaclava. Was this guy talking to him?

The ringing in his ears was slowly subsiding, and he started to make out the words.

"How many of you are there?" came a low voice.

Hugh shook his head, trying to stop the feeling that the room was spinning.

"How many of you are there?" came the voice again.

"Alright, alright," Hugo shouted, trying to overcome the stark fear coursing through his veins.

He glanced over at Pitman, who looked equally as disoriented.

"Who are you with?" the voice demanded with increasing intensity.

Hugo squinted, getting used to the light and trying to assess the situation while wondering how they had been compromised. Had they been spotted going in or betrayed?

There were three of them in the room, dressed in black with balaclavas covering their faces.

Hugo knew that he just needed to buy enough time for the virus to upload behind him and do its thing.

He glanced over at Pitman, who returned the knowing look.

"The rest of your team?" the leader of the trio demanded again.

Hugo ignored the question and assessed the man in front of him. Behind the balaclava, he saw an Afro-Caribbean guy staring back at him. The dark militia fatigues made them look like a ninja unit. He had no idea who they were, but their approach indicated that they were definitely Special Forces. What the hell were they doing here? They must have been tipped off.

The dude was turning Hugo's pistol around in his hands, studying it as if it held some clue to their identity.

"You don't look like a regular army or any security company, vato," Hugo said evenly.

The squad leader turned and spoke to his cuff into a concealed mic.

"Wolf 9, we have two captives. Keep searching. Be aware they are armed."

Hugo turned his head and glanced down at the laptop directly behind him. The progress bar was completed. He stared hard at Pitman, then blinked his eyes. Pitman understood.

Hugo then focused on the squad leader and began talking, stalling for time.

"What do ya think we're doing, ese? Do you even realise what this place is? Why are you chacales even here? If you're such a special force, why have you been sent here?" Hugo was well aware he was probably poking at a proverbial wasp's nest. He didn't even know who these guys were.

"Shut it," the leader grunted. He gestured at one of his men. "Take a look around. See what the hell they've been doing."

"Didn't you see those fields of antennas?" Hugo continued, "All pointing to the ionosphere over Asia. Know what's going on in Asia at the moment? Only the worst drought since records began, bru. You already know how many are dead."

The Special Forces guy looked confused for a moment.

"This place?" As Hugo's words finally registered an impact.

"Think about who you're working for, vato," Hugo added.

Then, there must have been a voice in the earpiece of his captor, and he was distracted again. The other two had moved away, looking at the server stacks.

Now was the time. He glanced again at Pitman.

They both moved with lightning speed. Hugo punched the squad leader with a well-aimed shot to the groin. The blow caught him off guard, and he doubled over with the contact. Hugo jumped to his feet and was out the door in a flash.

There was a shout as Hugo entered the dark corridor. He turned right, opposite to the way they had come in. Pitman followed right behind him, their feet pounding, echoing off the walls.

A single gunshot echoed through the narrow corridors, and Hugo glanced behind again but could still see Pitman running behind him.

"Come on!" he shouted. Hugo shoulder barged a set of doors, then took a sharp turn into another long, dark corridor. They got to the end and through more doors to a stairwell, where an emergency exit sign glowed like a beacon of hope. They began to ascend with a clatter of footsteps. Hugo could feel his heart hammering away in his chest. As his adrenaline spiked, a memory came to him of his gangbanger days back in South Central. Running from men with guns.

All they could do now was run. And keep running.

At the top of the stairs, Hugo unbolted the emergency exit doors and pushed them open. Gunfire followed them, and bullets ripped past them in the cold night air. Billy seemed to be slowing and pale-faced as he came to the top of the steps.

"Shit, shit!" Pitman grunted. "I'm hit!"

Hugo glanced down but couldn't see anything.

"Can you keep going?"

"Yeah, I..."

"Come on. We gotta get to the trees, vato."

They headed across the hard, snow-covered ground, running into the large field of antennas that crisscrossed the area, checking the building behind with quick glances. Ahead, the dark cover of the forest beckoned, but it was a good fifty metres of exposed ground. Dawn was breaking across a pink and blue sky, making the chances of him being seen that much higher.

Though, he didn't doubt those guys had NVGs.

The thick snow slowed their progress, and then, Hugo heard the exit doors crash open behind them.

More gunfire crackled across the field. Hugo dived to the ground and turned his head to see Pitman do the same. He spotted the dark figures of their adversaries, ducking down for their own cover. One retreated into the building.

Their pursuers were being fired at?

Hugo realised that Marty and Kate must have been alerted to the enemy's presence and taken up an overwatch position in the trees.

"Come on, keep crawling," he hissed at Billy.

The gunfire continued, coming in both directions over their heads. As Hugo and Billy got within a few metres of the tree line, there were thuds behind them, accompanied by a sudden eruption of billowing white smoke - a strategic deployment of smoke grenades that shrouded their escape. It was the cover they needed.

Hugo caught sight of Marty behind one of the trees, gesturing to them with a jerk of his rifle. Hugo didn't hesitate to run back to Pitman and lead him to the relative safety of the woods. When they got there, they slumped down behind a large tree as the gun battle continued.

Pitman was white as a sheet, strength seemingly draining from him by the second.

"Billy?"

Hugo slapped his comrade across his face, and his eyes flickered.

"The others?" he muttered, "what about the others?"

Hugo unclasped himself from Pitman's grip and looked at the source of dark red blood that was soaking Pitman's jacket.

It was the back of his right arm—a possible brachial artery wound.

He had lost way too much blood.

Not good.

"Don't worry 'bout the others, vato. They're watching our backs," Hugo replied calmly as he tore the hole in Pitman's jacket arm wider to get a better look. It was sodden and wet with blood. Pitman's eyes rolled as he wavered on the edge of consciousness, and then his eyelids flickered for a few seconds. His hands gripped Hugo's arm, and in a strained whisper, he mouthed the words "go" before his pupils dilated and his stare glazed over.

He was gone.

Hugo stared at his still face.

"Billy?"

He tried his pulse but already knew the truth.

"Fuck!" he shouted.

He sensed a figure moving across towards him, through the trees. Marty. He bent down next to Hugo, staring at their comrade. He put a hand on Hugo's shoulder.

"He's gone, buddy. Let's get out of here."

Hugo looked up at him.

"Just leave him here?"

More gunfire, closer now. Their pursuers must be moving across the field towards them.

Hugo nodded, the realisation of their situation becoming clear. They retreated into the woods while Copeland fired her last rounds across the field before moving back with them.

After a few minutes of stumbling through the forest, there was a distant series of dull booms.

Explosions.

Hugo looked across at Marty, who smiled back.

"Think we couldn't do it?"

Hugo gave the thumbs up, but he felt sick in the stomach about Billy.

One of their team was dead.

And someone must have betrayed them.

Chapter 35

Hugo and Pierce half-jogged through the forest but kept well apart. When they were within ten metres of the snowmobiles, Hugo signalled Pierce with a clenched fist, and their jog slowed to a cautious crouching walk. Hugo slowed his breathing and focused his gaze through the endless vertical lines of tree trunks and the position where they had hidden their transport.

Nothing indicated this position had been blown, and on the steep hill beyond, Hugo couldn't see any tracks in the snow. He then looked back behind him, straining his ears for any signs of their pursuers.

Now or never.

Hugo moved towards the forest edge and quickly found the snowmobiles while Pierce scanned the trees for any danger before joining him. Marty and Copeland ran to the second snowmobile.

"What the hell happened? With the ambush?" Marty said as he mounted his vehicle.

"I dunno, vato, but we got spiked, that's for sure. Follow B plan and exfil. However, you can," Hugo replied.

"Do we need to be worried about eyes at the airports?" Kate asked.

"I don't know shit. Assume there is, but I got the idea that it was a small, isolated team that hit us. Maybe surveillance ain't in place yet," Hugo offered

"Hope your 'idea' is right," Faulkner interjected.

Hugo didn't miss the tone of sarcasm in Faulkner's voice.

Both snowmobile engines fired up, and the group drove back up the steep field and the road to Tok airport. There, they handed over what gear they had left back to their contact there, who wasn't happy half of it had been lost.

Hugo didn't tolerate that attitude for a nanosecond. "We got set up. One of our guys is dead." Then, glaring in the man's face, he said, "You know anything about it?" That stopped any complaints. "If Joe hadn't vouched for this guy," Hugo muttered to Pierce, "I would've tortured the truth out of him right there in the aircraft hangar."

On the private flight to Fairbanks International, Hugo sent an encrypted text to Joe. It read: "Mission accomplishment complete but compromised execution. Bull5 has been KIA and left at location." It was a painful message to send and almost signalled complete mission failure to Hugo. He knew Billy Pitman had served with Joe in Afghanistan way back with some unit in the British Royal Marines. Throughout the rest of the journey, Hugo grew angrier as the implications of the screw-up of the mission sank in.

Under twelve hours later, Hugo and Pierce were back at their homestead in Tennessee. The following day, Faulkner and Copeland arrived, and the post-mortem began.

***

"All I know is they was waitin' – and we somehow got outta there. It was a fuckin' miracle we did. That crew that found us musta thought it was a false alarm and not expecting

235

anything. The only reason we got away – except for Pitman, poor bastard," said Hugo, chewing off the words with barely concealed anger.

"I knew it was a bad idea," John said quietly.

They were talking via an encrypted online meeting. Hugo from Tennessee, Rhodes from South America and Joe who had returned to the Andalucía base in Spain.

"It became a bad idea when it was compromised. How the hell would we know that was going to happen?" Joe said defensively.

"Well, it did. If there is a compromise in our network, you and Hugo need to deal with it!" Rhodes' voice grew irritated. "Now, I need to sign off and organise a few things and my trip. Joe, you need to keep me in the loop on this one."

Joe nodded. "I will." He looked as worried as Hugo now.

"Don't forget Michael will be visiting you in a week or so."

Joe grimaced. "All I bloody well need..."

"He's made everything we've built possible. Paid for it all. Don't forget that, and look after him."

"Don't worry, I will," Joe replied.

Rhodes disappeared from the video call, leaving just the two of them.

"Well, Hugo. Do you have any ideas where we need to look?"

Hugo shook his head. "The guy at the airport, maybe? I can't see it being any of my guys – the girl, Copeland, is a recent arrival, but—"

"Look into it. It ain't the guy at Tok. He's solid."

"Alright," Hugo replied. He trusted Joe completely.

"Was it on the news?" Hugo asked.

Joe shook his head. "They must've covered it up, and John didn't want any exposure from our end right now."

"Sorry it got screwed up," Hugo said.

"Forget that. You did a good job; you knocked out that facility, and it severely damaged their ability to continue the weather war. We stopped one of their crimes against humanity, at least. They'll be raging, that's for sure. Really pissed off."

"Yeah, sure," Hugo said but didn't feel convinced.

"Keep me posted, Hugo. Find that mole."

"Sure. I'll look into it, vato."

Hugo disconnected, shut down his military-grade laptop, returned it to his locker, and left the comms room. He half-jogged up the metal steps from the basement to the ground floor and made his way to the briefing room at the back of the house.

He would have to question every member of the base, not just the actual squad on the Alaskan mission. Marty and Hugo didn't always see eye to eye, but he was right in the middle of the mission. He helped blow the place. It couldn't be anything to do with him.

Josh Pierce? He had a relatively safe job of keeping watch from the forest, but he wouldn't have known that until Hugo told him. The others were all inside with him. Betrayal by them didn't make sense. No one else knew about it in the camp, not the details anyway. He thought that all he could do was go through the routine of questioning everyone, which was surely going to turn them against him.

Delaying the inevitable, he moved towards the kitchen at the back of the house. Lena, one of the crop managers, was there, making dinner for their section.

"Any chance of a coffee?" Hugo asked.

"Some in the jug," she said with a smile.

Hugo poured a mug and made some small talk with them,

but he was morose. His eyes drifted to the small TV set up on the bar. The president of the USA was speaking, but the sound was way down. The ticker bar at the base of the picture warned of increasing tensions between the West and the Russia-Chinese alliance. The ticker's words changed, and Hugo saw: 'Liberatus'. And moved closer to the screen to hear the audio.

"...Liberatus accused by intelligence agencies of attacks that can only be described as terrorist in nature." Then the programme switched subjects.

He grabbed the remote and turned up the volume, but the president was talking about China.

Shit! So they have identified it was us who did it. Better let everyone know.

Hugo saw a face that made him freeze as the frail president finished and moved away from the podium—a look of a man who appeared to be one of the presidential bodyguards but should be dead.

Hugo gaped at the screen, unable to believe his eyes. There was no doubt it was him.

Jamall Salazar.

The man Hugo was confident he had finished off with his 'flaming sambuca' at that farmhouse in Spain. He had terrible facial burns, and it was clear, even on the small screen, that Jamall had had surgery, which made him appear even more sinister than ever.

So, that puta is still alive?

Hugo felt himself staring at the screen, still disbelieving what he had seen.

Sonofabitch.

Chapter 36

Frustrating wasn't the word.

The intel from Darklight had been gold. There actually had been an assault on the Geo Weather Project. However, the small ground team that provided security had failed to stop that attack, and the facility was put out of action. But there was work to do, piecing together what happened and also to determine the identity of the dead assailant found at the scene. From the photo, Zak knew it wasn't his brother, Joe. He needed to speak to him, somehow. If Joe was going down the route of being involved in terrorist activity, that was bad news. Joe was his goddamn brother, after all. Zak had wrestled about whether he should tell his superiors about Joe, but keeping his mouth shut about all that he knew had always won out.

And now, Foster had moved him over to the Operations Centre for the Station 12 security to help work on a fucking drill. For the past few days, Zak Bowen worked through the documents for Operation Hallows, involving Western Government and intelligence agencies, their military command and various emergency response agencies. The exercise imagined a global scenario where a series of nuclear strikes, whether from terrorists or enemy states, simultaneously hit cities across the USA, Canada and Western Europe. Operation Hallows was designed to test the response to an absolute nightmare series of events and was so named as it was all to take place over Halloween.

Zak felt this had probably been prepared in response to the escalating situation in the Middle East and the possible Sino-Russian threat. At least, that seemed the most apparent reason, but who knew? Constant exercise drills imagined every possible grim and bizarre scenario under the sun, and Zak sighed as he scrolled through the countless pages, barely reading them.

Within twenty-four hours, it would all be over. Then, hopefully, he could get back to what he considered his real job. If Foster refused to allow this, Zak felt he would need to consider his future options carefully. Living in this massive and oppressive underground facility was getting 'old' pretty fast for him and his wife Rhonda, who wasn't exactly thrilled to be there either.

Zak looked across from the document he was reading on one screen and switched attention to the software on a second monitor that displayed a map of the USA and searched for the scenario modules to load into the programme but was then confronted by hundreds of folders. He found that within each one, there were seemingly thousands of files.

Bloody hell!!

Among the sea of screens scattered through the cavernous Operation Centre, Zak saw the guy who had been introduced to him as head of ops, Leone Kaine, and he waved a hand to get his attention.

"I'm not sure what I have got to do here," Zak said with venom in his tone. It was no secret he didn't want to be there. "These scenarios, and there are thousands of them, are far too many for me to open each one single-handedly. I need some guidance from whoever set this up."

Leone nodded. "Ah yes, that was Haleema. Unfortunately, she's unavailable right now. Let me see..."

"It would've been great to have some kind of handover. Is this Haleema in the facility? It would be good to talk to her," Zak said in a frustrated tone.

"Err, no. You'll have to ask Fagan." Leone glanced over towards an empty desk, where Zak assumed he would normally be sat. He gave Leone a questioning look, but he was focused on the screen and pointed to a folder labelled '_Code-Yellow-Delta'.

"Try that," Leone suggested tentatively.

Zak loaded it, and the map was overlaid with new data. A timeline moved across a section above the map in seconds, minutes, hours, and days. An animated red circle expanded out from the epicentres of four cities in the United States: New York, Washington DC, Los Angeles, and Chicago.

"Ah, this is an earlier one," Leone commented, apparently recognising the folder contents. Then, he continued, "Look, Zak, you'll just have to muddle through, but we need the scenarios that cover the entire US, so all the major cities are covered with the fallout and suburban areas. The worst cases. Okay?"

One of his other colleagues moved closer to them and gestured frantically at Leone for his attention.

"Look, do your best. I'm sorry – gotta go." And with that, he turned to walk towards the other man.

"Right," Zak said flatly.

As he was leaving, Leone turned back and said,

"By the way, if it's of any consequence, I have no idea why

you're here either."

"Thanks," Zak repeated in the same tone.

Leone disappeared, and Zak looked up at the extensive series of screens on the far wall. A countdown clock displayed 11:23 hours until the drill began.

Zak loaded a few more scenarios, but none looked right. The current one on his screen was the West Coast: from Seattle down to San Diego. He tried again from a different recently created folder. When he clicked the animated overlay, this one didn't seem to show blast radius or fallout. Instead, thick coloured lines spread across a map of the whole US and Canada. Interspersed among the lines were different-sized circles. As the animation played, the lines changed colour to red, and the map darkened as a clock timer spun by in a matter of hours.

This seemed like a different scenario, and Zak noted the file names.

He certainly needed some clarification and answers before the drill began. He scrolled through the staff directory and searched for HALEEMA. A record flashed up with an image of a young Middle Eastern woman. There was something familiar about her, and Zak tried to click through for more details, but a 'This file is classified' message was immediately displayed across his screen.

He stared at the face, straining to pull back at the recess of his memory. He ruled out anything to do with his work. This wasn't some terrorist suspect he had come across on his screen.

Something more personal. Closer.

He swung his chair around, away from the image and let his gaze sweep over the dark recesses of the command centre. The hue of screens and lights blurred.

A few desks behind, one of the operatives looked at Zak, then looked away, but he ignored them and circled back around.

Haleema.

She was a friend of his sister, Zoe. That's right!

One of her friends from university. They had met once in England. The face matched in his mind. He knew it was her.

What the hell was she doing here?

A feeling of unease rose in him as the cog turned. Pure coincidence?

The connection with Zoe, and possibly his brother Joe, threw a new dice onto the board.

Zak breathed out slowly.

He knew that there was definitely no such thing as coincidence in this game.

**

The lights flickered on again. Haleema turned on her bunk and tried to cover her eyes with her arm, but they were too bright. Her sleep patterns had been deliberately disturbed. Every time she had drifted off, the lights came on in the windowless cell. It was usually a cue for her to be dragged back into the interrogation room and quizzed about the leak of information by Fagan, who seemed to delight in making her life a nightmare.

She had denied everything. She claimed to be lost, but it was pretty clear she had been in that cupboard sending out information to the external internet. If it hadn't been for her only communicating via the highly encrypted Icarus, they would easily have tracked what she had been sending. But, as they couldn't find out, what would they do to her next?

243

It was very clear that Fagan badly wanted to know what she had been up to.

Would he resort to torture? It had been threatened on many occasions. At least, in theory, she wouldn't be killed.

Not yet, anyway. This was Haleema's hope, of course—pure hope.

She thought of her father. He would be worried sick. Had they told him what was happening to her? Was he a prisoner too?

Whenever she had asked her interrogators these questions, they ignored her and fired back their own.

Haleema waited for the click of the door lock and for the guards to come and drag her out. But they didn't come for now, and she drifted off, dreaming of the world she once knew – her home in Iran.

Chapter 37

The outside temperature had dropped significantly, and Zoe felt the encroaching hands of the cold air smother her like a heavy blanket as she fiddled with the controls on the central heating boiler trying to put some warmth into the radiators. The place she was staying was stuck between Battersea Park and the railway lines running up from Clapham Junction. The boiler was old, like the whole flat, and a far cry from the mod cons of her place. The flat was located in a gloomy, unobtrusive part of London, where trains continuously rumbled past the building, causing the windows to rattle in their frames.

John had set the place up for her, as he had done with Matt Fulford and the camera guy, who had also been told to lay low themselves. That had been the plan if things went wrong or took an unexpected turn, and that's precisely how it had panned out.

Oberman getting shot had truly not been part of the plan, although, apparently, Joe was happy with that result. The police wanted to interview witnesses, and, of course, the fact that she and Fulford had interviewed him directly before the incident made them 'people of interest' to the police.

However, if she did show her face, there was a good chance the hidden enemy behind the banking and weather manipulation conspiracy would be alerted. That, more than the shooting incident, was what worried Joe and Rhodes. The whole Faber and Xael mission must have, Rhodes had said grimly, made Zoe 'significant' somehow.

John Rhodes also told Zoe he was coming to London as the situation was becoming so delicate. Perhaps he could work with some of his old MI6 contacts face-to-face to try and resolve any issues. Zoe wasn't going to argue and agreed.

As far as the video interview with Oberman went, it made great content. The footage of an elite figure storming out of an interview would create a media whirlwind of interest. However, John ordered the release of the video to be put on ice until they could get a sense of how the consequences of Oberman's death panned out. This irritated Zoe no end. These people were connected to all that was happening in Asia, and she wanted to see some action.

She passionately felt that they should be hung out to dry, although perhaps Obermam's fate made that a moot point. It felt like divine justice had been served on him, the man who had signed off on the death of hundreds of people, including her fiancé, Ed.

Yet she felt he was so far up the food chain there were undoubtedly many others involved. She wondered who had done the deed and shoved Ed off the balcony because she was in no doubt that had happened.

All her own electronic devices, including her phone and laptop, had long been discarded, replaced with a simple Nokia burner phone and a new laptop. At first, she didn't recognise the distant chime, then realised it was a text alert on the old Nokia mobile hidden in her jacket.

She found it, flipped it open and read the text. It was from

CHAPTER 37

Fulford.

"Need to meet urgently. Can't discuss it on the phone, but I can come to you or nearby – tell no one."

Zoe inwardly groaned.

What now? Has something else gone wrong?

She paced around the main living room and paused at the sash windows that overlooked the street. In the distance, the four chimneys of Battersea Station peeked over the rooftops, and she thought of a café on Riverside Walk that skirted the Thames as a suitable meeting point. It was quiet. Tucked away.

She re-read the text.

"Tell no one."

That part made Zoe uneasy. The instructions from Rhodes were strict enough. Lay low, stay out of sight and have no communication until the all-clear was given.

But hunkering down wasn't going to give her any answers.

The café Zoe thought of opened early, and she began texting back.

"If you're certain, we should meet. Ronda café on Riverside Walk, Battersea, when they open at 6:30?"

There was an almost immediate response from Matt: "See you there."

***

It was a dark, cold autumn morning, and a thick fog clung to the streets. The type of morning best spent in bed, and Zoe wondered again if this was all a good idea as she trudged along one of the tree-lined pathways through Battersea Park. She zipped up her jacket and tucked her hands into the pockets to fend off the cold. The fog appeared denser, and a handful of other commuters and joggers seemed to appear out of nowhere

247

through the mist, putting her on edge.

She walked quickly around the boating lake and headed towards the park's edge. Behind her, faint footsteps taunted her imagination. Too loud and clumsy to be any tail, she told herself, but she sped up her stride.

She left the park at Chelsea Bridge and spotted Matt through the mist, sitting outside the café, smoking a cigarette. He acknowledged her with a nod, but his face was impassive. He looked stressed.

"Hey, Matt," she said, gingerly sitting down, shoulders hunched.

"Hi, Zoe." He smiled, but it was weak.

"Bit cold to be outside?" she volunteered.

"I'll finish this, and maybe we can go inside," Matt said, waving his cigarette. He didn't look like he intended to go anywhere, though.

"I'll go and order."

Zoe entered the modern cafe, grabbed a large Americano to take away, and then joined Matt outside.

"So, what's going on?" Zoe asked as she took a seat. She placed the disposable coffee mug, lid still intact, on the table outside the cafe.

Matt stubbed his cigarette and exhaled slowly. He seemed to be avoiding her eyes, remorse etched on his features.

"I'm really sorry, Zoe. I was left with no choice. My family, I've got kids and..." His voice drifted off.

"What? What's going on, Matt?" she said, a bolt of alarm passing through her.

Zoe felt confused, but, at the same time, a realisation was growing that she should have trusted her gut instinct and stayed away.

As if to confirm her fears, a figure came into view, walking towards them along the embankment. It was a woman in a long, dark coat and boots. There was a flicker of recognition, and then it all fell into place.

It was Eva Villar.

The realisation hit her like an elbow in the stomach. Matt had baited her out of hiding, not knowing her exact location, and she had fallen for it. It was a trap.

"Fuck! You lured me here?" she said, glaring accusingly at Matt.

Matt pulled back his chair with a scrape and stood up, still not meeting her eyes.

"I'm really sorry."

Zoe looked around with a mind to run like hell and stood up too.

Then, a well-built man with sandy-coloured hair appeared from the opposite side and walked straight up to their table.

"Don't try to run anywhere," he said in a monotone South African accent. Zoe sensed he was ex-military, and he had the professional killer look about him. She decided to do as instructed.

The woman was much closer now, and Zoe caught a glimpse of a pistol hidden in her coat.

"Hello, Zoe," she said as if greeting an old friend. "I'd recommend you take his advice," she added, with far more sinister intent.

The man took Matt by his arm and led him off towards Circus Road West, away from the river.

"What are you doing with him?" Zoe demanded.

"I'd be more concerned about yourself, Zoe," Villar said coolly.

"What's this about? Are you going to kill me? Out here in a public place?"

"If you want to know more about your boyfriend, you'll stay calm and behave," Villar responded in the same dispassionate tone.

"What do you know about it?" Zoe demanded, a flash of anger rising up within her.

"Get up. Let's walk and talk. This way," Villar ordered, jerking her head in the opposite direction to where the other man had taken Matt.

Zoe's mind raced.

She was in it now, right up to her neck.

Stay calm.

"Come on!" Villar snapped.

Zoe surreptitiously took her coffee mug from which she had barely drunk and began walking, holding it down by her side. She clutched the cup, taking comfort from the heat it offered as she was led along Riverside Walk towards the Battersea Station Powerhouse.

"I want to know why you broke into our building and carried out corporate sabotage – that's the charges we have against you."

Zoe shook her head. "I've no idea what you're talking about – why are you carrying the gun then?"

"Don't be an idiot," Villar said, "The CCTV and facial recognition points to you, even with that disguise you wore," Villar added, with a hint of sarcasm.

The other unspoken concern that crept across Zoe's mind, like a dark shadow, was why Villar had not just turned up with the police.

She must intend to kill her. That thought caused a cold chill to run through Zoe's body.

"I want to know what you're going to do?" Zoe asked, trying to keep her voice steady. She cursed her stupidity in coming. She should have stayed put as John had told her.

Now, she would be shot and thrown in the river and become one of those statistics of unsolved murders. Villar probably had enough influence to get the local police to label her death suicide. Just like those of the bankers' deaths, probably.

"Did you kill my fiancé? Did you throw him out of the window like all the others?" Zoe demanded.

Villar gave a short snort of derision. "I don't get my hands dirty if I don't need to."

"That's very righteous of you, I'm sure," Zoe said.

A jogger approached them, and Zoe wondered if she should grab him and beg for help. Scream and make noise.

The idea faded as quickly as it had come. Villar wouldn't hesitate to kill anyone who tried to interfere. It wouldn't help her to find out what happened to Ed. People like Eva Villar and her associates were more than capable of having their crimes wiped clean. They were part of this world but did not abide by the rules that governed it because they made those laws and rules for everyone else.

The young male jogger passed them by without a glance their way.

Zoe took in her surroundings, wondering if there was a way out because it wouldn't end well. Battersea Station, now a hive of luxury apartments, loomed overhead. On her left, a narrow walkway jutted out on the river, leading to an old jetty surrounded by tugboats that bobbed on the water. Ahead of them, behind temporary hoarding, was another construction site, one of the many development phases of the area.

Tall cranes protruded into the grey sky through the mist – skeletal-like monsters adding to Zoe's fearful state of mind.

On the far side of the river, the buildings of the Chelsea suburbs were still barely visible through the fog. It then dawned on Zoe that these isolated conditions might give her an advantage.

A temporary walkway took them away from the Riverside Walk towards Cringle Street and the dockyard warehouses that skirted the Thames.

"You said you had something about Ed? What was it?" Zoe asked.

"He's gone. Get over it. You need to worry about more important things, Zoe."

"So, you lied?" Zoe snapped back.

"Is that such a surprise?"

Zoe decided to change tack.

"Where are we going?" she asked more evenly.

"Somewhere a bit private so that we can chat. I want to know everything you know."

They approached a doorway with an electronic key lock set in the hoarding to the cordoned-off building site, where Villar pulled out her gun and pointed it at Zoe, "Here!" she said, and while covering her with the gun, handed Zoe an access card with a magnetic strip motioning her to open the door.

Zoe swiped it through the keylock on it, and a green light flashed, and then the door swung open. They both stepped through into a large building site that bordered the river. Directly opposite, a row of skips lined up in front of another hoarding wall. On the water's edge, a temporary office hut faded to grey in the mist. A concrete mixer lay dormant next to the groundwork for constructing a small building.

Zoe could tell that the place was deserted and devoid of activity or workers. It was early on Sunday morning, after all. Yet all this must have been pre-planned, and Zoe began to feel a rising panic in her chest.

"Keep walking through, over there!" Villar demanded, still covering her with the gun. Zoe looked around for the first opportunity to act as she clutched her palm around the still-hot coffee mug. With a deft flick of her thumb, Zoe peeled up the plastic lid before letting it drop unnoticed to the ground. As she did this, she glanced back towards Villar, who was still a few steps behind on her right side.

Zoe looked around again and spotted a gap in the hoarding between the last two garbage skips. Beyond it, she could see a series of warehouses and a sign that read 'Waste Processing Plant'.

Plenty of places to get lost in, she hoped. If she was going to die, better die trying to outrun this bitch.

Zoe swung around quickly and hurled the hot black coffee into Villar's face. Even before her cry of pain, Zoe brought down her boot heel hard onto Villar's knee and then ran.

She dashed for the space between the skips and hurled herself through the gap in the hoarding. She stumbled to her knees as Villar swore out loud curses behind her.

A sharp crack of a gunshot, followed by a ricochet off metal. Shit!

That sound made it clear: Villar was already in pursuit.

Zoe rolled onto her side and then propelled her body forward to the waste plant ahead.

Sprinting into an expansive yard and then along the side of a metal warehouse, Zoe moved her action up a gear. She came to a line of metal railings alongside a road, but the tall, high

253

gates were firmly shuttered. There was no way onto the street that way. Not quickly, anyway.

Just before turning the corner, Zoe glimpsed behind to see an annoyed-looking Villa appear through the gap, wiping her face.

Zoe ran along the front of the processing plant through an empty car park, then doubled back towards the river on the opposite side of the building. She scanned the high wall to the neighbouring site and considered climbing over. Then, at the end of the warehouse wall, Zoe noticed a narrow alleyway between it and another part of the plant leading back to safety and what she knew of this labyrinth.

A figure appeared at the end, blocking her way.

Villar had somehow anticipated her move.

Zoe continued, faster now. She came out in a more open space. A couple of forklift trucks and a lorry sat idle in front of an open warehouse. Under the roof, a giant mountain of scrap and twisted metal was piled up almost ten metres.

Zoe looked around her, assessing her options as her heart pounded. She looked back and saw Villar appear and raise her handgun again. Zoe took off, sprinting cross-diagonally in front of the mountain of scrap metal and out of Villar's sights.

She could see the river and the pier's edge on the far side. On the ground, spilling out from the debris of the scrap heap, was a short piece of iron rebar. Without further hesitation, she grabbed it and then continued her sprint towards the river bank.

To her right, a wall overlooked the mud bank stretched into the murky brown water. With no choice, she turned left along a line of trees that skirted a building. On the riverbank, tied up to the pier, was a large tugboat with shipping containers, two deep. Further along the bank, another moored transport barge, but high metal rails blocked her route.

The noise of Villar's pursuit behind triggered Zoe to move again. She ran across the pier, jumped over the small gap onto the deck of a tugboat carrying shipping containers, quickly rechecking behind her, but couldn't see any sign of Villar.

Then, with the iron bar firmly gripped in her hand, she slipped into the gap between two containers and crept to the end. On the other side of the boat, the river stretched across to the Northern bank and Grosvenor Road, and it seemed the morning sunlight was burning off the mist.

Could she swim across? She moved to the edge and looked down.

No.

The tide was still low, and a slippery mud hill would be like walking through a treacle to get to the water. She would be a stuck sitting target.

Her thoughts froze as she felt the slightest of vibrations under her feet. Villar had stepped on board.

Zoe moved slowly around the corner of the container facing the river and held up her iron bar, ready to strike. She moved along the boat's edge between the ends of the containers and the mud bank below. At the last container, Zoe moved back around to within a few steps from the pier. But she caught a glimpse of Villar, frozen in place, waiting for her.

A squall of seagulls circled overhead, disturbed by the blast of a horn from an unseen boat. Zoe felt her anxiety rising, and she sucked in long breaths to try and calm herself down. The adrenaline of the escape and chase was wearing off, replaced by fear.

There was a creak from the deck. Villar was moving! But she

wasn't sure where she was.

She looked up to the top of the containers. The door latches and enclaves in the metal looked like they made a half-decent climbing frame. Without another thought, she tucked the bar into the back of her jeans and began to climb up the container.

It wasn't as easy as it looked, and Zoe slipped several times, the cold metal burning her fingers as she climbed higher. She hauled herself up, prone to the container's roof, then took the bar into her hands again and drew more deep breaths.

Stay here and hide? Or attack?

If only some of that adrenaline would just come back, she thought.

Zoe crawled to the edge and saw Villar walking along the boat, peering through the container gaps. Zoe got herself up onto her haunches and moved to the edge.

Need to even the fight and get rid of that gun.

Villar passed underneath, and Zoe took a step to launch herself but scraped her foot as she stood up.

Alerted to the sound, Villar looked up and began to raise her pistol.

Zoe plunged, one foot smashing into Villar's shoulder while the other landed on her weapon-wielding forearm. They both collapsed over onto the flat boards of the deck like a sack of potatoes.

Villar yelled in pain as her pistol clanked against a rail, then tumbled overboard and onto the mud bank below. She rolled, pulling Zoe with her, and jerked her elbow back into Zoe's stomach.

The air sucked out of her lungs in an instant. Zoe grunted and loosened her grip on her assailant, gagging for oxygen.

Zoe's iron bar rolled away, and with it went any advantage

she had. Before Zoe could react, Villar jumped back to her feet and gave Zoe a hard kick in the stomach again, making Zoe curl up into a foetal position. Then, with one hand, Villar grabbed her by the scruff of her jacket lapel and, hauling her up onto her feet, began punching her.

"Enough of these games. Now, the others. Who else helped you?"

Zoe groaned, reeling from the punches.

Before she could say anything, Villar struck her with a fist that threw Zoe back down onto the ground with a jolt. The coppery taste of blood immediately wet the inside of her mouth, and her vision blurred for a few moments as Villar stepped toward her.

"Was your brother, Joe, involved? Where is he hiding now?"

"Fuck off, bitch," Zoe spat. The words in her throat made her cough and choke, but her anger was back – her adrenaline.

It took Zoe a few moments to realise her hand was resting on the same iron bar she had lost moments before, and she tightened her grip around the cold, rusty metal.

Villar pulled Zoe closer.

Then, with all the power and force she could muster, Zoe swung it hard toward Villar's legs, the closest she could get. Villar reacted, but it still caught her left knee.

There was a crack of metal on bone that drew another shout of agony.

Villar stumbled back and caressed her knee for a moment. She then sneered at Zoe and straightened up before limping over, and with her other foot, she kicked Zoe in the ribs, who again lost her grip on the section of rebar.

Zoe cried out in agony. A shockwave of pain shot through her. The fallen iron bar was now close to Villar's foot, and she picked it up.

"You don't get it, do you?" Eva rasped through ragged breaths. "You and everyone else will have a lot more to worry about after next week. There's a fucking war coming—"

She leaned closer to Zoe, gripping both her cheeks with one hand until Zoe was forced to look straight at her with screwed-up lips like a goldfish while holding the iron rebar menacingly.

"Beware the Hallows," Villar whispered slowly, a malevolent smile flickering across her face.

Zoe frowned. Puzzled.

Villar shoved her head backwards.

It felt like every inch of her body screamed in pain. Blood continued to well in her mouth, and she spat a gob of saliva and blood onto the ground.

"Let's start again, shall we?" Villar grinned with malice as she grabbed Zoe's shoulder with a hand and, once again, pulled her onto her feet.

Despite the limp, Villar pushed Zoe towards the waste disposal yard with the iron bar prodding at her back. A swelling cheek numbed the side of Zoe's face, and she clutched her ribs and stomach to ward off the pain coming from all directions.

Zoe vowed that if she was ever to get out of this, she needed to learn to fight better.

She wondered if anyone had seen what was going on. The waste management yard was still devoid of any workers. Even if it was early on a Sunday, she wondered if shift workers shouldn't be appearing.

Well, for some reason, there wasn't anyone. The whole place was deserted. She could shout and scream for help, but Villar wouldn't hesitate to club her with the bar.

They arrived at one of the storage area warehouses piled

with the metal scrap that Zoe had run past earlier. There were stacks of stripped-down kitchen units, old metal shelving, and electrical appliances like cookers and fridges all piled high up towards the roof like a towering city constructed from scrap. With a shove in her back, Zoe fell inside. She was then ordered towards a lone plastic chair that had been deliberately placed there.

"I was bringing you here for our chat earlier until you ran away," Villar rasped, confirming Zoe's thoughts.

"Take a seat," she ordered.

Zoe complied, but only through sheer exhaustion. Nearby, a stack of cookers and tall refrigerators stood upright. She was actually glad of the rest, even if it was a prelude to whatever this mad bitch had in mind.

Villar swung the iron bar around as if she were warming up for a ball game. She had an inner resolve and strength. Zoe could tell—something born out of a harsh and cold upbringing.

Although Villar had done research on Zoe and her family and was attempting to find out more, Zoe had also done some research of her own

She had read Villar's file with the data she had got hold of from Faban and Xael and had a glimpse of what these people had been put through for their masters. Joe had told her about the one called Jamall and how he had been brought up in a cage, trained, manipulated and transformed into a pure killing machine.

This Eva Villar was of a similar ilk. And then Zoe remembered some of the details.

"Do you think your parents were randomly murdered, Eva?" Zoe asked casually.

Villar blinked, seemingly startled by the question, but continued to swing the bar from hand to hand.

"What do you know about it?" Villar replied as she attempted a smirk, but Zoe could tell that question had dug under her skin.

"You don't think your masters did it? To control you, mould you into what you are?" Zoe continued.

Villar stopped still and stared down her nose at Zoe.

"I'm going to enjoy killing you, Zoe Bowen. When I get what I need."

Zoe coughed and spat out more blood.

"I've seen documents – you were taken after they massacred your family. You must still remember it?"

Villar stepped forward and slapped Zoe with her free hand. Zoe jerked her head to the side, taking the force and screwed up her face. A headache appeared out of nowhere, and her swollen face ached even more.

"No, I was saved. What the fuck do you know! Who else helped you plan the data theft at Faber?" Villar said, her tone low and threatening.

Zoe looked up at the woman with total disdain but kept her mouth shut and did not answer.

Ahead rose the rear corrugated wall of another warehouse building for the waste plant, along with the truck and forklifts that she had run past earlier.

Zoe considered her chances.

Villar had no weapon, and Zoe knew she couldn't outrun her, but then she wasn't exactly in top form after the punches she received. The foggy mist had lifted now, so any advantage it had offered was gone, but it was worth a try.

Then, there was the sound of footfall from the path alongside the warehouse, and a tall, burly man appeared. He walked down from the road end of the waste disposal station. Zoe recognised him as Kai, the thug who had taken Matt, and her heart sank.

Villar turned, and he nodded to her.

"You got the car parked up there?" she asked.

He jerked his head. "Yeah."

"Keep an eye on her. I'll get the rope. She's been a bit feisty. Tie her up if you can find anything."

"There's a rope on the back seat of the car."

"I'll get it. I need the meds and the tools," Villar said and held out her hand. He handed over his key fob, and she began limping off in the direction he had come.

"Sure, you don't want me to get it?"

"No," she said sternly.

Kai turned to Zoe and gave her an appraisal with his dark eyes without saying anything. Zoe glared back.

"What did you do with Matt?" she asked, voice full of scorn.

"I shot him in the head," he replied as casually as if he was saying he took two sugars with his coffee.

Zoe gasped and sank her head. "Fuck." Something told her he wasn't lying. "Bastard," she added under her breath, but she felt broken. The fight within her was fading again.

"His family?" she asked, almost in a croak as her throat seemed to well up.

"Same," he said. "Just like I threw your boyfriend off the balcony."

Zoe flushed. Her breathing stopped as she took in the words.

A flash of rage shot through her, and Zoe instinctively jumped up and threw herself at Kai, punching and kicking. He stepped back, ready for it, and shoved her over onto the ground with a single swipe of his burly arm.

She crashed down onto her rump and rolled to her side. He

261

laughed with genuine glee.

Facing away from him, Zoe caught sight of a piece of jagged metal sunk into the debris that littered the ground—a discarded tent peg. Rage still pulsing through her veins, she went to grab it with one hand. Then, a shadow came over her, and she felt her loose hair pulled hard, lifting her weight, so she ended up on her knees.

She cried out, yelling in pain.

With her right hand gripping the sharp metal peg, she thrust it with all her force into his thigh.

He screamed and let her go, falling backwards.

"Fucking bitch!" he shouted.

Zoe leapt to her feet and pounced at Kai, shoulder-barging him back towards the ditch of junk. He stumbled backwards, completely off balance.

And as he did so, his back slammed against the upright row of wrought-iron spikes on a discarded section of security railing.

There was a cry of anguish, and his face froze in horror.

Zoe stepped forward and realised the fencing spires had impaled his body, piercing his spine.

Kai coughed weakly, and dark blood spewed out of his mouth, speckling his crisp shirt. He desperately tried to inhale air with throaty rasps that grew faster with each rhythmic breath. Then, with bloody gritted teeth, he started to pull himself away from the spikes and reached out an arm towards Zoe, who stared back in shock.

Kai fell back, life ebbing away as he bled out into the trash and debris around him.

She stepped away from him, her anger now diffused and melting into a panic.

His chest rose and fell, the shirt reddening with blood, and then his desperate breathing subsided. His stare fell into a fixed gaze, looking right at her.

"Oh dear god," Zoe muttered.

Her first instinct was to help. But this bastard was a killer. She had no doubt. This was someone who had confessed to throwing Ed off his balcony and killing Matt and his family.

Fuck!

Zoe took one last look, then turned and moved off at a jog across the yard in front of the forklift trucks before moving along the exterior warehouse wall, parallel to where Villar had headed.

If Kai had come by car, perhaps now the gates to the road were open.

She got to the end corner and stopped. Villar was leaning into the car through the driver's door. It was parked just inside the grounds, and the main gate had been pulled open.

If she could get that vehicle, she needed the key.

Zoe moved quickly, running at a full sprint across the ground to Villar. She grabbed her by the shoulder, pulled her out of the doorway and jerked a stiff knee into the small of Villar's back, causing her to yelp in pain.

The key fob fell to the ground.

Zoe shoved Villar with all her strength and went sprawling onto the concrete. Zoe grabbed the key and jumped inside the car. The engine turned but didn't spark.

Shit.

Villar slowly got to her feet and turned around, a mixture of pure malice and hatred burning in her eyes.

Zoe turned the key again, and the engine growled to life this time. She slammed it into gear and let off the handbrake just as Villar suddenly moved like a springing cat and leapt at the rear door.

Zoe hit the central locking, but it was too late. As Zoe pulled away with a screech, Villar threw herself into the back seat.

The car screeched through the open gates and onto the street. Zoe spun the steering wheel, pulling up the handbrake as she did so, throwing Villar against the door. She slammed her foot on the accelerator again, and the car screeched off, speeding down the road. Zoe quickly fastened her seat belt, thinking only of how to make it difficult for Villar.

Her assailant in the back tried to slide an arm around Zoe's throat, but she jerked the wheel again and turned down a side street, slamming Villa's head against the rear door window.

A lorry pulled out from inside one of the countless building sites in the area, and Zoe swerved to avoid it and mounted the pavement opposite.

Hands again grabbed at her neck, accompanied by shouts from Villar to stop the car.

They zipped through a red light over a junction, and a car coming across slammed into their rear wing, enough to send it spinning until it smashed into a traffic island and came to a standstill.

Zoe unclipped her seatbelt and exited the vehicle fast, running along the road, constantly swearing under her breath.

"Shit, shit, shit!"

There was a shout from behind. A passing driver sounded his horn. Zoe glanced behind to see Villar already out of the car and jogging behind her, albeit with a slight limp.

She must have had her meds, she thought.

Zoe headed towards an underpass going underneath the railway bridge.

She took a left turn at an office building car park and broke into a steady jog parallel to the track, her only thought to just get as far away as possible from this bitch. Ahead was a striped gate barrier that led deeper into the office grounds.

Shit! She was cornering herself again. For fuck's sake, Zoe. *Concentrate.*

Set into a bank, high above her, lay the light-grey steel wall leading to the railway tracks. Zoe glanced back to see Villar turn the corner, still on her trail like a relentless long-distance runner forcing herself to the finish line.

Zoe jumped onto a parked car, climbed onto its roof, and then jumped up again onto the top of a parked van. The railway bridge wall still extended above her head, but it was enough, and she gripped the top of the ledge and hauled herself up, scraping her feet on the beams for leverage. She pulled herself onto the top and gritted her teeth as she pulled an arm muscle.

On the wall's far side were multiple lines of parallel railway tracks between Vauxhall and Queenstown Road Station. A five-carriage train, mostly empty, rumbled past. At one of the windows, the face of a middle-aged woman looked up from her book and watched Zoe curiously. Beyond the tracks, a line of some nondescript commercial warehouses jutted over metal parapets, and she could see the tops of lorries in a parking bay and, more importantly, her exit.

On one of the middle tracks, another train came from the Vauxhall Station direction, the yellow- and blue-painted carriages edging closer through the grey mist.

Zoe climbed down on the ledges in the wall and jumped onto the gravel by the first track. As she stepped over the first tracks, Zoe glanced from the train and then back to the wall behind her.

There was the sound of boots on the roof of the vehicles she had scaled before Villar's head appeared. She had easily scaled the wall before jumping down and yelling out in pain.

The red-headed bitch was gaining on her.

Zoe caught a glint of what appeared to be a blade in her hand and picked up the pace, but it was difficult to run across the tracks and sleepers quickly without the risk of a fall. She switched direction and ran along the track, shoes slipping off the sleepers, almost twisting her ankles in the loose railway chippings.

At a sound of ringing from the rails, she glanced up to see another train rumbling along the tracks towards her.

If she could get on the far side, it would put a wider gap between them both and give her breathing space. That's all she could think about in these moments.

After a few metres, she changed again and cut across the tracks, heading on a trajectory with the fast-approaching train. On the tracks next to it, yet another train came from the opposite direction. She needed to get behind both of them; otherwise, Zoe realised she would be trapped between the two fast-moving trains.

Zoe turned her head to check Villar and caught movement in her peripheral vision. Villar was closing right up on her, her hands reaching out to grab her shoulders, trying to pull her back.

Zoe shook her off, and the hands fell away.

Then, her focus distracted, Zoe's foot caught one of the rail tracks, and she stumbled and nearly fell across the tracks in front of the nearest train.

She looked wide-eyed at the approaching locomotive, its horn blaring, as she jumped across right in front of it.

Zoe fell, turning as she did so and landed on her back between the two sets of lines.

Villar was stumbling too, her own momentum dragging her forward into the train's path, and she locked eyes with Zoe a moment before the engine smashed her body away with a sodden thud, leaving a blur of carriages whizzing past.

The other train zipped by behind, and Zoe, in the middle of them both, held her head in her hands, screaming into the loud cacophony of noise as the wind buffeted her body.

Zoe started hyperventilating, her head spinning and her vision fading. Then the trains passed. The trapped feeling went as quickly as it had come. There was a hiss of screeching brakes as one train slowed to a stop.

Zoe scrambled back onto her feet.

Yes, she had really seen that. The bitch was gone.

She turned and stared at the mangled corpse of Villar further down the track. The train had carried it several metres before it had been dragged underneath. Blood glistened on the rails.

All Zoe could do was run again.

Keep running.

And she did.

Chapter 38

Even the jetting streams of warm water from the shower stung her bruised skin, but Zoe let it run and run to ease her aching muscles. She rubbed more shower gel over her body, leaned against the tiled wall, hugged herself to comfort her aching ribs, and sobbed almost uncontrollably. She was overtaken by waves of relief, mixed with bitterness at how this whole shit storm had played out, her thoughts lost in the nightmarish recall of what had transpired the previous few hours.

She couldn't forget the look of surprise on Kai's face, the killer of her darling Ed, as he found himself impaled. She wondered if he was still alive. She had found a rare working public phone box as she had stumbled back from the train tracks and called 999, anonymously giving them his location. It was just in her nature to do so, but she shook her head at why she did that for this murderous thug.

If Matt was dead, along with his family, he deserved to be left there. She would need to find out somehow.

And Eva Villar. The frozen snapshot, the look of complete acceptance of death on her face just before that train smashed into her. It was almost as if she didn't want to be part of this world anymore.

Or face what was coming.

What was it she had said?

'Beware the Hallow's Eve.' Like some line akin to that from some Shakespearean witch. Zoe almost laughed at that, but her smile faded.

Halloween was today.

Something was coming, something terrible. Zoe was sure of it.

She switched off the shower, quickly dried herself, threw on a gown, and found the burner phone she had stashed in the apartment before leaving for that fateful meeting with Matt earlier. She tapped in Joe's number and waited.

A woman's voice came on. It was his girlfriend, Hanna.

"Hey. It's Zoe."

"Oh, hi. How are you?"

Zoe tried to lie but couldn't. "Hmmm, I'll be honest, it's not been a great morning," she said with typical British understatement.

"Oh?" Hanna seemed to want more.

"Listen, I'm really sorry. It's very urgent. Is Joe around?"

"Sure, I'll find him," Hanna said flatly. Zoe was about to apologise for cutting her short, but she had gone, and then Joe came on the line.

"Zee!" Joe gasped. "What's happening? You OK? Hang on. I will put you through the VPN."

Zoe took a deep breath, and after five minutes of going through the morning's events, Joe swore over the crackly line.

"Fuckin' hell, Zoe. Thank God you made it," Joe said, genuine relief resonating in his voice.

"Thanks. I should never have left the flat, but the lesson's learned."

"Listen," she went on, "I've got no laptop here and just an

old phone. Can you scan the news? See if there's anything about Matt. Or even what happened this morning?"

"Sure. Give me a sec."

There was a pause and the sound of tapping.

"Oh Christ," Joe said under his breath.

"What?"

"Matt – he's been found in a car in South London. Shot in the head – police saying it's a suspected gangland robbery."

"No!"

So it was true. That bastard wasn't lying. She regretted calling an ambulance now.

"Any mention of his wife, kid?"

"She's quoted as being distraught in the story. Means she's alive."

"Thank god. Sick fuck lied about that bit then."

"I can't see anything on your friend Eva Villar or the other guy, though."

"Ok," Zoe whispered. She looked around the cold, empty flat and shivered.

"Zee, I'll get a flight over right now," Joe said, concern once more etched in his voice.

"No, no. I'm fine. Thanks. Really. Besides, John is flying in. Either today or tomorrow. I can't remember when."

"Ah yeah, of course. Good. Although his reason for being there is moot now, I guess."

Zoe nodded. That much was true with Villar and her hench-man dead or out of the picture. Whatever John had planned to do to help, perhaps it was no longer necessary. She would be glad of a friendly and trusted company, nevertheless.

"There's always more of them crawling out of the woodwork, though. We don't know. Maybe there's more John can do to smooth it all out. Like there's bound to be some witnesses from this morning."

"Just stay low. I don't know who John could trust anymore. There's Dad, of course—"

Zoe considered that. Her dad, Frank, had worked with the British intelligence agencies and had his fair amount of run-ins with them. He had also been a trusted agent for Liberatus for many years.

"No," Zoe said, "let's leave sleeping dogs be, eh? He's been through too much already."

"OK, If you're sure, Sis?"

"Yeah. Listen, there's something Villar said. It was weird. Like, Beware Hallow's Eve or something. She was indicating something about Halloween, I guess?"

There was silence on the far end.

"Joe?"

"Yeah, here. Just thinking. They ran these big operations named after the Horses of the Apocalypse: White Horse. We exposed them to planning a new virus based on the Spanish flu. Then Red Horse was their ignition of the Middle East to develop into a new world war – and I guess that's still playing out—"

Zoe mumbled an acknowledgement. She had heard some of this.

"Black Horse: the drought caused by their weather manipulation, which we've begun to deal with, but even so, the consequences might yet be a financial and supply chain collapse. I'm not sure we've seen that play out yet, either."

"So Pale Horse – you think that's connected with Halloween?"

"I don't know, Zee. I don't know what's coming, but it's

271

likely something is. Something bad."

The words struck at the pit of her stomach.

After the call, Zoe forced down some soup to combat the feeling of nausea that still churned in her stomach. She thought about herbal tea but opted for another coffee. After all, she thought she hadn't drunk much from the one she had thrown in Villar's face, allowing herself a mild smirk.

She found painkillers in the bathroom, swallowed two pills, took her mobile phone and coffee back to the bedroom, and peered through the closed blinds.

Birds circled over the rooftops in front of the bleak sky. The fog, such help that morning, had gone entirely, but the darkness seemed to be winning against a fading light, even though it was mid-afternoon.

Zoe curled up into a fetal position on the bed and drifted into a deep sleep, waiting for the call from John Rhodes.

***

Back in his office, Joe pushed himself back from the desk and rubbed his eyes. In the sprawling basement, now a makeshift comms room, equipment, monitors, and stacker servers dominated the space. He felt the pressure behind his eyes and sipped water from his metal container.

He wondered if he should have kept his little sister well away from all this. Maybe he should fly to London and make sure? Her ordeal had sounded like dicing with death too much for his liking. Then he shook his head and almost laughed out loud.

It was way too late to feel protective. If Joe had really wanted to keep her out of it, he would have done everything to stop Zoe from digging deep, especially going into the building like that. No, he had to admit he had been intrigued about how she would do. He had, subconsciously, at least, encouraged his kid sister to put herself in possible danger. He shook that thought away. Denying it immediately.

Liberatus needed good, brave people, and there was no more trustworthy than his own blood.

Then Zak came to mind, and Joe grimaced.

All except one.

He checked the Icarus app for any updates from John Rhodes. He should have landed in the UK by now, but Joe had heard nothing. His presence made Joe feel a lot less guilty about Zoe.

John would make sure the whole Faben and Xael episode was wrapped up to avoid more blowback in Zoe's direction.

Joe's gaze fell on the Quantum radio comms equipment that he had tested with Hugo. It had worked, which now meant a much more secure network between the central Liberatus locations in the US, UK and Europe.

He thought about other safe contacts for Zoe.

There was a good community of people he knew based in Suffolk who had come on to side with Liberatus. Danny and Bel Thorpe had organised a tight network in England and were wise to what was going on. Joe had served with Danny in the Marines back in the day. Although they hadn't been best buddies or anything, Joe knew he was a good guy.

Trustworthy.

Then there was Raj Singh, who managed a scattering of hives around South London and down to Addington. Joe sent Zoe a message on Icarus and shared these contact details with her.

His thoughts returned to what Hugo had told him several hours earlier in a frantic call. He had called him back on the Quantum radio to test it out. Hugo had said Jamall Salazar was

273

still alive and apparently now part of the presidential Secret Service.

This was worrying and sparked the worst feeling deep in his gut.

What the hell were they planning? Because with all the signals, he was sure something was about to happen and knowing the cabal, it wouldn't be serving humanity in any good way. It would be another blow in the relentless war against them.

The Horse operations. Operation Hallows, a massive emergency drill playing out that day, none of the signals were good.

He checked his watch. He needed to go.

The drive out to replenish the supply dump would do him good. Clear his head. It would be late by the time he got back, so he grabbed his camping gear just in case. It was a little ritual he occasionally did. Take off and camp out alone under the stars to remind himself of what freedom felt like because God knows what he faced down the road.

He left the basement rooms, gathered up a bag and camping gear, and threw it all into the back of the reconditioned army lorry parked in the makeshift car park at the front of the building. He walked outside the main building to the rear and onto an expansive terrace with tables and exterior seats set on tiled flooring. A wall of arches at the edge overlooked the patchwork quilt of fields and settlements below. Joe gazed down and saw a few figures working the crops. Beyond the fields, past the orchards, lay the long strip of dried mud of the riverbed that they sometimes used as a private airfield.

They had come far quickly, and Joe allowed himself to enjoy the scene for a few moments before moving off through the labyrinth of buildings and walkways that made up the compound. He bumped into Javier, one of the men who had helped Joe from the very beginning of the project.

"Hola, Javier. I'm just heading out to Cache 5. We were running low on a whole load of stuff last time I did an inventory, so I'll drop off supplies. I might camp out over there tonight, though."

Javier raised one eyebrow. "It gets cold, Joe. Are you sure about that?"

They both chuckled. The temperature had dropped, and there was talk of an extreme cold front coming in – a rarity for that part of Spain.

"Yeah, I'll survive one night, I'm sure."

Joe looked around. "Have you seen Hanna?"

Javier shrugged. "Not for a few hours."

Joe looked at his watch. "I need to go. Tell her what I'm doing, and I'll be back tomorrow."

"OK. See you, mañana."

Joe circled the other side of the main building back to the front track and climbed into the cab of the old reconditioned army truck. He started the engine and drove along the hidden route, through the woods and out into the hills of Andalucía.

Epilogue

President Woodside finished his speech to the group of students in the main hall at the University of Utah to polite applause. His stop there had followed a visit to the Primary Children's Hospital and the Salt Lake Regional Medical Center. The trip covering many of the states in the West was nearly over.

Woodside had been one of the most libertarian presidents since Kennedy, elected on promises to fix the corruption of a declining state. He had stopped short of calling out the 'secret societies' that Kennedy had focused on in his 1961 speech to the American Newspaper Publishers Association. However, Woodside had allies in the legislative branch of government and Congress and had set up a covert task force to investigate high-level corruption and links between some figures in Government and their intelligence and military apparatus, Ghost 13.

Jamall Salazar scanned the hall exits and glanced at his watch one more time. The final stop was at Utah State University in Logan, eighty miles north, knowing it would be cancelled at the last minute, and then the countdown to the carefully planned operation would begin.

"Coldfire, on route now. Transport's ready," said the low

hiss of the progress report in Jamall's earpiece, telling him what he could already see: the president, code name Coldfire, was now leaving the campus.

Jamall had been seconded from the CIA to the Presidential Protective Division of the Secret Service and was officially given the role of the Special Agent in Charge of the president's security detail due to his impressive skills as a field agent. It was an unprecedented switch, but such was the power of his masters in the cabal. Even the director of the Secret Service couldn't have intervened with the decision – if he had wanted to.

It had upset the existing close-knit team, but creating that dissent was also part of the plan.

There was one other key agent who Jamall could rely on, planted in place many years before. Special Agent Collins stood just a few metres from the president's podium in the side wings of the stage, his impassive gaze scanning the crowd. The president walked past him towards his aide, Kerry Holson, a demure but officious brunette in her early fifties. Jamall turned and headed towards the president as he shook hands with various professors from the university. Jamall took his position just behind the protectee as they made their way through the halls to the waiting motorcade outside.

Forty minutes later, the stream of black vehicles arrived at Salt Lake City airport for what most of the presidential entourage thought would be the last leg of the journey home.

Timing was everything, and Jamall had every time sequence and what exactly needed to happen when firmly locked in his head. Having checked his watch, he glanced at the interior rear mirror at the president, sitting in the back of the limo behind. Next to him, his aide, Kerry Holson, was finishing a call, looking concerned. She turned to the president and spoke. Although Jamall couldn't hear the words, he knew what was being said.

Their flight back to Washington would have to be delayed. Operation Hallows, a vast and complex national emergency drill, was now taking place across the US and Europe. An urgent Homeland Security conference call required the president's immediate attendance at a nearby secret USAF location.

The president looked tired and clearly annoyed. There was a small Halloween party at the White House scheduled later that evening for his family. He had really been looking forward to it, so why hadn't he been briefed?

Holson assured the president he would still make the party. They would take a helicopter straight there and then return for the Air Force One departure. There had been no briefing because of very recent global developments, and the reason for the last-minute location change would soon become apparent. It was a developing threat to National Security.

President Woodside accepted this with a nod as the driver, already apparently in the loop of the plan change, ignored the direct path to the massive Air Force One Boeing 747-200B that stood waiting on the tarmac, along with a group of men who looked confused as the presidential limo moved away.

Instead, the limo and the front and rear Secret Service vehicles headed across the airfield to a section of Salt Lake City airport maintenance hangars and a row of military helicopters. One such large helicopter had a pilot in the cockpit, the engine warming up and its rotors turning.

The limos pulled alongside, several metres away, and men in black suits exited all vehicles, assuming an outward focus on any potential danger from every direction.

278

Jamall called over Agent Bellini, the leader of the agents of the limo that had taken point. He pointed to another chopper nearby, where another pilot headed on foot.

"You and your team. Follow us in that."

Bellini's thick-set face remained impassive, but Jamall sensed his doubt somewhere in those craggy lines. Bellini began to say something but then nodded and turned to his three men who stood in a protective semi-arc around the president's vehicle.

Jamall opened the rear door, and the president got out and hurried over to the helicopter, his suit buffeting from the wind off the rotor blades, now spinning with momentum. He was closely followed on board by Holson, Jamall and Special Agents Elgart and Collins.

The side door shut, and the chopper ascended, heading out west from the airport. Jamall rechecked his watch from his seat and looked out at the city's skyscrapers below without interest. Only the finer details of what he needed to do ticked like a watch in his brain.

This was the most important mission in his life, and he was more than ready. He realised now that every day had been leading to this point in time, all through the guidance of his masters. Once completed, his personal power would ascend to greater heights in the new world order that was now so close.

It was less than thirty minutes of flight time before the apparently disused USAF depot came into view, tucked into the peaks of East Utah. The fenced and well-protected area was the size of around five football fields laced with small roads connecting a series of buildings and cut in half by a long runway. The chopper headed towards one of several helipads by a two-storey nondescript building situated at the north corner. It became apparent there were already men on the ground and another black transport helicopter.

The president glanced down at it with interest.

"Who are they?"

"That'll be the CAT unit, Mr President. They will have secured the area ahead of our arrival," Holson told him.

He nodded. "Of course."

The counter-assault team of the Secret Service was the tactical support for the Presidential Protective Division. Jamall also glanced down at the scene as they descended. The operatives of the CAT unit were fanned out in an arc around the helipad, their assault weapons trained outwards towards the directions of potential danger.

Jamall knew it was a deception. They were actually an elite unit of Ghost 13 dressed as Counter-Assault soldiers.

Loyal to the cabal and the Council of Thirteen.

Not to the president.

On touchdown, Jamall spoke in his lapel mic with a brief. "Coldfire coming in now." He swung open the door and gestured to President Woodside, who unbuckled his belt and stepped through the door and onto the helipad.

The agents quickly ushered him into the stone brick building via steel doors. Inside, they all moved down a long hallway with exposed brick walls and stark lights overhead, waved through by men in uniform until the president was ushered into a large meeting room.

Jamall ordered Elgart to stand guard outside the door while he and Collins went inside. A large oval table in the middle of the room had a large teapot and crockery. A large screen displayed the presidential seal logo on the main wall.

Holson took a seat next to the president.

280

"I'll try and brief you as much as I can."

From the back of the room, Jamall watched as she took out a laptop and proceeded to log into an intelligence database, following instructions.

"We have an International Emergency drill now in full swing, Mr President: Operation Hallow—"

Jamall checked his watch: 19.55 hours. He glanced over at Collins, and they acknowledged each other without even a nod, and then Jamall slipped quietly out of the meeting room.

Standing on full alert outside, Agent Elgart looked over at him and nodded. Jamall walked back towards the main foyer area that led out to appear to do one last check of the general situation. He could already hear the distant low buzz of the second Secret Service chopper.

Time check. 19:56

It was going to be tight.

Through a row of windows looking out at the helipads, darkness had fallen quickly, shadowed by a first-quarter moon. The surrounding hills and mountains were dark shapes against a deep blue and purple sky dotted by stars. He could make out a few of the CAT unit soldiers in hidden positions around the outlying buildings and hangars.

The few USAF staff who had been on site had already left by the road, as ordered.

He turned around and returned to the briefing room, past Elgart again, and quietly slipped back inside.

"—all major cities would be centres of chaos, Mr President." One of many faces on the screen, a bald man in military uniform, spoke. Jamall did not recognise him but assumed he must be a general on the Chief of Staff.

It wasn't his concern.

The chopper engine was audible, even from within the room, and then the crackle of gunfire began.

Holson turned to Jamall, eyes wide. "What the hell is that?"

A voice from one of the meeting attendees on the screen. "What's happening? Is that gunfire?"

"I hope in God's name this is part of the drill," the president said, incredulous yet fearful. He turned to Jamall for reassurance, who raised his hand for silence and spoke into his mic.

"Report, Agent Elgart. What's happening?"

"Unclear. Appears we're under attack," Elgart replied. "One hostile bird incoming," he added breathlessly.

The truth was the incoming Secret Service chopper would be receiving fire from the alleged CAT unit soldiers from their hidden positions, but there was no way Elgart could see what was happening.

"Go check it out."

The lights and screens died instantly, and the room fell into darkness with a single distant crack from somewhere in the building.

Right on time.

"They cut the power?" said Holson, her voice shaking.

"Stay calm," Jamall said reassuringly. A mini flashlight came on somewhere from the form of Jamall's body, and he moved it around the room.

"There is a secure safe room downstairs. We're going to head to it, and I will lead. Do you all understand?"

"Yes," came the scared voices.

"Agent Collins, I'll take point."

A thunderous boom shook the whole building from outside, followed by a repetitive clatter of loud, sharp crashes that vibrated under their feet.

Jamall opened the door, and a flickering orange glow streamed in across the walls and a dead monitor screen from the hall. It was the light of a large fire coming through the window down the corridor, accompanied by occasional bursts of gunfire and shouts. Elgart had disappeared, having headed outside.

Jamall led the president and Holson away from the entrance and commotion, and they headed down the dark hall, following the flashlight. They went through double doors and arrived at a stairwell, the sound of gunfire and roaring fire fading behind them.

"We're going down several flights, then we'll be at the safe room," Jamall said calmly before descending the concrete steps.

When they reached the bottom, the light revealed old rusty pipes along the ceiling and thick cable wiring running the length of the hallway. Jamall kept moving along, commanding the protectees to do the same, reassuringly but sternly. Wide steel doors lined their route, and then Jamall stopped and swung one open.

"Inside, quickly." Jamall moved the flashlight toward the president's face. His eyes looked from Jamall to the darkness of the unseen room and back to him, confused and frightened.

"Inside, there?"

"Please – for your safety."

The president stepped in through the door as commanded.

In one swift, almost casual movement, Jamall raised the pistol he had taken out from his shoulder holster and fired a single shot into the back of Woodside's head. The body fell and slumped lifelessly down onto the hard floor.

He turned and brought the light up to Holson's face, frozen

in shock. Then, a loud crack and a red hole appeared on her forehead, and she dropped to the floor. Behind her, Collins lowered his weapon.

"Drag her inside, too," Jamall ordered. Collins put his weapon away, grabbed her ankles, then pulled her body into the cold dark room and dropped her unceremoniously alongside the corpse of the President of the United States.

The torchlight scanned their bodies.

"Check they're both dead," he said.

Collins got down onto one knee and checked the president's pulse.

"Yes. He's dead."

He then moved to Holson and did the same. After a moment, he nodded and said. "She won't be telling anyone shit."

"Right, let's go."

Collins stepped out, and Jamall closed the door and clicked a rusty padlock closed over the latch. The two figures moved through the pitch-black void and up the stairwell.

A fire still raged, burning out the husk of the Secret Service chopper that had crashed down onto the tarmac runway a few hundred metres from the building. The flames eagerly licked the metal shell, and inside were several corpses, still in their seats, slumped forward. Burning and smouldering metal fragments scattered around the crash area in an arc of destruction.

On the ground lay the twisted body of Agent Elgart. Shot as he had exited, possibly during the firefight between the Secret Service helicopter outside and the ground-based CATS.

The president's helicopter was still intact, and men from the CAT unit were busy preparing for exfil and laying false evidence. It was all going to look like one well-coordinated terrorist assault. Several bodies had been brought from the advanced covert helicopter that the Ghost 13 team had arrived on, hidden under the metal-shielded hangar.

These were to ultimately identify them as 'The terrorists'.

Two of the Ghost 13 soldiers lay the bodies amongst the debris, which would inevitably be identified as known terrorists if any investigation ever got that far.

On any typical day, the real CAT, made up of the elite members of Special Forces units, would be assembling somewhere to counterattack the threat to the president.

But today was no ordinary day.

Today, chaos reigned.

Free Thriller

Exclusive offer. To grab your FREE Novella eBook, head to:
www.jaytinsiano.com/secret-access/

PLUS, you'll get access to the VIP Jay Tinsiano reading group
for:
Free Books and stories
Previews and Sneak Peeks
Exclusive material

Also Available

For updates and a full list of retailers for each book, visit www.jaytinsiano.com

Pale Horse (Dark Paradigm #4) Coming in 2024.

ISBN: 978-1-9162397-7-7

As the world hurtles toward the brink of collapse, the key figures of the freedom-fighting faction known as Liberatus find themselves thrust into the very apocalyptic future they both anticipated and dreaded.

In the heart of London, Zoe Bowen, still grappling with the scars of her past encounters and her climactic battle against Dr White, embarks on a desperate quest to locate John Rhodes amidst the escalating chaos gripping the British capital.

Meanwhile, Joe Bowen, far removed from his Spanish stronghold, faces a perilous journey to reunite with his comrades.

Within the Tennessee Liberatus enclave, Hugo Reese gains a tenuous grip on their dire predicament, unaware of the treacherous betrayal brewing within his own ranks.

Deep beneath the surface in Station 12, Denver, Zak Bowen finds himself at the epicentre of a massive emergency simulation that, to his horror, transforms into a chilling reality.

As the shadowy cabal executes its devastating agenda, the world teeters on the brink of collapse. Hold tight as this pulse-pounding apocalyptic conspiracy thriller hurtles toward its electrifying climax.

White Horse (Dark Paradigm #1)

ISBN: 978-1-9162397-4-6

Half a world away in Spain and running from his past, a Los Angeles gangster unwittingly takes a train that's headed straight into a terrorist attack. He survives only to face an even deadlier threat.

On that same train: a virologist with clues to a deadly epidemic. Did his secrets die with him in the strike?

Raging in the aftermath, a foul-tempered police chief with a daughter caught in the attack thirsts for revenge. But against whom?

An orphan child without a name disappears down a dark, illegal CIA mind-control programme. Now trained in the ways of death, he prepares to do his master's twisted bidding.

From its first pages, the relentless techno-thriller White Horse drops you with a thunderclap in the middle of these colliding worlds. This tale of a global conspiracy that threatens humanity itself will keep you guessing whether anyone can survive.

Red Horse (Dark Paradigm #2)

ISBN: 978-1-9162397-5-3

A hacker's mission to find her missing father leads her into a deadly game of political intrigue and danger in this electrifying techno-thriller.

Haleema Sheraz, a skilled cyber hacker for the Iranian government, receives devastating news: her father has disappeared without a trace. With the authorities dragging their feet, she takes matters into her own hands and uncovers a shocking conspiracy dating back to Operation Paperclip during World War II.

Meanwhile, her brothers have joined an ISIS-inspired uprising, plunging Iran into chaos and leaving Haleema no choice but to risk everything to save her family.

As the conflict escalates and the stakes grow higher, Haleema calls in old allies Joe Bowen and Hugo Reese to help in the desperate struggle for survival.

Red Horse is a pulse-pounding, action-packed thriller that is a must-read for fans of high-tech espionage and gripping suspense.

False Flag by Jay Tinsiano. (Frank Bowen #1)

ISBN: 978-1-9997232-2-4

1991: A plan to destabilise Hong Kong is emerging; the key players are being put into place, the wheels are in motion, and innocent people will die.

Frank Bowen is a Londoner on holiday in tropical Thailand.

Half drunk and strapped for cash, he's the perfect bait for a political plot that will leave him running for his life with nowhere to turn.

Pandora Red by Jay Tinsiano. (Frank Bowen #2)

ISBN: 978-1-9997232-3-1

Frank Bowen's mission is to find a GCHQ whistleblower, but in doing so unwittingly risks everything, including his own family's safety.
As part of a covert team assigned to dangerous missions, Bowen believes he knows what he's up against until a team of Russian mercenaries are thrown into the mix, leaving everyone and everything hanging in the balance.
It's a race against the clock to save all that he holds dear and uncover the dark truths behind his mission.

Ghost Order by Jay Tinsiano. (Frank Bowen #3)

ISBN: 978-1-9162397-0-8

Frank Bowen attempts to piece together a fractured life at home but finds himself pulled back into the dark state once again. Only, this time, he's playing both sides.

Blood Tide by Jay Tinsiano.

ISBN: 978-1-9997232-6-2

Detective Douglas Brown transferred to Hong Kong to forget

his past and the dark memory that still haunts him—Richard Blythe.

Blythe, an explosives expert gone rogue, had terrorised London and outwitted Brown, leading to the deaths of countless innocents.

Now the detective's worst fear has come true. Blythe is free from prison to wreak havoc and lead Brown on a deadly cat and mouse game in the city of Hong Kong.

Blood Tide is a gripping terrorism thriller from Jay Tinsiano.

Blood Cull by Jay Tinsiano & Jay Newton

ISBN: 978-1-9162397-2-2

A series of ritualistic killings.

A retired detective inspector desperate to save his wife.

A horrifying secret.

Detective Inspector Doug Brown has retired to Scotland, but when his wife falls ill, there is no choice but to take on a private contract offered by an old acquaintance.

Soon he finds himself on a dark path, tracking down a ritualist killer of affluent men who has so far eluded the police.

But as the merciless killings continue, Doug is unknowingly getting closer to unveiling a sickening conspiracy.

About the Authors

Jay Tinsiano

Jay was born in Ireland but grew up on the flat plains of Lincolnshire surrounded by cows and haystacks before moving to the city of Bristol, where he has lived, apart from far-flung nomadic excursions, ever since.

He is the author of the Frank Bowen thriller series and, in collaboration with Jay Newton, the Dark Paradigm Apocalyptic thriller series, Doug Brown and the shorter Dark Ops stories.

Jay is an avid reader, specifically of crime, sci-fi and thrillers, with occasional non-fiction thrown in. He can be occasionally found in a Waterstones bookshop café or perhaps a quiet pub, furiously scribbling notes and whispering to himself.

Jay Newton

Jay Newton practices and teaches martial arts, is a keen cyclist, manages a band and is an avid fiction reader.

He is currently working on the Dark Paradigm and Dark Ops series with Jay Tinsiano and lives in Bristol, UK, with his family.

Printed in Great Britain
by Amazon